There Goes The Neighborhood

S. REED

First published in the United States of America 2022 by Lake Country Press & Reviews

Cataloging-in-Publication Data is on file with the Library of Congress.

ISBN 978-1-7377679-8-5

Author website: https://sdreedauthor.wordpress.com

Publisher website: http://www.lakecountrypress.com

Proofreading: Borbala Branch

Cover: Emily's World of Design

Formatting: Dawn Lucous of Yours Truly Book Services

BOOKS BY S. REED

There Goes The Neighborhood

Kerwall Town

DEDICATION

v

This novel is dedicated to two very special people who are no longer with us. Firstly, James, you were always the brightest smile in the room, now you're the brightest in the sky. Secondly, Charlotte, you left this earth before I could call you my mum.

QUOTES

You're only given a little spark of madness. You mustn't lose it.
-Robin Williams

I could build a castle out of all the bricks they threw at me"
Taylor Swift - 'New Romantics (1989)'

AUTHOR'S NOTE

Dear friends, fellow Earthlings, and other worldly beings, hello again, it's nice to see you. How have you been? I hope it's been good for you. I cannot thank you enough for joining me on an adventure and once more and trusting me to entertain you with one of my stories in exchange for your hard-earned money.

I've always believed that there is something else out there, among the stars and in other galaxies, at least I've always *wanted* to believe. What you are about to read is a work of fiction. Names and places, events and everything in between has been made up to entertain you.

I first thought of this story back in my first year as a specialist teaching aid whilst in an English class, and it's been telling me to write it ever since, but as ever, life got in the way.

I'd like to remind you all that all my novels are connected in some way, and I'm invested in long term storytelling. I'll say no more than that.

Now, sit back, relax, and enter a time from long ago.

Your friend,

S. Reed

PART I

They say there are only five kinds of alien contact...
Seeing a UFO from around 150 Meters... 1st Kind
UFO leaves evidence on ground or in the sky, as in scorch marks... 2nd Kind
You can see visible occupants in the UFO... 3rd Kind
You're taken into the UFO and experimented on... 4th Kind
Direct contact and communication with the Alien... 5th kind
But what if there is a 6th kind...
Befriending one.

Chapter 1

Underapreciated

Poppy Field Lane is like any typical American suburb of the 50s... but it's the mid-90s and the (mostly) terrible fashion notwithstanding, the Lane is a time capsule of life in Upstate New York before the feminist movement. The men go to work, and the women stay home and look after the house. The men have all the fun, and the women clean up afterwards. The men set all the rules, and the women abide by them... except when the men are out of town. None of these rules apply to eccentric widowed billionaire Ignatius Feltrap who is as young as she is rich.

She lived in the biggest house – a mansion, really – the biggest in all of Poppy Field Lane, but one day, she decided she no longer liked her neighbors, so she paid an extortionate amount of money to have her house moved to the beachfront. Not because she liked the view, but so it would spoil the stunning vistas for her abhorrent neighbors, Carol and Frank, the Lilinsters (there are better names that Ignatius likes to call them by, but none of them are polite). Ignatius is convinced they have risen from the fiery depths of hell just to try and ruin her life; try to, anyway. It also gave her a chance to throw even wilder parties without the worry (not that she did) of a noise complaint from said neighbors. In fact, if it weren't for them, most of the town wouldn't mind her. And don't think she doesn't take pleasure in their indignation. Carol, especially, lived for calling the cops to Feltrap Manor, although she would never give it that name. She'd usually say something like "That woman, I believe her name is Ignatius, yes, the *widow*, well, she's throwing an illegal party again", and she would purr over the word 'widow' and let it hang in the receiver's ear like a moldy piece of fruit. Ignatius hoped taking that power away from the vile witch would make her melt, but it only seemed to exacerbate the tension between the two of them. To Ignatius's disdain, Carol and her brusque husband tick on. How she loathes the ground they walk on. If you ask her, the Lilinsters are to blame for her being outcast from the rest of Poppy Field Lane. If it weren't for them, she would be accepted by the town, despite being 'new money'. And despite her rambunctious atti- tude, she does want to be accepted, but she will not conform to the Lane's outdated ways.

There is an unspoken understanding that they and Ignatius are civil toward each other in the street... However, only one of them got the memo and read it. The other, it seems, set it on fire... with a flamethrower.

"Good morning, Igni. Lovely day, isn't it?" chimes Carol as she power-walks past her, assaulting Ignatius's eyes with a jarring mesh of garish and florescent Lycra. She also knows full well that Ignatius hates people calling her Igni, especially Carol. The way Carol says her name sets her teeth on edge. Even from the very first day Ignatius moved in with her husband (oh how she misses him dearly), Carol has been funny with her. Ignatius tried a few times to get on Carol's good side, to try and bring peace even, but there was something not quite right bubbling away under the skin of Carol and in the end,

Ignatius decided she no longer cared to try and be civil with her.

"It was, until my eyes laid upon you," she replies with a smile, showing her full set of pearly white teeth, and finishes off the mocking with a wave that turns into a one fingered salute.

Carol manifests a disapproving grunt and strides off; clutching her imaginary pearls as she goes.

Ignatius can't recall how her feud with Carol started, but she sure as hell knows how it's going to end. It'll be either driving her six feet into the ground with her pettiness, or one of them move, whichever comes first – and Ignatius is damn sure that won't be her. She does know one thing, though: Carol is bad news. With some people, their true colors always bleed through in the end.

Along with moving her house to the beachfront, she brought with her the entire front lawn and most of the back-yard, too. The house is complete with a three-foot high, gleaming white picket fence that stretches the whole way round. She is known for growing the most amazing flowers, too, most notably poppies in every hue. Those are what she was attending to when Carol interrupted. Her hair is tied up in a rainbow bandana, and her denim dungarees are stained with fresh soil. Her white sneakers are also stained, as well as her white tube socks. Looking like this is another middle finger not just to Carol, but to the whole of the suburb. The women are supposed to dress a certain way and act a certain way, but Ignatius couldn't care less about their expectations. They would never dream of driving her out of Poppy Field, as they rely on her for her donations to the restoration and upkeep work, and whether they like it or not, for the entertainment, too. The world is her oyster, and she has enough money to buy the town almost two times over, which is a grand feat consid-ering this is one of the more opulent suburbs of all of North

America. And it's just another reason why everyone else in Poppy Field Lane would never try to force Ignatius out.

Even before her late husband perished in a fire many moons ago, she was under-appreciated by all in the town. They thought she was with him for his money and nothing more. It didn't help that he was more than twelve years older than her, but she didn't care. The fact that she was a successful business-woman in her own right either never crossed their mind, or they just refused to believe that a woman could be just as successful as a man. Everything she did had an Asterix next to it; often leaving her wondering what life was like if she was a man - as she thought her accomplishments will come with praise instead of indignation.

Perhaps the biggest reason for her always feeling under-appreciated is the fact that no one seems to take her seriously as a woman, is she has no children. She often observes moms with multiple kids being clutched close to their side as she walks past them, and she even catches some of them make the sign of the cross. The 50s style attitude rears its ugly head in more ways than one and these looks, although Ignatius doesn't show it, often feel like a dagger in her heart. She's been half surprised that she hasn't been committed to the Pembroke Asylum under the guise of female hysteria.

The early morning sun is a bright fiery sphere in the sky and threatens to bake anyone who stands in it too long. Despite this, it would still be a beacon to all the sun worshippers in Poppy Field Lane. Ignatius's sun-kissed skin has always been the envy of all of the suburb, and yes, especially Carol. She is everything Carol wants to be, but there is no way Carol would admit it, or even be able to attain it, because after all, everyone is unable to escape the clutches of time. You can make yourself look younger on the outside, shove fat from your ass to your face in an effort to look like you're in your thirties, but there is not a chance you can change the age of your insides. If Carol could bottle youth, most notably Ignatius's, then she would get drunk on it all in one night.

Ignatius gets up from the flowerbed and dusts herself down, admiring her morning work and heads inside. she manages to get one sneaker off before her only company, a three-year-old black Labrador named Alife, leaps on top of her as soon as he sees her and licks her face while wagging his tail. When Alfie is stood up on his hind legs, he reaches the top of her shoulders.

"Alright, alright, Alfie, settle down. I was only outside," she says as she sets him down, his big brown eyes full to the brim with happiness as his head cocks to one side. She takes this moment to take off her remaining sneaker and and places it neatly by the other one on her pristine floor.

He tries to jump up again, but she gives him a look, and he covers his face with his paws, his eyes peeking out, one of his ears flopped over to the side. Ignatius rolls her eyes at the sweet pup, a warmth settling in her heart. She taps her chest, making him jump up once more, continuing the lick-fest for another few moments before setting him down again and heading to the kitchen, Alfie following closely.

Her kitchen is huge and decked out like her favorite diner, from a small town in England that she once dreamed... or thought she dreamt of. There's a chrome Island in the center of the spacious kitchen, and in the corner, a red leathered corner unit with cream piping, complete with another table and authentic mini jukebox finishes the look. She can't remember the name of the diner from her dream but thinks it begins with a 'K'. When she thinks about that dream, there's a slightly uneasy feel to it, like it may not be a dream at all but a place she's been to or needs to go at some point. She knows it didn't belong to the time period, though, which is why she vibed with it; that's how she feels about her life here, and the whole suburb, too. The way she decked out her whole house—most notably her kitchen—was to try and recapture something she had lost from childhood. Most of it was spent watching her parents argue over petty things while she gawked at the happy people on TV. The kitchen always seemed to represent the heart of the home. Perhaps that's why the color scheme is red; it offers a sense of warmth.

Everything Ignatius has stems from never having anything as a child. She wanted a better life, one that she could be proud of. It's why she worked harder than anyone else around her to attain all she has now. But the one thing she truly wanted is no longer here now: the love and affection from her husband. There isn't a day that goes by where she doesn't miss her Aiden. His smell - like fresh daisies and sandalwood, his touch - light but firm, comforting, his voice - soft and the sound of home. Some days, she forgets he's no longer here and calls his name only to be met with crippling silence. She has long suspected that her husband's demise was due to foul play. She had dedicated her time trying to convince the police department of that, but all they came back with was 'a freak accident'. In Ignatius's mind, there was nothing accidental about it, but with no proof and no evidence, she had no case. 'No body, no crime' was also touted about - but there was a body - she was the one who had to identify the charred ruin of her husband on a cold slab in the morgue. And there most certainly was a crime.

She brews herself a coffee and sits on the red leather and cream piped corner booth, gazing out the window and admiring the view of the golden beach framing the blue ocean. Alfie is sat on the other side, also admiring the view. His tongue hangs out the right side of his mouth, yo-yoing a line of drool from his lips to the floor. The radio plays in the background, the soothing yet haunting sounds of her favorite song, Mr. Sandman by The Chordettes. She taps her fingers to the rhythm of their pleas, wishing the sandman would bring her a dream, and hums along to the words. It's a song that played at their wedding, which may be an odd choice for some, but it's just another way Ignatius stands out from the dull and drab crowd. The dream to them was being happy in each other's arms, and they had managed to make it a reality. Now, the dream is just to hold Aiden one more time.

The chime of her doorbell interrupts the morning silence, making her burn her tongue on her coffee. She gets up and strides to the door, which doesn't put the visitor in good stead. If it came down to a foot race, Ignatius used to run track at school and would always place in the top three.

"Hell...o," she says as she opens it, her hand clasped on the frame of the royal blue door, but no one is there. She furrows her brow, a tug of annoyance pulling at her stomach, and her mouth droops into a frown. Before she can shut the door fully, the doorbell rings again, making her go from mildly annoyed to almost vexed when she opens it to find no one there, still. She slams the door with force, making the golden door-knocker rattle on the mahogany. When the bell rings the third time, she ignores it and stomps her way back to the kitchen, her slipper clad feet making dull *ffft ffft* sounds on the highly polished, bright stone floor. Her radio now plays some other song, a current one she doesn't know nor care for. *At least the ringing has stopped*, she thinks. *It was probably one of the local kids playing knock door run or something stupid like that*. If she truly felt threatened, she has two options: Option A) Alfie, who would scare the shit out of anyone if prompted, and option B) Her nail bat, which would also scare the shit out of anyone. She's never had to resort to either of them before but isn't afraid to either. Her late husband had trained her in many things, including how to look after herself. He was a black belt in Krav Maga, which is the perfect karate discipline for self-defense. It was one of the things they did together, and he would never admit it, as he was just as competitive as her, but she became better than him at it.

Chapter 2

The Intruder of Poppy Field Lane

A cluster of huge Colonial and Georgian houses stand in a parade of wealth on the ten tree-lined streets of Poppy Field Lane. Home to one thousand residents —both young and old—the lane exists behind the protection of giant golden gates, keeping the riff-raff out. Or, as Ignatius sees it, the semi-normal people who could pop the crystal entrusted bubble the rest the housewives live in. God forbid they let in another rule-bending feminist... the husbands would revolt. One was bad enough. No, best to police the border, requesting reasoning for every passer-through instead. Though very few reasons are ever good enough for the council of homeowners. On the gate hangs a sign that, from afar, reads Welcome to Poppy Field Lane, but up close, its true meaning is evident. Although it doesn't say it, the fancy, gold lettering on a clean white backdrop might as well read: Come on in those with the status or prosperity needed to be seen near such a prestigious suburb, or else hit the bricks and don't come back. Most of the time, the on-duty security guard is Darren Rose, a middle-aged and balding man whose face shows the number of years he's worked. He speaks with a soft, southern accent and is known as the gentle giant to those who took the time to become his friend. To those who didn't bother, he is an intimidating man, standing just shy of 6'5".

He is on duty today, too, and like everyone else doesn't see the intruder even though it walks right under his nose. The moment the intruder walks past him, the monitors cackle and freeze for a moment, but Darren sees none of this because he's reading a Phillip Pullman novel and his feet are on the desk in front of the monitors. The intruder has time to look into the little booth of his and see all of this, and even gets close enough to smell Darren's cologne. *Old Spice.* So strong, it smells like he took a bath in it. The intruder sees how tall the man is, and if it so wanted to, could reach out and touch him. Instead, it passes by, whistling its favorite song about a sandman bringing a dream.

Elsewhere in Poppy Field Lane, people are going about their business. The men are out at work, and the women are busying themselves with whatever choice of chore their hearts desire on this hot day. The intruder takes it all in with avid curiosity. It's not the first time it's watched people go about their mundane day, and it certainly won't be the last either.

It watches Janey Thompson make fresh batches of cookies for her three children, the hell raising fourteen-year-old twins, Aaron and Dan, and the little angel, twelve-year-old Cadence. They all share Janey's corn yellow hair and brown eyes, and Cadence is a spitting image of her mother. Their father, Carl, is hardly ever home. He's a high-ranking sales executive for a big tech company and is often on the road, sleeping in motels along the highways. Janey and Carl fell in love when they were just seventeen, but last summer, Carl's loyalties faltered, and he had extramarital coitus with another woman named Harper. Neither woman knows of his infringement, and even though it was just a summer thing, Harper hasn't forgotten about his deep blue eyes and soft hands.

Two of the newer homeowners of Poppy Field Lane, Mark and Sharon Smith, moved over from England a number of years ago after giving up hope of ever finding Mark's father, Terry - it's also the middle name of every male in the family. At the time he went missing, he was in his mid-eighties, and that was almost twenty years ago. He lives in a small town, but for the life of them, they can't seem to recall the name. Their two kids, who aren't kids at all now, Jack and Donna, come and stay for a few weeks at a time when they're not busy with their work. It's the kind of work that begs a lot of questions, but no answers are ever forthcoming. You would only have to look at Jack and Donna's harrowed faces to understand what they might have gone through or do for a living; it's the look of pain. Mark and Sharon don't share that same look. They have a look of wealth and happiness, but behind those eyes, sorrow lurks. Mark and Sharon are considered 'new money.' They struck lucky on the lottery years back and decided to escape to America where they acclimated into Poppy Field Lane like they were born to it— becoming fast friends with Ignatius and catching the wrath of Carol in turn, they're often missed from her event invite list. But no matter, everyone knows Ignatius's parties are the ones to be invited to. Carol's parties have a cold, sterilized feel to them where Ignatius's feel inviting, and you actually feel welcomed.

The intruder watches the Smiths on their wrap-around porch, taking in the sun on deck chairs, Sharon in an oversized white sun hat and stripy yellow t-shirt and white shorts, Mark in a light blue t-shirt and black shorts. The intruder smiles at them, revealing four sets of sharp, white teeth, two on each row, and it gives them a gentle wave, too, knowing full well they can't see what it is doing. It then moves on, still humming its favorite song, with Mark and Sharon being none the wiser. It's a relief being out of that awful place again, partly due to its powers being at full strength once more. And one of the dastardly things they could do was stop it from turning invisible in certain sections; that was mostly due to all the medication and the fear they instilled into it.

Poppy Field Lane is known for its exclusivity second and Ignatius first, which rubs a lot of the homeowners the wrong way - well Carol, mostly. They came here to escape the exposure, but with the local celebrity around, all eyes are always on the neighborhood. The media speculate on what she's going to do next and who she's going to have at her next party. The headliners for the last one were *The Spice Girls*. Ignatius had flown them in from England to play one song, and after that, they became regular guests. They're not the only high-profile guests come friends Ignatius has, as painter Jackson Pollock is counted among them, too - that is, until they start playing cards and she, more often than not, loses.

One of the most popular pass times for the people of Poppy Field Lane is to speculate on what she's going to do next and who she's going to have headlining her next party. Lord knows she can afford anyone she wants, from the Spice Girls to Elton John or even Jonny Cash. Hell, she can book 'em all and have a festival or concert on a random Tuesday if she wants. Ignatius could throw a thousand lavish parties over the next hundred years without blowing through a quarter of the money she has. Some say that's why she's so rambunctious; a burning unfulfillment itching at her that money can't scratch. Sometimes, when she throws parties now, she's not even there herself - mentally, anyway. She's off in the arms of her husband and then something will bring her screaming back to reality.

The main hub of the neighborhood is *The Smoke House*, the finest eatery on all of the east coast, which turns into a piano and jazz bar at night. Is run by Daniel and his wife, Loraine. The restaurant come diner can seat more than eighty people, and on the evenings, it's almost always full. The decor is light and homely with splashes of color, and above the door is their family motto: *'If you can be anything, be kind.'*

Other notable sites of the area are the three-mile-long gold sand beach, which is always uninterrupted by tourists, so it remains free of litter, and the Poppy Gardens, which is situated in the heart of the neighborhood. It boasts all kinds of flowers, two huge fountains, and a mini lake that is popular with the local bird population.

It's fair to say that if you live here, you have a very good life, and if you don't live here, you should certainly aspire to. Poppy Field Lane *is* The American Dream.

The intruder continues to watch the affairs of this neighborhood, and by the time the moon has taken over as the sky's evening entertainment, it finds a place to rest. It's had a long day absorbing all the information. It lies its strangely shaped head on the golden beach and falls soundly asleep within moments. It has been on the run for as long as it can remember, and this is the first place it has felt truly safe – too safe in fact, and if it had been more alert, it wouldn't have taken to rest in such an open space. But the allure of the soft golden sand was all too much, and its eyes were ever so heavy, as if weighed down by two elephants on a string.

At around 11 p.m., Ignatius jolts awake from a deep sleep by the constant barking of Alfie. Her eyes adjust to the darkness, and her blonde ringlet hair stands up like she's been electrocuted as her heart beats unsteadily. She reaches for the nail bat from underneath her bed, grasping it from the heavily taped end firmly in her hand. Alfie has been taught to bark when there is danger or an intruder. He's on his hind legs, tail straight, ears all the way back and alert at the window.

"*Shhh, shhh*, ok, boy, ok, I'm here, now keep quiet will ya? Quit your hollerin'," she says in a sleep-laden voice and wraps her dressing gown tightly round her.

Chapter 3

An Unearthly Discovery

On the other side of the country, somewhere deep in the Nevada desert and past huge chain link fences with warning signs about being shot on sight, there is an underground facility where all the world's secrets are held. The building stretches for miles, and the parts that are on top of the land, the bit that everyone knows about, is only the tip of the iceberg. There is a well-known saying '*You can't handle the truth*'. Well, in this case, it may be right. If people found out what was truly down there, it may send them insane.

The whole operation is run by one man, and he has more authority than the President. The man in question is almost 6'8", bald with an immaculate, bushy black beard. His narrow eyes are like tiny lumps of coal set into tanned skin, and his voice is low and laced with menace. The facility call him '*The Captain*'. His real name is classified - not literally. He is sat in his minimalist yet spacious office behind his steel desk, in his high back chair. The only sound is that of the clock on the wall that reads 11:48 p.m. Stood in front of him, in his usual weasel demeanor, is his second in command, John Mercer. A bead of sweat runs down from his thinning strands of hair onto his hook of a nose. There is a sheaf of papers in his shaking hands, which he lightly places on the desk before taking three shaky strides back with his gaze firmly planted at a spot on the floor.

"What is this?" The Captain asks, staring a hole right through John, who visibly trembles. Any moment, weasel John is going to soil himself, and it wouldn't be the first time.

"I... I... It's the f-file on... on..." He starts, but his mouth has gone so dry, he's unable to form a coherent sentence.

"I didn't ask you to stutter... I *asked* you What. Is. This?" Each word sounds like a gunshot in John's head, and he squirms. A tiny bit of warm piss trickles down his leg, and his face goes bright scarlet. The uncomfortable and clammy warmth in his underwear matches the warmth now prickling his cheeks.

"We—well, ok, we've lost the Alien... sir," he puts his tiny hand to his head in a salute gesture while still looking at the floor, which now has a small, yellow puddle. The smell reaches his nose, and he gags despite his best efforts to stifle it.

"What do you mean *'lost the Alien'*? It's not a pair of fucking car keys! It's the most valuable asset this country has, and YOU'RE TELLING ME YOU'VE LOST IT?" he screams so loud that spit flies from his mouth.

The Captain snatches up the papers from his desk and looks over them with furious urgency. After a few moments, he stands up so quickly, his chair falls to the floor in a crash, making John leap into the air and squeal out in fright.

He then walks around his desk and slowly approaches John, who stands still, shaking as if he's been left out in the cold for a week. The Captain looks down at the piss-puddle and smirks. He puts his hands, which are the size of glazed hams, on either side of John's face, making him pout his lips. Tears roll down John's face, and a bubble of snot forms in his right nostril that pops and runs down his philtrum.

"John, John, John. Relax, I'm not going to hurt you," he says in a soothing tone that sounds anything but soothing to John. Stroking a hand through John's thinning hair, he makes hushing noises, that sound more like a snake than a human.

"Now, give me solutions and not problems, ok? You don't want to give me *problems*, do you?" He shows John a full set of teeth. It's like a shark smiling with a set of pearly whites, unnatural and wholly unsettling.

"No," he snatches at the word so quickly that when he speaks it, it makes him jump.

"Good, now fix this mess... For The Facility," The Captain says, looking directly into his soul. After a moment, he lets go of him, and John scurries out the room so fast, one would think someone strapped a rocket to his ass and lit the fuse.

"I'll get you this time, you little blue bastard. And this time, I'll watch you take your last breath." The words echo through his office, and he goes around his desk and picks up his chair before sitting down and straitening his tie.

The *little blue bastard* has been the bane of his professional existence for as long as he can remember, and he was a pain in the ass for his predecessor, too. In fact, since the ship crashed in July 1947, the '*little blue bastard*', as The Captain deemed it, has been quite a menace to this whole facility. At first, it cooperated, contributing to all manors of what we now call modern day tech, but since some time in the 70's, it's become... *aloof*.

The Captain caught it once, and of course, tortured it for getting away, much like he did his dog when he was fourteen. Somehow, it managed to slip away from him a second time, and The Captain almost lost his job for it until he said he'd bring its head back on a polished, silver platter. That was a couple of years ago. He's been trying to track its movements ever since. For weeks, months, if we're telling the truth—The Captain was following a stray cat that ended up in New Mexico. The *little blue bastard* removed the tracker and dumped it on the unsuspecting cat, making one of the world's most technologically advanced facilities look like preschoolers.

The Captain looks over the papers once more and lets out a guttural roar, then rips them into tiny pieces and chucks them on the floor.

"Pamela!" he yells into the intercom.

"Yes, Captain?" Her voice comes back in a static, hesitant squark.

"Get in here and clean this mess up. And bring in the bottle of vodka. The good stuff, not that shitty, watery crap you get out for the visitors. Hurry up!"

"Yes, Captain, right away!"

She comes in moments later with a wastepaper bin and the special vodka he requested and sets it down on his desk. She hasn't even put the first scrap of paper in the bin before he's torn off the cap and taking swings from the bottle, neglecting the glass and ice for the time being. He's been known to pour it into his eye, too, on the rare occasion.

Once she finishes clearing the room of rubbish, Pamela stands at his desk, her ginger, curled bob in slight disarray, and straightens the shoulder pads in her tweed suit. She's not one for wearing high heels, but The Captain said she looks like an unwanted scrub without them, so now she wears kitten heels as a compromise. She remembers the time when she had *the audacity,* as he put it, to wear casual clothing that didn't accentuate her breasts. Which is why she now wears suits with low-cut tops or semi see-through blouses. He has objectified women all his life and shows no signs of stopping. For all the words in the world, sometimes the simplest and most blunt ones are best when describing people like The Captain— people who are wrapped up in their own misogyny, sexism, hatred, racism, and it begins with a capital 'C' and rhymes with *runt.* The trouble is, people like him often get away with it as they are in a position of power, and others are scared that their legion of brainwashed followers will also attack them, which has been the case a handful of times. They were quickly shown the exit thereafter and are now on the streets in some one-horse town, begging for scraps of food.

Ignatius and Alfie have scoured the house from top to bottom and can see no signs of a break-in. Alfie, however, keeps going back to the window.

"What is it with this window, Alfie?" she asks, growing concerned. He barks in return.

"You want us to go out there, don't you? ... Fuck." Ignatius isn't scared of the dark, *per se*, but she would rather not take the chance going out to the beach in the dead of night when everyone knows that's the time vampires and witches and all other monsters come out to play. Hell, she even hates her house being in darkness, so the outside is taking it to the next level. At least she has her dog... and her nail bat.

The late-night sea breeze is harsh on her skin and plays with her blond hair, making it a little hard to see as her locks cover her eyes that are wide and alert to any sense of incoming danger. Alfie is almost belly flat to the floor, his snout inches away from the soft, golden sand. His body moves in snake-like movements as he tries to get the scent of the intruder. In the darkness, Alfie's black furred figure would be impossible to see if it wasn't for his luminous collar and leash. In fact, if anyone were to look from their window, or from the top of the beach, they might see something resembling floating fluorescents bobbing up and down in unusual directions.

"Ok, boy... where is this thing you're so desperate to get? I swear to all that is holy, if it's one of your missing toys, you'll get no treats for a week." That's a lie. No way she could ever be mad at Alfie—he's her best friend. She leans down and ruffles his fur, mostly for her own comfort. If there was a choice to give up all the parties and all the money in exchange to have Alfie forever, she'd take it off your hand so quickly, only a bloody stump would remain. Alfie, after all, is her only living connection left to her Aiden.

After a few moments, her flashlight trains on something farther down on the beach. It's too dark to see from this far away, so with jelly legs, she moves closer to it. Her heart threatens to beat out of her chest, and Alfie, who was full of gusto a moment ago, has tucked his tail between his legs and digs his hind legs into the sand in an effort to plant roots and never move.

4

Chapter

Beach Buddies

Ignatius is almost on top of the thing in the sand, close enough with her torch to see that it has almost burrowed its - and she was unsure she was truly seeing this color but - milky-way, almost galaxy-like body. She heaves out a deep breath, which drifts away in the night air instantly. She slaps the side of her face gently, psyching herself up and then, thinking she is brave enough to reach out a hand and touch it, she recoils instantly from the warmth.

"It's alive! It's fucking alive!" she exclaims in a harsh, scared whisper. It doesn't register with her that when she said it, no words came out, only a tiny squeak. Alfie is a few paces behind her, still trying to dig his back paws into the sand. He's whimpering a bit, but not too loud, out of fear of the thing on the beach. She shines the torch up the rest of the thing's... body.

She moves the light up to the thing's face and screams.

The thing, in return, opens its eyes, its eyelids opening from the side. It blinks once, twice, and sees what's in front of it, then screams, too. Alfie joins in with a howl and starts to run in circles as if he is chasing his own tail.

"*Hvad Fanden!*" the thing says in a strange accent.

"No! Don't kill me! Wait, please! I'm sorry!" Ignatius collapses on the sand, covering her eyes with her hands.

"Oh, ok, you're American. Sorry, wrong language there for a second!" it says, shooting its hands up in the air, hoping this mad woman bestows some mercy on them.

"You... you..." she starts but can't quite finish.

"Talk? Yes, yes, I talk, I sing, I dance, I'm a freaking legend. Now, mind telling me what you're doing out here in the middle of the night with a death hound and a flashlight in my face? Don't you know that's rude?"

Silence is the only response from Ignatius. In fact, she's gone the same color as milk, her beautifully tanned skin nowhere to be seen, her eyes staring at the... the...thing with cerulean blue skin that shimmers the most beautiful shade of blue she's ever seen when the moonlight hits it. It shines and sparkles, and she could swear it swirls gently, too.

"This is where you're going to faint on me, right? Ah jeez, I hate it when humans do this. It's the exact reason I try to stay hidden," it says in its faux American accent.

"No," she manages.

"No? As in no you're not going to faint?" It exhales a sigh of relief and rests a hand on its left hip. "That would be doing me a world of good. It's a whole other process if you faint, and I'm just not ready for that kind of commitment this late in the night."

Ignatius can see that it's about four feet in height and maybe a few inches but nothing more than that. It's the most peculiar thing she's ever seen. There is more, too. If its voice wasn't in a deeper register, she would not have been so sure on its gender at all. One thing is for sure, though: Ignatius is completely fascinated by it; from its big eyes, slender frame, and wide hips to its skin, so out of this world in a literal sense, too. But above all of that, she finds its aura the most fascinating.

S. REED

It feels kind and warm, like an old friend. "What are you? ...I won't faint. You're the strangest man I've ever seen!" she says, taking in this strange creature but not entirely believing what she's seeing. Everything else in the world has gone silent. There are no waves crashing on the rocks, no owls hooting. Nothing. It's just the sound of Ignatius's voice and this strange being. Alfie has retired to behind her legs, his body low, his eyes full of wonder.

"Man? Wow, ok. Just because I look like a male, and sound like one, it doesn't mean I am one. It's not cool that you assume that. I forget that on your planet, you're a couple of lightyears away from tolerance and acceptance, but c'mon, gotta keep teaching, right?" Their tone, which is meant to be scolding, is betrayed by their eyes, which are full of humor and mischief. It's missed by Ignatius, though, whose mouth flies open in shock. They know full well what humans are like, but this one, yes, they can tell she's different. It may be in part because they haven't pulled a gun on them yet, or maybe it's something else.

"My... planet?"

"Oh, jeez, yes, your planet. You know, teeny blue and green thing called Earth. Been in the solar system for a couple million years. Mine, where I come from, is Meta Outta Rim Klet - section 78. But for ease, we just call it M.O.R.K78."

"So... You're an alien?" Her brain is trying to catch up with what her eyes are seeing.

"Ding ding! She's got it, folks! I am, indeed!" They makes a slightly mocking bow gesture and reveals their extra sets of teeth.

"Oh *gawd*! You're not going to probe me, are you?"

"What? Absolutely not! Why does everyone think that? I mean, I can if you're into that kinda thing, but... What am I talking about? Of course I'm not gonna probe you. Pray tell, exactly what information am I going to gain from your ass?

How well you wipe when you shit? I don't think I need to know that."

"Sorry... this is... I don't know... so strange."

Alfie, who has been looking up at the alien with huge, curious eyes, now bolts upright next to Ignatius.

"I'm sure it is... Hey, mind if we go inside? I don't really wanna be attracting attention, if you know what I mean." All of a sudden, they feel as if a thousand eyes are staring at them and the woman with her dog, and it sends a shiver down their spine.

"Are you a murderer?" she asks just above a whisper.

"Of course I'm not. I just don't think it is wise for a human and an alien to be out talking on the beach in the middle of the night. Also, I'm pretty hungry... got any snacks?"

5

Chapter

Paging M.O.R.K78

Once in the house, Ignatius shuts all the blinds and locks the door, then ushers them into the kitchen. The lights emit a dimmed, warm white hue, thanks to her still stylish, brass 80s dimmer switch.

"Sooo, what do I call you? I think we should get that out of the way first, right?" Ignatius asks hesitantly as she re-tightens her dressing gown.

Alfie is still staring at the stranger with big eyes, but he ventures no further than the side of Ignatius.

"My name is Rumvæson, but my friends, if I had any, would call me Væson for short and maybe even Væ for shorter, you know, if they're in a hurry. How about you? I mean, I could read your mind and find out, but I rather not cross any lines," they say with an irresolute laugh.

"You can." She lets out a sigh that is filled with awe and bewilderment. "*Sheesh*, this is gonna take some getting used to. I'm Ignatius." She extends her wary hand.

Væson returns the gesture, wrapping its long, bony figures around her hand, and Ignatius takes in how different their hand is to hers. She takes Væson's hand for the time being and gives it a gentle shake, being extra careful with it as she has no idea how fragile it might be.

"Isn't that a man's name?" Væson asks with a wry smile, knowing exactly what they're doing.

"Weren't you the one just giving out lectures a moment ago? Practice what you preach!" Ignatius's face flashes red, then calms when she sees Væson laughing. It sounds strange coming from this other-worldly being. Stranger still, she kind of likes Væson already. Ignatius stares off into the distance for a moment, as if remembering something from her deep past. After perhaps a few moments, she speaks. "If you must know, my dad, also called Ignatius, wanted me to be a boy. My mum wanted the same, and they both loved the name, so it stuck... But I'm sure you already knew that, right?" She turns around and finds Væson is no longer there.

For a moment, Ignatius wonders if she's dreamt this encounter, or if perhaps she's finally snapped like everyone said she was going to—the booze finally seeped its way to her brain. Oh, how Carol would revel in her breakdown. She might even throw a party. Funny, the things that go through your head at breakneck speed.

"You got cable? I'm sure you do in this big, fancy house of yours!" Væson yells from the living room. They're eating what looks to be their sixth cup of creamy chocolate yogurt, and their long and thin intergalactic feet that have four toes joined at the bottom by web like skin, are hanging off the side of her antique, green armchair. There's also half a gallon of milk on the oak coffee table, and the TV is on so loud, she's surprised she didn't hear it sooner. They took the moment to get the snacks when Ignatius was telling her story, looking in each cupboard and fridge like it was an all you can eat buffet. They haven't seen food like this in a long time, and their highly sensitive tastebuds were watering at every single delight. Ignatius never had kids, but looking at this scene, she feels for every parent who has ever dared to take their eyes off their toddler for more than five seconds.

Væson hangs their head from the arm of the sofa and hollers, "Do you always stare off into the distance like that? I wiped the drool from your face, by the way. You're welcome. So, where were we on the cable situation? There's a game I wanna watch. Well, it's a soccer game, it should still be on, right?" While on the run, they caught snippets of soccer by looking from the outside into humans' cozy living rooms.

Væson keeps talking as Ignatius storms over and yanks the remote out of their hands, pushes their feet off the armchair, then turns the volume down on the television. It all happens so fast, Væson almost ends up upside down on the armchair.

"So, I take it that's a *no* to the cable?" They ask with their lips mushed to the chair. Then, they rises up like some marionette puppet and hover in the air for a moment, turning themselves the right way around in the process. Ignatius stares with wide eyed fascination, and Væson smiles at her from their new, lofty position before slowly coming down to solid ground.

"How did you...?" she says before actually fainting this time, her body falling to the floor in installments. Her lips looks as though she's kissing the floor, and a little trail of drool leaks out of her mouth.

"Well, at least you look peaceful," Væson says as it takes the remote back.

Væson stares at Alfie, and Alfie stares back.

You killed my human! Alfie shouts into Væson's head.

Relax, no I didn't. She'll be up in a few hours to give you dry ass food and pick up your shits. Come and sit on the couch, but I swear, if you lick me, I'm putting you outside. Væson looks at the four-legged animal, and Alfie's big eyes stare back, tugging at Væson's hearts. They try to reassure the animal by saying: *It's a sedated shock caused by, well, me being awesome. Don't worry, every precaution has already been taken. She's not in any danger. You're just going to have to trust me on this.*

Alfie tilts his head and thinks about testing the boundaries for a moment but opts to respect this intruder thing and does as he's asked. After all, he's a *good boy.*

Væson isn't the fondest of dogs, but they can tell by Alfie's aura that he's going to be no trouble.

They sit and watch the soccer game for a while. During the second half, Ignatius sits up, holding her head, confused as to where she is for a moment. She grabs one arm of the couch for support and pulls herself up with a slight grunt.

"Aww, look who's up," Væson glees and moves off the sofa with a slick glide.

"S-so, I didn't dream it?" Holding a hand to her head, her words come out in a haze.

"Nope... *oh,* unless this is all a dream, and when we're asleep is when we're actually awake. Now, that's a hypothesis I can get behind."

It looks like Ignatius's head might explode at the thought of processing all of this. Before this evening, she was the most talked about woman in town, the woman who threw the biggest and best parties. She was the most interesting, and she was never left speechless; and now, words are failing her. Hell, the concept of everything she thought she knew has slipped through her hands like lathered soap. Yet all this only adds to Væson's charm.

"Ok, ok, can we zoom back to the start for a moment?" she asks, trying to get a foothold back into reality.

"The very, very start? As in, before time?" Væson asks a little confused, their voice lilting up in pitch, face turning to one side.

"No. Goodness no! I mean, from when we met."

"*Ah,* ok. Well sure... I told you I'm Rumvæson, and my

friends if I had any, would call me Væson. And then you told me your name is Ignatius, an—"

She holds a hand up to stop them. "I got that bit. You're difficult, you know that, right?" An exasperated smile hides just behind her ruby lips.

"So I've been told."

She lets out a frustrated sigh. "I mean like, what do I call you? Earlier, you said you aren't a man, so... I'm sorry, this is still so new, and you should give me credit for not freaking out about having an *alien* in my house."

Alfie shifts his head from Væson to his master as if watching a tennis match. In a way, he is, but they are verbal volleys instead of his favorite thing: tennis balls.

"Well, you did faint."

"You LEVITATED! Of course I'm going to faint from that!" She puts a hand across her brow and tries to ask the question again. She can see that Væson likes to wind people up. "Anyway, so gender?"

"For us, on Mork-78, we don't have genders. We simply are. We see no point in labels. You are what you are, you like what you like, and no one really cares as long as everything is above board. See where I'm going with this?" Væson states matter-of-factly.

"You make it sound all so simple."

"It is, that's why. No point making something you can't control complicated, is there? Remember, labels are put in place to make you fear what you do not know."

Ignatius doesn't reply to this but silently contemplates it. After a moment, she nods in agreement.

"So, I don't even know why I'm asking this... but... do you have any other *powers* other than levitating?"

"I thought you'd never ask." A smile spreads across Væson's face in excitement.

They interlock their long fingers and crack them, then crack their neck too in an effort to either limber up or do a musical number.

"What can I do, you ask? Let's see, there's the telekinesis, that's moving things with my mind, of course. And my mind, well, this brain is super smart. Then there's the regeneration, and I can change my appearance at will..." Væson does this to demonstrate, turning into the king of voices, Robin Williams, rather fittingly. The likeness is uncanny, except for the fact that Væson's periwinkle eyes remain the same and their eyelids still retract the same, strange sideways direction that she is slowly getting used to. Then they shift again—into Jennifer Aniston, perfectly capturing her Rachel haircut from the show they'd caught glimpses of.

"And to top it off, I can talk to animals telepathically. I can pass that one onto you if you'd like. That way, you can hear what the murder hound is thinking about you... You're getting that pasty look again. Let's try to avoid passing out once more, shall we?" Væson pleads.

"You think you have me figured out already, don't you?" she says, laughing in spite of herself, which actually aids her nauseous feeling. Væson nods eagerly in agreement. "Just a lot to take in... So, you're like a Doctor Dolittle?" Ignatius tries to gather her thoughts around yet another new concept. She takes a seat in the corner booth of the kitchen, just in case her legs buckle under her again.

"Dolittle? I do quite a lot, actually."

""No, no, it's a book, and film, about a man who can talk to animals," she says, hoping this will sufficiently explain what she means.

"Ooooh, ok. Can he pass on that power, too?" Væson asks eagerly.

"Well, no..."

"Hmph, so he's not as good as me?" They extend their hand, (which is remarkably like their feet but without the webbing and with an extra digit, making it a human looking five), look at their long and finely shaped nails, and blow in a way they have seen other humans do when they are trying to put an exclamation mark on a point.

"It would appear not," she replies. Now, the smile on her face is in full bloom; she can already see a lot of herself in them.

"Good, I'm kinda competitive," they say as if it's a deep revelation. Væson hovers from one end of the kitchen to the other, being careful not to bash their head on the expensive looking light fitting on the ceiling.

"I'm starting to see that. Are you always this confident borderline cocky?" Her hands go up to her golden bunch of ringlet hair, as they often do when she's deep in thought or annoyed. Thankfully for Væson, in this instance it's because she's deep in thought. Ignatius's mind goes to Aiden and what he would think of her new friend. Her hand touches the locket around her neck. It's a small, silver heart with his picture in it. Inscribed on the back are the words '*When I'm not with you, I'm close by —. X.*' She strokes it absentmindedly.

"Cocky?" Væson's voice brings her back to the kitchen. "I prefer to use the term endearing, and yes, yes I am." Their smile once more reveals those extra set of teeth, and Ignatius stares at them, wide eyed herself, her eyebrows disappearing into her fringe as she tilts her head to try and see the extra row of teeth in her visitor's mouth.

"I see you staring at my gnashers," Væson briefly chomps up and down and then gives Ignatius a wide grin and big eyes, "and before you ask, *no*, they're not for eating humans or any other morbid thing you can think of. Cool though, right?" Væson extends their smile further, so all of their pearly whites are on show. They have seen humans do this many times and try to mimic the behavior.

"Well, that's a relief," she breaths out heavily and moves a

THERE GOES THE NEIGHBORHOOD

blond strand of her hair out of her eyes with a puff from her mouth. It's another tick she has; this one when she is either nervous or in deep thought, or it seems, when she's listening to an alien talk about all the things they can do.

As if struck by a heavy object, Væson staggers back and holds their hand to their head, brow wrinkling in both pain and shock. Their features flatten into a serious deadpan glaze, followed by an internal wrench of the gut, as if some invisible force had sucked all the wind out of them and drenched them in guilt. They dash from one side of the kitchen to the other at a speed Ignatius has never seen before. Alfie watches on, mesmerized.

"What? What is it?" Her rosy cheeks turn ashen.

"I should really try to make contact and send a page to my planet to let them know I'm ok," Væson sits on the arm of the couch.

"When was the last time you contacted them?"

"Oh, twenty-five years ago... give or take. It's the first chance I've had since then." They finish the last part feeling a little guilty - knowing it was of sorts a half truth.

"Twenty-five years?" Ignatius's tone inches up an octave. "How old are you and what have you been doing all this time? Please tell me you're not in any kind of danger." The way her narrowed eyes bore into Væson with speed means she's expecting an answer. Væson holds up a hand in an attempt to dismiss her worry.

"I'm old enough to know better than to not answer the question about my age, but young enough to not have one of those senior discount cards your lot gives out. As for the danger part, well, that ties in with your second question. I've been held hostage by a couple of bad humans for a while, but I'm free now, which, as it turns out, has *kinda* put me in even more danger... I guess that's the price of freedom, *eh*?" they say with a sheepish shrug while levitating down into the seating opposite her.

"Not in any good world I know." She runs a hand through her hair, worry etched on her face for a being she barely knows. Her eyes and ears fixate on them, making sure to not miss a word as she sips more of her drink that's gone cold. But that's of no concern to her. She prefers her drinks cold—it's become a habit of hers, getting lost in other things and then remembering about a once warm drink only to discover it's now beyond lukewarm. It used to bother Ignatius, and she'd put it in the microwave to warm it back up, but it's never the same.

"I guess you haven't opened your eyes long enough, then. Your world is full of danger, and the freedom that comes with it," They say with an all too knowing tone heavy in their voice.

"All right, calm down, preachy. How serious is the danger, like on a scale of one to ten?" she asks, trying to lighten the mood.

"One to ten? That's a little silly. How is ten a dangerous number? Seven maybe, but that's about it," Væson says in what Ignatius assumes is a serious tone.

"Why is seven a dangerous number? Is it something to do with your home planet?"

"Didn't you know? It was in the news! Seven *eight* nine!" The corners of Væson's mouth twitches upwards, trying to keep a straight face, but it's too much. They burst into a good and hearty laughter; the full and true kind that comes deep from the gut as it rises up and spills out into the air. Ignatius scowls at first but then joins in. Alfie watches on with curious fascination. "It took me the longest time to understand that joke. Someone told me years ago," they say, reminiscing about one of the other good human interactions they've had.

"I have to ask, when you saw me earlier, you didn't know what language to speak?" Her tone pitches up in confusion, and her head lilts to the side, wanting and needing to know more.

THERE GOES THE NEIGHBORHOOD

"I can't just assume that everyone speaks the same language. Trust me, I've made that mistake before," they say.

Hearing this and knowing that Væson has been hurt by people of her species before for innocent mistakes makes her heart sag in her chest. Her eyes fill with tears that teeter on the edge of falling, but she composes herself. She hasn't felt this urge of protection since Aiden passed.

Væson turns their left forearm over and pushes their wrist with their right index finger. Almost instantly, their left arm lights up with miniature screens, a keyboard, and even a small clock.

"What in the world!" Ignatius's voice is on the cusp of breaking for a second.

"Oh yeah, my arm is like a supercomputer, too. Standard stuff for the species on my planet. I'm sure it will be on yours, someday. May be like 2042, though, so don't hold your breath. Trouble is, because I've been locked away so long, it's on the fritz a little. I need to let it re-boot or something." Their mind briefly drifts to their home planet and wonders if they are looking for them.

"When you said page, I thought you meant one of these." She grabs her small, black pager from the wooden sideboard behind the booth she's sitting on. Væson looks at it, takes it in their hand, turns it over, and laughs.

"I... What in the— Do you throw it at people? Is that how it works?" Væson twirls it in their hand and tries to push the buttons.

"Give it here!" She snatches it back. "This device, I'll have you know, works by... well, it just works, ok? Trust me, when all else fails, you can count on a pager," she finishes as she clutches it to her chest protectively.

"You two need some alone time, or?" Væson asks with a raised eye. Ignatius squints her vibrant, viridescent eyes at Væson. How strange it is, she thinks, that she's more at ease around an alien than she's ever been around her neighbors. It's almost like Væson is an old friend, a kindred spirit, that she's been searching for. Perhaps a cosmic force is responsible for bringing them together. The notion is a soothing balm to her chest. Whatever it is, Ignatius is glad for having met the little blue ball of energy.

The supercomputer on Væson's forearm beeps into life, letting them know that a diagnostic check has been taken and the reboot was successful.

Væson taps away at their forearm, and Ignatius notices that none of the letters on the alien's arm are ones she's ever seen before; it is quite literally an alien language. After a few moments, Væson declares that the message has been sent, and that it will take a couple of hours for it to reach them. Væson tells her that they let their planet know they're safe. They would have told her anyway, but her eyes looked like they were going to plop from her tiny human skull if she wasn't told right away. Væson doesn't mind, though. She's the first human they've ever trusted, thanks to most of the other ones trying to torture them, so the bar is pretty low. Hell, she's the first human they've seen not in an authoritarian uniform for many years.

She makes Væson a cup of cocoa. By the look on their face, it's the first hot drink that has passed those strange lips and mouth in a long time, and their eyes, those big, strange eyes, look heavy with heartache and sorrow. Ignatius knows there and then that she would do anything to protect this other-worldly being. What's more, she feels it's her duty.

Chapter 6

July 1947 - The Alien's Crash Landing

The central console lights up like a Christmas tree as soon as the asteroid strikes their ship. Væson's head hits the window, then the array of screens and levers, knocking them in and out of a state of semi-consciousness. The co-pilot, Jenson, is left to man the ship single-handedly. The ship makes a plethora of sounds, all of them bad. It veers from side to side, hitting more asteroids in its path. Smoke billows from the back, and Jenson holds onto the steering sphere for dear life - trying desperately to steer the ship back on course - but it's all in vain. The ship collides into more asteroids, as if they were a pinball in a machine which wreak havoc on their once trust ship.

Smoke from the cracked console clouds Væson's vision. The ship's computer glitches and warning alarms blare as an electronic onboard assistant sputters something in Morknolian.

Væson's vessel recalculates, flashing emergency coordinates.

"Earth." The soulless voice of the onboard assistant announces in what feels like desperation.

More alerts and stats flash across the ship's screens.
"Earth: Surface Livable
Status: Hostile
Species: Primitive
Cloaking Shield: Activated."

"Klargën! Klargën! Klaaaaargën!" Jenson screams into the emptiness of the ship. It's an old Morknolian word for *shit.*

"New target found. Emergency coordinates activated. Brace for impact of planet called E.A.R.T.H. Warning: Planet extremely hostile. Primitive species. Proceed with caution. Activating ship's cloaking device." The onboard assistant says the word 'Earth' with extreme caution, sounding out each letter to make sure the pilots hear.

The mission was supposed to be simple. The asteroid belt wasn't even meant to be here. Jenson and Væson have done this route a million times and can do it in under seven parsecs, having found a shorter way than most. The mission was an uncomplicated watch and observe one, much like they have done before. They were scoping out a nearby planet to see if it was advisable to do a trade deal with them. Jenson isn't sure what went wrong first: the navigation or the ship itself, which is an old and cantankerous thing, anyway, and is certainly due for an upgrade to the new, deluxe model that the rest of the trade advisers have. Jenson and Væson are very much attached to 'Betty', though, and refuse to give it up or trade it in. It was one of the very first things they had bought together as crewmates. They picked it up from a planet that specializes in recycled junk. The planet in particular smelled like microwaved eggs and looking at the place, you'd think it was where the rest of space dumped their unwanted goods. It was one of the very first times Jenson and Væson had visited a planet together, and they saw everything through rose tinted glasses. When they clapped eyes on the rust bucket, all they saw was potential; much like first time buyers of a house who are blind to all the cracks and how strenuous the re-build will be. When Jenson saw it, their mouth opened and formed a perfect 'o' shape.

"It's beautiful!" they said, rushing over to it; Væson, hot on their heels, agreed with the sentiment. The words on the side were faded with age and years of travelling through hyperspace. The only legible letters were 'B.E.T.T.Y', and that's where the name came from. Inside the ship, there was more dilapidation that they didn't see. The seat cushion's padding was leaking out the top, and the dashboard was cracked. The harnesses in the cargo container were threadbare, and the kitchen needed a complete remodel as every single cupboard door was off its hinges. Over time, they had fixed most of the things - the urgent ones, anyway. They forgot to fix the pilot's chair, though, which inevitable would be a costly mistake. When the ship was parked in the bays at the offices, it stuck out like a thumb with puss oozing from the sides. Some of the higher ups don't take too kindly to this as they think the ship gives the company a bad image. One in particular, a long-jowled, hard-faced M.O.R.K citizen called Flagant, one of the heads of the company they work for, took umbrage with the ship, and them too, and set about teaching them a lesson. Flagant covered their tracks because if this indiscretion is found out, their head would be put on a spike in front of the Capital building; much like all the fates of the traitors. For a peaceful planet, this is an extreme action and has always been a last resort, after a lengthy and detailed trial process.

Jenson looks over to their long-time co-pilot and best friend and manages to kiss Væson's forehead. Standard protocol is to make sure your co-pilot is safe. Jenson does just that with the swipe of a button, activating a protective shield. The bluish, transparent bubble makes a whooshing sound as it cocoons around Væson. On Earth, humans would mistake it for a jelly-like substance. Now that their co-pilot is safe, they deftly move their hand to their own switch. Jenson is not at all surprised to find that the bubble shield for their chair is broken. Panic attacks their chest, but they do not show it on their face. It would be a dishonor to panic in such a situation, and worse, to leave Væson, their co-pilot and best friend, with the image of their fear as a final memory. Instead, they look over to Væson and smile.

"*Gaboe.*"

Not being able to do a single thing to help their friend hurts Væson more than any physical pain could ever achieve. They try to stretch a hand out to Jenson with one of their final bits of strength, but the seat belt and the bubble shield restrict them so they are agonizingly out of reach. Then they finally drift into unconsciousness.

Somewhere in the distance, more alarms go off, more smoke fills the ship making it harder and harder for Jenson to breathe, and Jenson thinks they hear a strange singing sound but can't decipher where it is coming from. It's the sound of females singing about a thing they call a 'sandman', and Jenson wishes that the dream they bring is a happy one.

Væson awakes a good few hours later, their eyes blurry, shifting around the unfamiliar, cold room. They have never felt coldness like this before and manage to look down to find the clothes they were wearing have been stripped from their body and replaced with just a thin, white sheet. The room is small. Too small, and there isn't a window in sight.

"*Slum? Sluuum? Slum...*" Væson calls out in desperation. The words echo in the room and sound unfamiliar and unwelcoming.

Behind one of the walls is a two-way mirror, and on the other side are about fifteen scientists in white coats and clutching clipboards - when they hear their patient speak, they scrawl things down at lightning speed, desperately trying to decipher a meaning. There are some army personnel looking on in gawped fascination too - chests puffed out and arms behind their backs, watching this peculiar creature and straining their ears to try and hear what it's saying.

"What is it saying?" asks one of the smaller army men, curiosity filling his voice. His uniform hangs from his body, two sizes too big, his hands barley peeking out of the cuffs, and he has a face that looks like it's often found up the boss' ass.

"Sounds like some sort of S.O.S call to me," says a man with a thick white beard and crazed, curled hair, rightfully nick-named 'The Mad Scientist.'

"Make no mistake about it... that *thing* is a threat to our nation. To our people. We will find out what it wants, and we will find out what it knows. Proceed with extreme caution, but don't go easy on it. I want to see what color it bleeds," a man says in a harsh voice, void of all emotion. He is known around these parts simply as '*The Boss*': a man with a gruff, harsh voice that can be hard to understand, but no one has ever dared to ask him to repeat himself mostly because he has a physique reminiscent of a brick shithouse. Standing at 6ft5, his intimidating glower sends fear down the spines of anyone unfortunate enough to find themselves under the scrutiny of those piercing blue eyes. He scrapes a deeply tanned hand through his standard crew cut and growls under his breath. *God help the alien*, the mad scientist thinks, *it doesn't stand a chance*. And he's right. The Boss is ready to tear the thing limb from limb for pleasure disguised as 'National Security.' Anything could be covered up with those two words. Even murder. He's killed many a man, even women, in cold blood—once just for sneezing on him, and never has he faced a single charge. How he loves his job.

The boss pushes a button on the desk and a door *whooshes* open. He enters the room with the alien, standing above the strange, cerulean colored creature as the door closes behind him. The Boss looks at the fear in the alien's eyes and smirks. He walks over slowly to the captured creature, savoring every echo of his footfalls.

The alien tries to sit up but can't, due to the iron shackles around their arms and legs, and frighteningly around their neck, too, restricting any and all movements. They swallow, hard. Every movement is met by a clank of the metal, making Væson even more uneasy.

"*Myid?*" The alien asks as the human comes within an inch of their face. It's a word that means help, but Væson isn't sure this man speaks M.O.R.K. In fact, they have no clue where this place is or where Jenson is, for that matter.

"Are you threatening me, you little shit?" The Boss mocks, standing over the frightened Væson, who looks up at the man's imposing frame and tries to shrink away, but the metal chains pull them back forcefully to the hard wire bedframe; it doesn't even have a mattress, and when they are forced back onto the springs, one of them pierces their skin. Luckily, it doesn't bleed. The Boss watches this with glee—seeing pain on the faces of others makes him tingle all over.

The alien's brain quickly analyzes the speech pattern, translates it, and downloads all of the words in the correct language.

"No...No... I was asking for help," Væson panics.

"So you *can* talk English... you were being an ignorant little fuck and refusing to speak the language you fled to. Well, let me tell you, this is AMERICA. Here we speak ENGLISH!"

"Isn't that a little confusing for you?" Væson asks before their brain has time to tell them it's a bad idea – *stupid,* in fact.

"A smart guy then, eh? Let's see how smart you are when I gut you like a fish!" The Boss says, but with his accent, fish sounds more like 'feesh'.

"Like a feesh?" Væson asks, confused.

"Feesh! F.I.S.H."

"Ooooh, a *fish*. Sorry, your accent is hard to understand." Their strange eyes look up to the hulking human with honesty and pain but most of all, with worry. Their words continued to bounce off the walls and echo round the room. It makes them uncomfortable, but they tried their damnedest to not let it show.

The Boss balls up his fist and punches Væson in the left eye twice in quick succession. The sound is dull and decisive, as human flesh meets the squishy big eyes of the alien. He goes to punch them in the right eye but pulls back, making Væson flinch. More springs dig into their body, and they try not to wince in pain.

"How's that for hard to understand?"

Væson stays quiet.

"Exactly what I thought. Now... Where are you from?" He waits a moment before asking the next question, making sure he gives the alien enough time to answer. "What do you want from us? And if you bullshit me, trust me, I'll know, and you'll regret it." His words bounce off the walls, somehow making the room feel smaller. He's already been embarrassed once by this thing and is damn sure to not let it happen again.

Væson swallows hard and realizes this thing in front of them means business. If they are to get out of here alive, it would be best to cooperate.

Væson, alone with this hulking human, is scared beyond measure, but with all the resilience they can muster, they try not to let it show on their face. They wonder what would happen to them if he found out about all their neat abilities and the technology they have on the ship. Hell, just the knowledge alone would advance this primitive species a couple hundred years. The need to cooperate and the need to stay alive battle in their head, weighing all the pros and cons. For now, the alien concludes it's best to listen and absorb all the information that is thrown at them, and when the time is right, run.

Chapter 7

The Secret Neighbor

The bright sunlight rushes into the grand living room, painting every inch of it the rare hue of aureate, making everything it touches drip in opulence. It disturbs Ignatius from her unusual sleeping position on her black leather couch. The hot material snatches at her skin greedily. She looks around to see if her visitor - it's probably too early to say *friend*- is still here and is relieved to find them sound asleep on the dark green fabric armchair. It was one of the first items she and Aiden bought together, and she can't bear to part with it even though it doesn't go with her updated color scheme of black, white, and gray accents in the living room. The TV is on quietly in the background, and some early morning news program spouts unimportant nonsense.

She gets up from the sofa and heads to the kitchen to prepare breakfast for them both, pulling a pink floral satin robe around her, when a thought dawns on her: *What kinda food does he... they eat? Eggs and bacon?*

"I love eggs and bacon. Count me in," replies Væson, sitting up.

"How did you... Oh, right. Remind me to never think of anything overly personal in front of you." Ignatius pours water into the coffee pot and opens the fridge to retrieve the eggs and bacon, putting them in two separate frying pans.

"I certainly will not. I gotta have at least some fun." Væson grins as they levitate beside her in the kitchen.

"I just won't think ever again, then."

"Do that, and you'll be President within a month," Væson jests.

Ignatius levels them with a look, which quickly turns into laughter. She finds it hard not to laugh with this strange being around her. Her life has been soulless parties and endless men since her husband died. Neck deep in depression, parties and destructive behavior have been the imperfect antidote. No one seems to care about your feelings if you're throwing them a party they'll never forget or supplying them with free alcohol. Equally, no one seems to be around when the times get too real or too tough for them - moving onto the next socialite with tons of money like the party leeches they are. Ignatius has seen many friends come and go. Come when the parties are loud and go when she wants to talk about her fraying mental health. The parties she throws now, there is hardly anyone she recognizes. They are all perfect strangers. Even the people in her gated community—save for a small handful—are strangers to her. This is why she has built up a brick wall, so people can't hurt her anymore. She knows this is unhelpful, but she's at peace with that. That's what she tells herself, anyway, in an effort to keep the waves of crippling loneliness away.

While Ignatius and Væson eat breakfast and chat about life on M.O.R.K-78, The Captain is blowing gaskets left, right, and center in The Facility, and Carol is at her net curtains, peering through the gap, keeping an eye on the neighborhood events. She's already called Darren Rose at gate security about Janey not putting her bins out in time for collection. That was none of Darren's concern, but Carol told him nonetheless and went on about it incessantly for a good fifteen minutes. Carol would have gone on even longer had he not interrupted her saying he had an emergency. It's an excuse he's used before, and each time, it sends excitement down her body. She always asks what kind of emergency, but his reply is always *'Need to know'*, which increases her excitement. She has a phone tree, and within minutes, the whole neighborhood is ablaze with news of an emergency in sleepy Poppy Field Lane. No one ever doubts the truth of what she says, even though there is never any evidence, as no one wants to get on the wrong side of her. She is the head of all organized events—excluding the ones organized by the neighborhood rebel, Ignatius. The last person to cross Carol was August-Lynn Barrett, the shy housewife of respected doctor and owner of the local medical practice, Doctor Kent Barrett. August had forgotten to R.S.V.P. to an event in a timely manner, so she was put on litter duty for the next three social events of the season. What Carol didn't know was that she was battling with depression after a miscarriage, and the last thing she wanted to do was go to yet another socialite fete that put money into the coffers of one of Carol's many events. August had plenty of ways in which she could R.S.V.P., and all of them involved balling them up and shoving them somewhere the sun was less likely to shine.

Once Carol finishes with her phone tree and alarmist duties for the day, she goes into what she calls her *"control room"*, which is where she keeps track of every single member of the community. Many years from now, it would go against all privacy acts, but not in the 90s and not in Poppy Field Lane. There are two steel filing cabinets in one corner of the room detailing each person's infringements, their likes, dislikes, how many times they have volunteered for things, and what jobs they have. On the main wall is a huge map of Poppy Field, and each member has been assigned a colored pin that marks the location of their house. Ignatius's pin is black and not as pristine as the others. The edges of the pin look like they have been chewed a little.

At the far end of the room, surrounded by a bay window, is an old oak desk with sheafs of papers and documents and plans for any and all eventuality. You can say a lot about Carol, and people do, but you can't say she doesn't care about her little slice of heaven... even if her form of care is borderline neurotic.

I gnatius has heard the rumors of Carol's den of perceived inequity and wondered, with great amusement, what color pin she would use for Væson and then panic strikes her... What is going to happen when the neighborhood finds out about her little blue friend? There is no way she can keep Væson a secret, but also, she may just have to.

"If you're worrying about me being discovered, don't be. I've got it covered," Væson says, dragging Ignatius out of her thoughts again. She'd been moving the last pieces of her food around the plate with her fork, and the sound of the scraping was starting to jar Væson's nerves.

"Ok, new rule, or reaffirming the rule: don't read my mind please." It comes out a little sharper than intended, and Ignatius tries on a tight-lipped smile to soften her words; but Væson doesn't notice or mind.

"No can do, sorry. Can't help it. My brain is like a huge radio signal, and thoughts are just attracted to it." Væson shrugs and smiles.

There is just the egg yolk left on Væson's plate. They wash the meal down with two cups of coffee—something Væson hasn't had before and now thinks is the greatest invention the humans have ever made. They even tried to eat the coffee beans raw as if they were smarties but quickly discovered that was perhaps the worst idea they'd had in a rather long time.

"Got a straw?" Væson asks, levitating above the chair.

"What on earth would you want a straw for?" she asks, perplexed.

"To suck up the yellow thing on the plate, of course."

"...I'm not even gonna ask. Top cupboard, left side behind the sauces." Ignatius sits back in the wooden chair, wondering what her alien guest is actually going to do.

"Saucer? How'd one of them fit in that teeny tiny cupboard? Perhaps I've underestimated the technology here," Væson ponders.

"Sauces, as in ketchup and mayonnaise. Goodness me, you don't get out much, do you?" she asks, not realizing at all the harrowing conditions Væson has been kept under for so long.

"I get around," Væson says coyly.

Væson opens the cupboard and gets a plastic red and white striped straw out, closes the cupboard, then brings the bendy piece of plastic over to the egg yolk and sucks it up, all without lifting a finger. They send the straw around the whole plate, slurping up every last bit of food. Once there is no more, they drop the striped tube and let out a good, hearty belch; the smell of the smoked bacon and egg yolk hangs in the air for a moment or two.

"Feeling better, are we?" Ignatius asks in a bemused yet slight awestruck tone.

"Much." They pat their stomach, and another burp passes

their lips, which garners a look from Ignatius that's half amusement and half shock—due to the loudness of the burp. It sounded like a car backfire in an alleyway.

"Right, now the fun part..." Ignatius says, a smile blooming on her face, revealing all their pearly white teeth that wouldn't look out of place in Hollywood.

"Fun part?" Væson asks.

"Yep, I cooked, so you get to clean up."

"*Pah*, that's easy. But I would be hesitant to use the word fun," Væson says. "There's no way you can have fun with anything for less than five minutes."

"Oh, I can think of a few things." Ignatius says to herself and smiling- thinking of a memory of her Aiden, this one bringing a warmth to her instead of the usual sadness.

Within seconds, the faucets are running in the sink, the smell of the apple and cherry washing liquid filling their noses. The bowl is filled with suds, and the items used to cook are dancing their merry way around the kitchen to be washed. The whole process takes no more than three minutes, including the drying and putting away. Væson conducts it all like an orchestral conductor of Swan Lake. Childhood memories of Fantasia rush back to Ignatius, and another piece of her heart warms to them for rekindling a wonderful memory of a simpler, happier time.

"Right! From now on, you're on that duty. That was incredible!" Ignatius leans back in her chair, eyes wide open and mouth slightly ajar.

"You should see what I can do with a hoover." Væson hovers up and off their seat excitedly.

"Why, are you as quick!?" Still processing what she's witnessed. Ignatius sits back in her chair and runs a hand through one of her golden curls.

"I dunno, never tried it, but you should see it." Væson smiles, tossing her a wink.

"Wait, was that meant to be sexual?" She laughs and gets up from the table, the food resting heavy in her stomach. She can still taste the egg yolk and streaky smoked bacon on her tongue and chases them down with her still warm coffee. The sunlight is fully breached now, making its way through the huge French Patio doors. With the doors open as they are this morning, waves of sea air waft into the kitchen, lingering with the other smells, but the sea air is most certainly the more dominate being as the house is so close to the beach. It often leaves a salty taste in her mouth that she's long gotten used to.

"What, no! What is it with humans and taking winks as sexual? Is this sexy to you?" Væson winks again, the eyelid on their left eye opening and closing sideways like automatic doors in a supermarket.

"Well, not *that*, but here, on Earth, yeah, winks are meant to be flirty."

"You're all a bunch of weirdos."

"Oh really? Well, what constitutes as flirting on M.O.R.K-78?"

"Chocolate starfishing, dur.. What it is, is you pull down your pants, bend ov—"

"*Woah*, okay, no thank you! I'm good. I got the visual! Thanks for that!"

"You sure? It's very romantic!" Their eyes enlarge with the romancing of the memory and a smile stretches across their face.

A bit of sick rises in Ignatius's mouth, and she leaves the room.

"See, turned you right on, that has!" Væson laughs.

Ignatius doesn't know nor care to know if Væson was joking about this, but it reminds her of how dogs greet each other, and that summons another visual and another wave of nausea.

8

Chapter

Væson's Past

The first time Væson escaped the clutches of The Facility was back in the 60s, and it lasted all of seven months before The Facility caught up with them.

For weeks, Væson had been monitoring the goings-on of the place, logging when people started and finished their shifts and documenting their weaknesses, all in their supercomputer of a mind. Væson also managed to build up a tolerance to whatever drugs they were pumping into them.

For years, Væson assisted them with advancing their technology and gave them detailed information about other life in other solar systems, even going into detail about which ones were hostile and which ones were friendly. This didn't exactly break intergalactic law, but it was a close line, and Væson was careful not to cross it. The trouble is, there is an old saying, "more often wants more" - which in essence means the more you have, the more you want, and The Facility had an insatiable appetite for power and control.

The hardest part of it all was not being able to communicate with their family back home, as the last thing Væson wanted was for them to know anything about their family or any personal details. And they were eternally glad they had not told them about Jenson... But they also worried that The Facility hadn't brought them up either, but those are thoughts for another day. It was hard for Væson to imagine Jenson being tortured and information being extracted from them. It was one of the thoughts that kept them awake at night. thinking their best friend was so close and yet being so far away at the same time. Another thought often chased that one - and that was the one they didn't care to think about - they didn't want to think that their best friend was dead. That The Facility had pushed too far and killed them. No If they were to get out of this they would think only positive thoughts about Jenson and hope against hope that they were just fine - maybe living their best life on a beach somewhere - Jenson always loved the beach - any planet they went to, they always made time to sit and stare at the ocean and build tiny flying saucers from the sand.

The only thing they revealed about themselves was the fact they could levitate, and the members of The Facility soon found out about their ability to regenerate cells at a rate they had never seen before. For a small mercy, they actually put this information to good use, and thanks to Væson's blood and DNA, there have been a plethora of medical advances, most of which would have still been lightyears away if it had not been for Væson. However, they were deeply afraid of what The Facility was up to in regard to all the other information. Thank goodness The Facility knew nothing about alien weaponry.

Whenever The Boss got frustrated, he would take it out on Væson. He found it more satisfying than hurting animals and other humans because Væson just took the pain and punishment no matter how deep the blades went in or how tight the chains were or how long they deprived them of food and water. These were exclusive testings that only The Boss was privy to. Once or twice, Væson felt as if they were on the very brink—

they had gone a week with no more than a few glasses of water and scraps of food. They were only kept alive because they were still useful. It was in those long, delirium filled moments that Væson could have sworn they had heard Jenson calling out to them, guiding them to stay away from the bright light, willing them to go on and find some inner strength.

Væson's escape happened so fast, it was a blink-and-you-miss-it kind of deal, *and they blinked*. Within moments, Væson was breathing fresh air, and The Facility were fumbling with their asses, trying to figure out who to blame first and which lamb to send to the slaughter. It would be an hour before the whole Facility knew what had happened, and the culprit's head would be rolling shortly thereafter.

The adrenaline of the escape lasted all of five minutes for Væson before it turned into panic. They were on an alien planet, with no defense or direction. The only thing on their mind was finding the ship and Jenson. Væson refused to think that anything had happened to them; they had been knocked out when the shields went up, kind of like a built in safety measure of the ship. They had been best friends since birth, and in some circles on this planet, they would also be considered partners.

Sand kicked up into their face, forming a kind of bulwark with their arms to protect their eyes and mouth made things a little more bearable. They had no idea how dangerous the golden grains were. After walking and levitating for what felt like hours, Væson stumbled across some sign of life. They were instantly drawn to the colors, and it made a welcome change from the industrial grey they had been seeing for years on end. Back in school, they had one brief topic on distant planets, and one of them was Earth. It was spoken about in hushed, fearful tones. There was also laughter in those voices, as they were thought to be primitive creatures with huge anger issues. Of course, there were the TV shows they watched, which contradicted this. Væson was fascinated by those, and they always wondered what life would be like living with a nice human family.

Væson did their best to blend in and transformed into a human around the age of twenty-two. With a finely cut jaw line, a tangle of black hair, an immaculate black suit, and velvet bow tie, they looked stunning and ready for business. Entering the busy street with huge signs and flashing lights, there was an assortment of structures and adverts, all saying the same thing and offering promises of riches. Although the paths were wide, they were still teaming with humans, all minding their own affairs to notice or care they were in the presence of an extraterrestrial. There was an electric energy in the air, which Væson loved and was instantly drawn to. Væson made their way into one of the buildings and was instantly accosted by a large man in a suit and dark shades on his eyes. Væson thought the man looked like a walrus wearing a suit.

"What are you doing here!" The man shouted, a bit of spittle flying out of his mouth and almost onto Væson's cheek.

"I... I..." was all Væson could manage, their wide alien eyes expanding in shock; a memory came back to them from when they were at school and the teacher announced there was an impromptu test. They had panicked so much, they asked to be excused from class. That wasn't an option today, though, so they inhaled deeply and tried their best to act as human as they possibly could. *It's showtime,* they say to themselves to psych themselves up.

"Get to your table, people are waiting. Time is money! Go! Go! Go!" Spittle flew from the man's mouth and landed on Væson's lapel. They stared at it, almost longingly. When the man was out of sight, Væson wiped it with their finger and licked it.

Time is money.... That's a new one. Is it really money? Do the humans really do transactions with time? Strange things.

Inside the building, they were greeted with a wall of pande-monium—from lights and sounds to cheers of jocundity which was swiftly followed by cries of agony and despair. Væson could feel it all; it radiated off the humans like a pulse and reverber-ated their core.

Væson eventually made their way to the croupier table, weaving in and out of the brainless crowd. They observed some of them sitting on stools and pulling on leavers while lights flashed in their eyes. Some of them bent down and scooped up some money from the bottom - *oh, they must be time coins!* Væson thinks and is immediately pleased for the winner. Others moved on, then the stool was taken by someone else who pulled the lever and was rewarded by sounds and lights and the drop of even more coins. They watched others at more tables, too, all with different expressions on their faces but all dressed immaculately. They asked someone who had a similar attire to them where *the table* was, and they were directed to a man waving his arms. Væson made their way to them and apol-ogized to the humans for their absence. They scanned the human brains for the rules, and it was instantly downloaded into their memory banks. The large man in the suit, who was not unlike the walrus man at the door, watched for a moment, then moved off. No one seemed to notice Væson wasn't human. Blending in was easier than they expected, and within days, Væson became one of the most popular croupiers, even learning how to do card tricks and extravagant shuffles.

Within weeks, they made that particular Casino the most popular one on the strip, and no matter how many people sat at their table, not one of them mentioned the strange eyes or the way they blinked. They were following the money and, as they say, money talks. Væson got good at schmoozing with the patrons and became familiar with the regulars.

Væson also began to imitate how they spoke and how they dressed, too, even going as far as wearing different wigs and dressing up as a *teddy boy* when out of their work attire—the British invasion of culture was alive and well in this little bubble of the United States. During their downtime, they played the piano in the local jazz clubs and were also known to sing, too, all by reading a couple of books and watching a few pros. Væson's mind was the most absorbent of sponges, and they longed to entertain and make the good people happy.

However, one of their favorite things to do wasn't the jazz clubs where they sang or dressing up as a teddy boy with some people they knew, but it was again exploring their feminine side and dressing up as a flapper girl. They had seen them on stage one night, utterly transfixed by their feather dresses and strange bonnets on their heads. What they loved most was their confidence. One night, while in female form, they went behind the curtain after one of the shows and straight up asked them if they could join in. The woman put her hand on her hips, pursed her lips and said, "Come back tomorrow and let me see what you got." The very next day, they did just that. They turned up early, and the stick thin woman once again looked at Væson's curves with an evil grin that was missed by Væson. The woman, whose name turned out to be Daniella, had come from Russia many years ago and built up a mini dancing empire in the desert. Daniella had assembled the rest of the dance troop to watch what was about to unfold; but they had no idea what they were about to witness. Væson stepped onto the stage, a single spotlight their only company, and for a moment, they hugged their body, feeling like too many eyes were on them. Then they took a deep breath, looked down at their emerald green feather dress—they wanted black or white but couldn't find one on such short notice—and then looked directly at Daniella who was dead center in the auditorium, hands on hips. She had a face that looked like she sucked lemons for a living.

"Well, are you going to dance or are you going to stand

there like fat swan?" She was smiling, but her words were ice cold, and it took a moment for Væson to realize Daniella wasn't being too friendly.

Væson, who had stayed up all night studying the fine art of dance, started slow, and when the band behind them kicked in, they decided to step it up a notch. Daniella's jaw hung from her face, and her eyes were utterly transfixed. She was perplexed and ever so slightly jealous at how light on their feet they were, but the dollar signs appeared in their eyes. She knew right then that a star was born and she was going to be the one to nurture it.

When the audition was over, Væson made their way to the edge of the stage and sat down, feeling out of breathe.

"So, was I ok?"

"You will do. But more training is needed. You will need to work harder than you have ever done before." She said with her arms folded and barley glancing at her newest star. Daniella came from the school of tough love and it had paved the way for her own success and saw no reason to not dish it out on others too - it was her form of saying 'you're accepted.'

It didn't take long for Væson to become accepted by the dance troupe, and Daniella even softened on them. She felt a sense of protection over them. They began to spend more and more time with the dance company. If they had done this from the get-go, things may have turned out slightly differently.

Leading a double life as both a male and a female human was hard, testing work, and they found out that they were treated extremely differently depending on which gender they were. They were fully engrossed in both versions of themselves, and it was part of the reason why they forgot to communicate home as often as they should have... If you can count once being often, that is. Their communicator had told them they hadn't received the message yet, anyway, but they didn't think to check if it was a fault on their own end or their home planet's.

While they were on stage, all their troubles melted away, and they got complacent. And that was where it all went downhill...

The owners moved Væson from the croupier table to black-jack, and that was where they became a real star because they injected so much energy into each play. Væson had more money than they knew what to do with, so they decided to rent an apartment and stash it in the walls. The apartment was under the name of Bruce Parker, which was the alien alias they gave themselves. It paid homage to two of their favorite comic book characters. Things were going swimmingly until they decided to advertise 'The Amazing Bruce Parker' outside the casino. Not long after that, The Boss got word of it; one too many of his staff were bragging all too loudly about actually 'meeting' this great magician. The Boss turned green with envy and decided to take a look, since the amount of buzz a simple worker was creating was a huge red flag. They weren't like the usual celebrity magicians that were a dime a dozen in Vegas, or so it seemed, anyway. Besides, The Boss felt a sense of betrayal from his staff. He was meant to be one they cooed over and respected, not some magician in a casino. The Boss had become frustrated that the staff at The Facility had been stumbling in blind drunk most of the time, and when he demanded to know where they had been, they simply said, "the best casino on the strip" before resting their weary heads on the desk.

The Boss had staked out the casino they were all on about one evening. It was easy, really. It was the only table in the joint that had a huge line. He didn't recognize his little blue bastard at first as they were disguised as a human - but he had spent long enough with the creature to know its mannerisms - espe-cially the way their eyes blinked - it was like he was like he was the only one who could see through the finely crafted facade. Once he identified Væson, he waited for the escaped prisoner to finish their shift, then pulled a black bag over Væson's head in the alleyway and shoved a six-inch needle in the alien's neck. Væson's arms pinwheeled for a moment before their colourful world faded to black.

Within the hour, Væson was once again an unwilling resident of The Facility, dosed up on toxins—new ones that they weren't immune to yet. Stuck in a room that wasn't fit enough to be a regulation jail cell, Væson sat on the end of their bunk and cried. Not because of where they were, but for the freedom they'd lost. Væson vowed to get out again and again and make something of their life while stuck on this planet... There was a real possibility that their stay here on Earth was to be indefinite.

But the odds were on Væson's side, and the house always wins.

Væson wiped the tears from their periwinkle eyes while The Boss inconspicuously looked on. When Væson smiled, it sent a shiver down his spine.

It was not the first time Væson had been captured and held against their will. It had happened once before, back on their home planet. But at least on M.O.R.K-78, they didn't torture them and actually gave them edible sustenance.

Chapter 9

Ignatius's Cousin

After Ignatius discovered Væson's power of transformation, the two of them decided to tell the neighborhood Væson is her cousin. There is no way they could keep an alien secret in this town. Some towns have secrets, this one has none... well, now it has a big one.

"Ok, this is great and all, dressing up like one of your cousins, but surely someone is gonna point out my eyes. We're not in Vegas anymore... or California, for that matter, we're in Upstate New York."

"Vegas or California? The saying is Kansas, and here I was thinking you were smart," she jests.

"They are stories for another time. And you're talking about that book with the girl who murders a witch's sister, right? Lovely horror book. I read it back in the 80s."

"That's not a horror book! It's a classic," she says a little defensively as she tends to feeding the impatient Alfie who is tap dancing with his big paws on the kitchen floor.

"Oh really? And everything I just said, that's not a horror? Again, humans are weird."

"You're twisting the truth of a book aimed at children," she argues, exasperated.

"You read that to kids?" Væson whistles while moving their index finger in a circle around their temples.

"Anyway, forget that. You're my cousin from... just out of state. I picked you up last night, late, and Darren didn't see you because you were asleep in the back seat. Sound good so far?"

"Yeah, sounds good to me. Ohh! Can I be an eccentric cousin, one who is still grieving the loss of their wife so they do extravagant things and just say crazy shit for the sake of it?"

"No. I think you should be mute," she says, a little more forcefully than intended. There is no way Væson meant to draw parallels with her own life, but it hurt like wiping lemon juice on a papercut.

"Mute? You can't silence my golden words and winning personality. Bruce Parker shall never be silenced!" Væson exclaims dramatically, then ponders for a moment. "Actually, Bruce Parker should be silenced. That name, it's too high risk. I'll just use your last name and my name. We can say it's foreign or something. From what I've seen here, the people don't seem to be all that smart."

"Væson Feltrap it is, then. By the way, there are a few smart people here." Væson raises an eyebrow at that statement. "Well, semi-intelligent," she corrects, trying to sound nice. "Ok, some of them won't be bringing home any awards." She pauses, feeling exasperated. "Fine... if most of them had another brain cell, it would die of loneliness."

Væson crosses their legs while levitating and meows, pretending to claw the air.

"My, my, aren't we catty... I love it!" Væson laughs.

"On a serious note, though, I've already warned you about Carol, but I'm warning you again. That woman is crazy!"

"I *do* like crazy."

"Not this kind, you won't," Ignatius says.

"Why? Don't tell me, don't tell me," they say, coming down from their levitating position and sitting back on the wicker kitchen chair in the corner. "Let me guess, you 'stole,'" they say this bit with air quotes as they aren't too sure if it's real or not, "her husband, and she blames you for his death and for taking her out of the wildly inflated inheritance."

"You know, I would have been impressed if you didn't read my mind... but yes, that's why she hates me. However, not everything is as simple as that." She sits awkwardly in her chair, not wanting to recount this tale but feels it to be necessary. "Firstly, as you can see, I'm a lot younger that Carol. Aiden was, too. And technically, you can't steal something that the other person never had. She likes to make up her own version of events - and to keep myself guarded up, I, too, have locked away what really happened, but I can and will say with absolute sincerity that when I got with Aiden, Carol wasn't even in the picture." She nervously plays with a ringlet of her hair. Thinking about Carol is a nasty chore, and thinking about *her* with Aiden is like cyanide to her insides.

Væson pretends to protest about the mind reading but then says, "And you say she has the whole neighborhood by the balls? She really does sound like my kinda woman."

"Keep. Away. From. Her. That simple enough for you, space person?" she punctuates in slight annoyance. "Right. Let's see it then..."

"See what?" Væson asks, eyes moving down to their crotch.

She smacks a hand to her forehead. "Not *that*! I mean let's see Væson Feltrap."

"Oh, oh, ok, give me a sec. Hmm, let me see. Ah, yeah." Væson stands up and within seconds, their mysterious yet beautiful blue skin and strange, alien body morphs into a tall, tanned, blue-eyed stranger right before Ignatius's eyes. The sun that breaks in from the kitchen window adds a slight shine to their skin, as if they are made of brilliant diamonds.

"How do I look?" they ask, smiling with a normal set of teeth that are dazzling white.

"I...oh, my," is all she can say while staring back at their eyes, which are still Væson's but now they are set behind tanned skin and accented by light stubble and dusty brown hair. She is lost for words. "I mean, you were great before, but..."

"But you prefer this human form. I get it I get it," Væson says, dejected and hurt.

"No, no, it's not that! Honestly," she says, trying to convince herself and Væson.

"Listen, just save it, ok. I'm going to go for a walk and hopefully, when I come back, you won't be so prejudice." They get up, leave the kitchen, and head out the door before Ignatius can say anything.

She runs after them, and when she opens the front door to shout their name, she's grabbed by someone from the side. She screams, trying to peel away. When she finally does, she sees her assailant is laughing hysterically. When she realizes who it is, she punches them in the arm.

"You should have seen your face," Væson says, trying to hold back more laughter while tears are streaming out of their eyes.

"You're not funny, you know!" she shoots back, her lips curling up in a smile.

"Then why am I laughing?" Væson asks, clinging onto her for support.

"My, my, my... who is this handsome devil and why are you keeping him to yourself?"

The strange voice cuts through their laughter like an axe through butter, and they both swing around to see the face of Carol. Ignatius's smile turns into a frown. Carol stands at the bottom of the porch, one hand on the rail and moves slowly up - like a dung-beetle finding a new piece of shit. - except Væson was anything but shit - Carol on the other hand, the jury is still out.

"Not that it's any of your business, but this is my cousin, Væson. They'll be staying with me for a few weeks. They came in last night."

"Howdy ma'am, pleasure to meet you," Væson says in a southern accent.

Carol's face turns a bright red, and she lets out a flirtatious giggle and moves so close to them that her breath can be felt on their neck.

"Well, let me say that the pleasure is all mine." She slides Væson's hand into hers.

"Don't you have a husband?" Ignatius asks.

"Don't you have a place to be?" Carol claps back.

"Ladies, ladies, settle down. Carol, I am flattered, but I would never advance on a married woman. I'm sorry, but that's just how my momma raised me," they say with their smooth, southern drawl.

"Hmm... at least that makes *two* of us," she says while burning a hole into Ignatius.

Ignatius laughs a strange tin laugh with an emotionless face.

"Can I count on you to turn up to the events planning meeting later?" Carol asks, eyes still on Væson.

"You know I don't go to those," Ignatius says flatly.

"I was talking to Væson. Not everything is about you, honey," she says, looking her up and down like she was some filthy roadside attraction's trash.

"Oh, I, erm, don't think I'd be much use," Væson concedes, flashing a look to Ignatius for assistance.

"Nonsense! I'm sure you'll have valuable input," Carol insists, batting her eyes and giving her mouth a flirtatious pout.

"Well, if you insist—" Væson says. There's an uncomfortable aura surrounding Carol, but Væson can't quit put their finger on it. It feels like a box of wasps that has been shaken a couple hundred times.

Ignatius elbows Væson in the chest. "No, we're busy. Sorry." She attempts to shut the door, but Carol puts her florescent sneaker in the way.

"Not all day, surely. See you both at twelve. Don't be late. Ta-ta now, mwah, mwah!"

She skips off merrily in a ball of Lycra and luminous colors, leaving Ignatius and Væson dumfounded about what just happened.

Chapter 10

Væson and the Meeting

Væson, now in their human form, wearing acid wash jeans, black boots, a plain white t-shirt and hair pushed back with a red bandana, is almost vibrating with excitement as they enter the meeting room with Ignatius. She, on the other hand, hopes this ends quickly and without much fuss. Although dressed better than most with diamond earrings, pearl neckless, a blue blouse that comes off the shoulder, high waisted jeans, and maroon boots, Ignatius put money on the fact Carol would still have something spiteful to say behind her back.

She tells Væson not to get used to this with the side of her mouth but isn't sure they hear her because as soon as the two of them enter the room, everyone rushes over to greet them. News travels fast in this neighborhood, and even faster if the news is of an eligible bachelor walking around.

Væson does their best to listen to all, but they all insist on talking all over each other and it becomes a fruitless task.

"Alright, alright, let the newbie breath, ladies. We don't want to scare him off before he's made it four paces in the doorway," Carol says with a jarring smile. "I honestly don't know what gets into them sometimes. Come, take a seat at the front of the hall, you can bring your growth, I mean, Ignatius with you. Don't look so shy, not all of us bite." She holds their hand and weaves in and out of the crowd, managing to dodge the rueful look from Ignatius. She can't help but make the off-handed comments to her, and the constant tête-á-tête between her and Ignatius is what keeps her young – at least that's what she tells herself, anyway.

The hall drips with opulence and grandeur and is where a lot of the money goes. The walls are pure white with gold leaf accents, the chairs are white wood and some kind of satin, and in the corner stands a white piano that is seldom used - but is free from dust - the whole place is like a show home. At the front, where Carol does her talking, is a mini platform and white wood lectern with a poppy etched into it in full color. The red looks radiant against the pure white, as if it was on a soft bed of snow. Along one wall is a giant glass patio door and just beyond that is lush green grass and a fountain with white benches around it. Past that are interconnecting flower beds in the shape of a poppy. It is Carol's pride and joy, and no mercy extends to anyone who tampers with it or forgets to water it. She is the longest reigning chairwoman of the committee and has also gained the distinguished, and wholly made-up, title of Life President. Which means, even when she's not doing active duties later on in life, most of the things have to pass by her desk before they get approved. Not many people know that, but it's in the fine print that barely anyone reads. Throughout the years, she's made deep roots, and they'll be there long after she has gone. For all intents and purposes, she *is* Poppy Field Lane, and there's no way she is ever going to give it up.

Væson uncomfortably looks around and notices that all eyes are still on them, making them slouch deeper into their seat.

"Psst, can I ask you something?" Væson whispers.

"Suuure..." Ignatius replies hesitantly.

"Why hasn't anyone noticed my eyes? Not that I *want* them to notice - even though they're obviously stunning, but don't you think it's a little odd that not one person has mentioned that my eyes look, well, inhuman?"

"I wouldn't read too much into it. This whole town is self-centered. If they do mention them, though, just say it's a genetic thing... or you could just wear some jaunty sunglasses and say it's your thing?" she suggests with a shrug.

"Ladies, ladies... oh, and haha, *gentleman,* of course. Let's get this meeting started, shall we?" Carol bangs her gabble to get attention. Dressed like a husk of corn in a long, green dress, her brown hair representing the roots, completing the look. Today, she has chosen to wear bright red lipstick to match her bright red shoes, and there's a small red mark on her front tooth where the lipstick has smudged. She notices it in her compact before addressing the audience. "One can't always be perfect." She laughs off the small faux pas.

Væson is still slouched in their seat, knowing all eyes are still on them despite a new speaker in the room addressing everyone.

"Why are they still staring? Don't they all have husbands, or wives, or a murder hound or something?" they whisper.

"You're the new toy... I told you not to come here, but what do I know?"

"Not a lot, but more than some," Væson concludes with a shrug.

"Now's not the time to be a smartass, *cousin.*"

"It's always time to be a smartass, *cousin!*" they say in a southern drawl. One of the women behind them hears it and sighs longingly.

Ignatius shoots Væson a look that says more than any words could, and they take heed and close their lips.

"...So this year, I thought it would be delightful if we hosted a Grand Christmas Fair, one bigger than ever before. When people think Christmas, they will now think *Poppy Field Lane*. There'll be booths for you all, but make sure you sign up to the event you want quickly. No dilly dallying, or you'll be left with something rotten, and I'll have no sour faces at this event! We all know how important this event is for the neighborhood and how much money it brings in. It's also the only time of year where we let... *outsiders* in, but don't worry, as always, it'll be held both in here and on the central lawns, and no one will be able to wander to our houses. Darren and his team of experts has made that quite clear, so put your worries in a bottle and send them on their way." She punctuates this with a two-beat high pitched laugh.

This garners some intense chatter amongst the crowd. They haven't seen a fundraiser proposal like this in a long time, and a Christmas one to boot, well, that just put the cat among the turkeys.

Daniel Cummings is sat just in front of Væson and Ignatius and turns around to speak to them. His hair looks like auburn serpent coils as they swing from side to side in a comedic fashion. His green eyes are fixed on Væson's unique, inhuman ones.

"Nice to see another guy around here. Hi, I'm Daniel. Some call me Dan, others call me 'SmokeHouse Dad.'" He extends his chubby hand to Væson's faux human one and squeezes it in a manly handshake. Væson tries not to wince.

"Sorry, I've got a gamers grip!"

"Ooooh, good, I thought it was a wanker's muscle!" Væson quips, making Daniel laugh in a *heehaw*, breathy way. They don't entirely know what the word means and have only heard it a handful of times via one of the shows they watch... or used to watch back home. Sometimes, when they download all the words in a specific language, some words get lost to local vernacular.

"You're funny, new guy! We should game together some-time!" Væson decides not to correct Daniel on the improper use of the pronouns just yet but will do so if it continues to be an issue. They think about telling Carol this too - but already know it will be met with confusion and stern bristles - like a garden broom in the snow.

"As long as 'game' isn't a euphemism for something, you can count on it. I've been tricked by that before, and trust me, it's always awkward. Especially when the eye contact from the partner starts to linger a little too much."

"No, sir-y, I mean good old fashioned Game Boys and a battle... or six on the SNES with Mario Kart. I like to think of myself as the undisputed champ of that game but, seeing as there is no way to play against others in the world, there's no way to prove it. You'll just have to take my word for it."

"You just said a lot of words I don't actually understand, but all of them excited me sexually. Just putting it out there!"

Daniel *heehaws* again and grips Væson's arm in a friendly way.

"... As you are all aware," Carol continues from the stage, "Christmas is not only about giving, but about family and friendships. And let's not forget the man who started the tradi-tions, Christopher Claúse, way back in the small village many moons ago."

"Is she for real?" asks Væson in a conspirator tone, turning to Ignatius.

"She sure is. I think she has a shrine to him in her house," she replies in the same tone.

"Ohkay, then," Væson says in thin whisper.

Without any prior warning, Væson's arm vibrates and begins to flash in rhythmic patterns. They try to hide it as best as they can with their other hand. The sensation lasts for around thirty seconds, and it's not unpleasant, but it's certainly not human behavior.

"What the hell was that?" Ignatius asks them just above a whisper.

"You saw that?" Væson asks sheepishly.

"Uhm, yeah!" she says, quickly looking round in quick bursts to see if anyone else had seen it; she misses Daniel as they were too busy scraping their jaw off the floor.

"Do you think anyone else saw it?"

"Ooh, ooh, I did! Looks like you've got some gnarly tech under the hood," Daniel exclaims excitedly.

Væson waves his hand over Daniel's eyes. "You saw nothing." Sadly, Jedi mind control isn't in their wheelhouse of powers.

"What are you doing?" Ignatius asks.

"I'm improvising."

Daniel waves his hand over Væson's eyes and says, "Yeah I did, and it was cool, man. Hey, you gotta come to my house after this. I won't take no for an answer."

"What is it with you humans and your insistence on not taking no for an answer? Are you just taking it out of your dictionary now or something?"

The rest of the meeting goes by quickly, but Daniel's eyes are fixated on Væson's arm hoping it does that strange, inhuman thing again. If this was the future, they could pass it off as a new *body* feature—that's if it was noticed at all. Technology would have advanced so much that people would be more interested in a screen than the humans around them. For all they would know, aliens could already be among them, and in office, too, much like Vampires, but they wouldn't even know it as they wouldn't look farther than their screens. Perhaps this is why Væson is getting along with these humans so much. Back on M.O.R.K, as lovely and idyllic as it may be, there's very little connection. And it's this connection that Væson really craves, and what separates them from the rest of their home planet.

The people filter out of the meeting in drips and drabs, Væson and Ignatius leading the pack, hoping to give Daniel the slip.

"So, are you going to tell me what that was or...?" Ignatius asks as soon as they're breathing fresh, suburban air.

Væson rolls up their sleeve and sees there is 'one unread message' in green writing in their native language.

"I appear to have a message," Væson says.

"And? What does it say?" Ignatius shoves the words out of her mouth with feverish curiosity.

"One second, one second, no need to be so impatient," Væson replies with a smirk that they know will just wind Ignatius up.

Væson taps on their wrist and reads the message out loud:

Rumvæson,
Thank you for making contact with us from your location of Planet Earth.
Proceed with caution and continue to observe all events. This is your new mission.
The life of M.O.R.K.-78 are counting on you.
You can consider this a promotion, too.
We will now expect a minimum of two weekly check-ins.
We are sorry to hear of the loss of Jenson. Their family has been notified.
Until our next correspondence,
Œstegen

"Ok, that's exciting!" Væson says in a giddy tone.

Unknown to them, Daniel is trying to read the message over their shoulder. They're too preoccupied with trying to digest the information they don't hear his heavy breathing or see his eyes that are filled with wonderment and curiosity.

"What, who is that?" Ignatius asks, trying not to sound ignorant.

"That is the President of my world."

"You only have one person to rule the whole world?"

"Sure. Why would you need so many when we all get along, anyway?"

Daniel gasps and says, "You're a... you're a.... alien! Oh, my!" before he falls to the floor in a thud.

"How long has he been there?" Ignatius enquires hastily.

"Why do they always have to faint?" Væson asks, they want to make sure Daniel doesn't go too far under, like he did with Ignatius back in her home - they touch Daniel's head to settle the brain, letting him fall to a peaceful rest.

Daniel's theatrics have gathered a small crowd, and Ignatius does her best to shoo them away, which all of them comply with, apart from Carol, who insists on helping.

"I am a trained first aider, I'll have you know. My being here is vital," she states with self-importance, staring at Væson the whole time.

"As am I, so stop crowding the patient and get out of here!" Ignatius snaps at her.

Carol does that weird fluster huff that most extremely wealthy women do - turning her lip up in a curl of annoyance and makes a high pitched *hm* sound in three quick bursts.

"I didn't come here to be insulted!"

"Oh, where do you normally go, then?" Væson asks in a deadpan voice.

"Well, I never!" she exclaims, arms pistoling up and down in the air as she storms off.

"Grab an end with me, will you?" Ignatius tells Væson, who elects to grab the legs.

Væson doesn't actually need Ignatius's help and carries Daniel over their shoulder, fireman style.

"His house is only a little bit farther. Hopefully, his kids are home to let us in," Ignatius remarks halfway down the street.

"Hey, did I ever tell you about the time I carried a baby troll for twenty miles on my back?"

"I don't believe we've gotten to the weird facts part of our friendship yet."

"Then you're in for an absolute treat!"

"Oh, great," Ignatius states with feigned annoyance.

It's a short story that's told in all by the time they reach their destination. With every story, she feels ever closer to this strange non-human, this alien.

Her friend.

Chapter 11

Suburban Alien

Luckily, Daniel's kids are home, but his wife, Loraine, is still out, which is good because the house is a hive of chaos. Væson gently lowers the incapacitated human on the sofa in the cluttered living room. His son, Danny Junior, and his daughter, Skyla, who are still both clad in their sleepwear watch in amazement. The toys they've been playing with all morning leave a long trail of destruction from the living room all the way up to the stairs, and there's empty cereal bowls on the fading wooden table. In the kitchen, there's evidence of them making said cereal thanks to the milk being left out on the side, with the cap off, obviously, and a small pool of it on the floor. That was Danny Junior's doing; he's not the most dexterous.

"So, who knocked out Dad?" Danny asks, not at all surprised. The first thing Væson notices about him is his ears. They're bigger than any satellite orbiting in space, but Væson chooses not to say it, as they know how humans can be with harsh truths.

"He just had a slight reaction to something he thought he

saw, that's all. He'll be fine. Do you have any smelling salts?" Væson asks Skyla, hoping she's the brighter of the two. They try to remain as nonchalant as possible as they don't want to alert these tiny humans to what is really going on here. In all their years of study, they've found that the smaller humans are often the brighter of the species, and they have a higher capacity for believing things and accepting other humans as they are.

"No smelling salts, but I've got a pair of Danny's smelly socks. They'll wake the dead!" She cheers with confidence, a grin stretching across her face. Skyla lives to help people. At school, she's known as a teacher's pet. At home, she's known—to Danny Junior, at least—as little miss perfect.

"That'll work perfectly. Grab them as quick as you can," Væson says with excitement. They take a quick look around the room while Skyla is gone and notice Danny Junior staring at them in a strange way, as if he was trying to figure something out. Væson gives him a smile that is all teeth, hoping it's friendly. It must have been, as Danny Junior gives him one back in return.

Skyla runs out the room and within seconds, she returns with a stiff looking sock.

Væson takes the sock in both hands but is sure to keep it away from their face. Despite the effort, they still get a good waft of it and gag at the stench. It smells like it's been doused in strong vinegar and something else that Væson can't put their finger on. Væson puts the putrid smelling sock under Daniel's nose, and the result is instantaneous.

Daniel bolts upright, gasping for air, looking around confused. His eyes adjust to the familiar surroundings, then he notices Væson and hugs them tight, almost squeezing the life out of them.

"I knew you were real," he whispers in their ear. "Thank you." And he lets go after one final squeeze.

"Is Dad gay now?" Danny Junior asks the room, which elicits a firm glare from his sister.

"Don't be so stupid. Dad can't be gay. This must be, I don't know, his..." she starts but can't finish.

"His lover! This is so cute. I wonder if Mom knows."

"I'm not gay kids, but I'm glad you wouldn't care if I was. Your mom and I have raised you right, that's for sure."

Daniel is able to sit up more and repositions himself on the red couch that has probably seen a few better days.

"I just want to say that what you think you saw and what you think you know about me isn't true," Væson addresses Daniel directly.

"Hey man, it's all cool. Your secret is safe with me, with us... well, us and my wife. But she's cool, don't sweat it."

"Dad? What are you talking about?" Skyla asks, getting frustrated at this situation. She always wants to know all the facts right away.

"We are in the presence of a real, living *alien!*" Daniel says in wonder. He tries to stand up but all the excitement rushes to his head, and he sit back down with the assistance of Væson.

Skyla and Danny Junior exchange a befuddled look and shrug. They knew sooner or later, their Dad was going to stumble into some huge life changing discovery and have even practiced their shocked faces for when the inevitable reveal came. Their dad is always on the AOL forums chatting with other people just like him, but he takes the extra step of going to the supposed crash landing sites and doing stakeouts when he isn't working at The Smokehouse, of course. Slapping their hands to their cheeks, mouths open in a huge 'O' shape, they both utter the words, 'no way' in perfect unison.

"Oh, is that why your eyes are all strange?" Danny Junior asks. Inside, his excitement is effervescing, but a look from Skyla tells him to remain cool, calm, and collected.

"Our dad is right. We won't tell anyone, but... you don't

look like an alien. Why aren't you green, tall, and slim with black oblong eyes and really long fingers?" Skyla asks, interrogating them with her cold, hard stare. She wants all the facts and what she's seeing right now doesn't match up with her imaginary rolodex in her mind. She straightens her auburn hair with her right hand, a thing she does when she's thinking hard. At this point, neither she nor her brother believe Væson to be an alien, but it doesn't stop them from wanting to. And besides, this isn't even remotely the strangest thing their dad has brought home. That is, unless his guest does turn out to be an alien. Then it might make the top three.

"I'm *not* an alien. I'm just a regular person with an eye condition. Your dad just got over excited, that's all." Væson tries to back away from her gaze, but her deep brown eyes are too much. If Væson didn't know any better, they'd think she was a vampire, with a stare that intense.

"I know what I saw, and it's totally cool. You're our very own *secret* suburban alien!" Daniel says, now finding the strength to stand up. His Jurassic Park t-shirt rides up, revealing a portly and tanned belly with a wire nest of hair. He pulls his t-shirt down quickly before revealing more of himself and scaring off his new friend.

Væson and Ignatius exchange a look and shrug. *What else can they do?* It's not like they could go back in time and stop Daniel's curious peepers from spotting Væson's arm. Besides, she's pretty sure she can trust the Cummings clan. Though part of her wants to be selfish and keep Væson to herself and Alfie.

"Ok then, but don't go fainting on me again. And I swear to your god and mine, if I see my picture on some strange forum, I'll blast you... and yes, I check the forums," Their stare is intense, trying to be menacing, but a small smile creases their lips.

Væson rolls up the sleeve on their left arm and taps a

button which instantly changes them from human to extra-terrestrial.

"Holy Shit! You really are an alien!" Danny Junior yells.

"Watch your mouth, we're in the presence of the most awesome thing on the planet. You're not gonna probe us, though, are you?" Daniel asks, his hands immediately flying to his butt.

Væson double face palms themselves and drags their fingers all the way down their face. "Seriously, what is it with you humans and probing? I mean, I'll probe you if you want, but it's not all that enjoyable. Everywhere I go, it's always the same. You know what? One day, I just might probe a human, though there's never enough lube, but that's another story," they say, trailing off into another thought. They look at each of the humans that mean them no harm and speak their truth, hoping that this time, it really is different. "... Yes, I'm an alien... no, I'm *not* from Mars, so don't ask that one, either. No, I'm not going to invade your planet, and no, I'm not going to abduct you or your cows. Now, can you keep your word and not tell a soul outside of this family home? And trust me, I'll know if you have. I can read minds as well as explode them," Væson warns. Ignatius gives Væson a look as if to ask if they can really do that, and Væson shakes their head in the negative.

They go through what powers they have, and by the end of it, Skyla says they are basically a tiny Mary Poppins from a distant planet. This elicits a laugh from everyone. They also brief their new friends on the proper pronoun usage and a bit about life on M.O.R.K.-78. Daniel and his kids listen in wide eyed fascination and curiosity. Væson, who is fond of the theatrics, tells their story while floating in the air with their legs crossed.

They all have a million questions afterwards, and Væson answers them all with patience. They enjoy being themselves around humans and were getting tired of hiding their true self.

"Last question, I promise, but it's the most important one of all: can you still play Mario Kart with me?" Daniel asks.

"Sure thing. What is that, though?" Væson asks with piqued curiosity.

"Before you play your little games, maybe close the blinds first," Ignatius says. "You know what this neighborhood is like, and I'm sure a levitating blue alien will cause some people to raise the red flag. Who knows what'll happen to you, then!"

They all agree, and Skyla pulls the blinds.

Daniel takes Væson into his man cave, and although Væson has no idea what all of that is, their breath is taken away. It's perhaps the largest and cleanest room in the whole house. In the center of the room are four bean bags of various sizes and colors. On the left wall are three full sized arcade consoles: Space Invaders and Mr. and Ms. Pac-man. On the right, stretching the whole wall are gray shelves stacked with games, consoles, and retro memorabilia. At the back of the room is a mini bar that is adorned with more gaming and even wrestling memorabilia. The final wall is taken up mostly by a huge projector screen, and just below it is a Nintendo 64 with four controllers already plugged in. There is even something that Daniel calls a *PlayStation,* and something called a *commodore.*

"Welcome to heaven, my alien friend," Daniel says, full of pride.

Danny claps Væson on the back and says, "It sure is!"

Skyla chimes in agreement, too.

"I... I love this. I'm never leaving," Væson says in wonder. Ignatius shoots them a look, but it goes unnoticed. The green-eyed monster is rearing its ugly head, and she tries her best to quell it, but isn't successful. She still wants them all to herself but knows that she can't cage a bird as rare and as wonderful as Væson. Then a weird sensation enters her head. She hears the sweet melodies of their voice in her mind.

You're still my favorite, don't worry. You're my first human friend, don't forget that. Now, let's beat these chumps at Mario Kart!

How did you?.... Never mind, I'm just glad I'm still number one. Sorry for being selfish, she says back.

While this internal conversation is happening, Daniel has set up the game and is leading Væson to a bean bag. The sensation is strange to them at first, and they fight the feeling of sinking into it unsuccessfully, which makes everyone laugh. Daniel helps Væson out, and after a few moments, they get the hang of it.

Væson resist the urge to scan their brains to learn all the rules and the tracks.

The first ones to play are Daniel, Væson, Skyla and Ignatius. Danny says he'll take the loser's spot unless that happens to be Væson. Then he'll take the person who places second to last.

Væson picks the character that looks most like them, Yoshi, and explains their reason as such.

"Ok, understand the rules enough?" Daniel asks.

"Yep, hit the racers with stuff and make sure to come first. Sounds pretty simple to me!" Væson replies.

The game starts, and Væson is last off the line and attempts to go backwards around the track. Everyone is shouting instructions at them which prove unhelpful and gets them even more confused. Væson continues to resist the urge to scan the rules, and once they head the right way, they finish a whole two minutes after everyone else.

This happens for the next two races, and Væson is becoming vexed.

"Ok, this last map is the hardest of them all, so I'm just warning you. It's called Rainbow road, and trust me when I say this, it's the most frustrating map ever. No one will begrudge you for coming last. Hell, I'm just stoked to be playing games with an alien... Am I the first person to do this?" Daniel asks.

"You are," Væson says through their two sets of teeth.

THERE GOES THE NEIGHBORHOOD

"And am I the first person to *beat* an alien at a game?"

"Obviously...Now hurry up and start it, I'm gonna win this one," they say.

"There is no shame in losing. Chill, Væ... I can call you that, right?"

For the first time since crashing on Earth, Væson feels warm and welcomed by humans. It's different to any other time they escaped the dreaded Facility. They finally friends and have a nickname, one thing they never thought they'd have. Well, back in The Facility, it was always *the thing, that,* or *little blue bastard.* Væson takes a moment to appreciate this step, and their stomach fills up with warm feelings, something else they have sorely lacked during their time on Earth.

With a clear mind and a look that is the total opposite of what they're feeling on the inside, Væson says, "Yes..." with gritted teeth, and then a smirk blooms on their face as they scan the rules and the track.

Væson is first in line and races ahead of the pack. They don't fall off once and play like a lifetime pro, even doing the trick of keeping a shell behind them, in case of incoming enemy shells. Væson finishes a full minute before everyone else.

They drop the controller onto the bean bag, stretch their legs, and fold their arms behind their head.

"I think – although I'm not sure – but I *think,* that is how it's done. You can bow down to your all alien, nonbinary ruler at your leisure," they gloat and do a mini victory lap around the room, soaking up as much annoyance from everyone as they can muster.

"You cheated!" Daniel complains.

"I didn't. I simply read the rule book and brought myself up to speed. We can play again if you think that." Væson smirks.

"You bet we're playing again!" Daniel cheers.

The result is Væson winning all four maps with plenty of

time to spare, and they crown themselves the unofficial champion of the game.

Daniel declares that Mario Kart time is over, takes out the cartridge, and replaces it with his favorite game, *WWF No Mercy*. He doesn't bother explaining the rules as he knows Væson is just going to scan them.

The man cave is filled with laughter as they all beat the pixels out of each other. This turns out to be Væson's favorite game, and they play it until they hear Loraine shout from the hallway that she's home.

Ignatius tells Væson to quickly change back into their human form, and they duly oblige, not wanting to frighten her.

Loraine enters the man cave, and her eyes are drawn to the visitors.

"Oh, Danny, I didn't know we were having guests," she says.

"They just came by to game after the meeting," he explains, pausing the game and turning round.

Væson stands up and walks over to her, extending his hand.

"Pleasure to meet you. Your husband and kids have told me so much about you. My name is Væson, and I'm an alien... I mean, a human, I... I mean, what I'm meant to say is that I'm Iggy's cousin, from out of space... town," they struggle, face turning a deep maroon.

"Danny, darling...can I have a word with you in the living room for a moment?" she asks through thin lips.

"Of course, dear. Excuse me everyone... Don't un-pause the game. I know where I am."

Daniel and Loraine exit the man cave and go into the living room.

"Who the hell is that, and why did you let that weirdo near our children!?" she squarks.

"Woah, woah, trust me, Væ is a good soul. And you won't believe what he... *they* really are!"

"Ignatius, too?"

"No, no, it's a pronoun thing. Trust me, you'll understand soon enough," he says, holding her shoulders.

"Well, you better start explaining pretty darn quickly, and if you've brought someone dangerous into this house, god help you, Daniel Cummings, I will hit the roof quicker than you can say, well, anything, as a matter of fact." She hates sounding like this, it's not her style, but her kids are her everything, and she will rightly defend them with every last fiber of her being.

"... It'll be better coming from Væson, but you know all those TV shows we watch about aliens and stuff like that? Well... Væ is one of them. They are a living, breathing alien, and they couldn't be cooler."

"How much have you had to drink, Danny?"

"None, I swear!" Daniel pleads.

Loraine purses her lips and puts her hands on her hips as if she was some crazy, sitcom wife.

"*Are you high*?" She raises an inquisitive eyebrow.

"God no! I haven't touched the stuff since high school. C'mon, I know it's crazy, but you gotta just believe me."

Loraine exhales with effort and eyes her husband suspiciously.

"Let me smell your breath." She points an index finger at him with one hand and the other remains firmly on her hip. Daniel knows this look very well and ordinarily, he would succumb to it, but today, he decides to play with fire.

"Let me smell *your* breath," Daniel says before realizing what a fatal mistake he has just made. Loraine's left eyebrow arches up, daring him to continue. Daniel gulps and backs down. His wife's look has gone from 'try me' to 'don't test me' in mere milliseconds. He heaves out a hearty laugh and grasps her hands, holding onto them softly, rubbing his thumb along her knuckles to try and calm her down. "Look, you don't have to believe me, but maybe you'll believe Væ," he says, trying to keep hold of her hands, but she bats them away and puts them back to her hips. He shouts Væson's name, almost deafening his wife. She puts her hands to her ears and gives them a rub.

A few moments later, Væson pops their head around the corner. Ignatius is standing behind them, worried and cursing herself for putting them both in this situation.

"Væson, oh new buddy of mine, please tell my wife that you're a... you know," he cups his hand to whisper, "an alien."

"Wow, ok, I... an alien? Gosh, are you feeling ok there, Daniel? I mean, we've only just met. I'm so sorry, Mrs. Cummings, I think your husband has had a bump on the head."

Loraine gives him a look that only a wife can give a husband who has done something monumentally stupid.

Ignatius jabs Væson in the arm and mouths *what are you doing?* Væson tips her a wink.

"Honey, honey! They're joking... they're *joking, aren't you,* Væson? Ok, fun's over, turn back into the awesome blue creature that we all know and love."

"I think he's crazy," Væson whispers to Loraine who in turn rolls her eyes at her husband.

Væson discreetly jabs Daniel in the ribs playfully and gives him a smirk.

"What are you doing?" Daniel whispers, eyes wide, his serpent ringed hair almost standing up held by invisible strings.

"I am so sorry. Sometimes, my husband has weird alien fantasies. I mean, sure, it would be great to see one, but this is the 90s. And why would an alien visit Earth, anyway? Would you both like to stay for dinner, as an apology for my husband?" she offers, softening a little.

Loraine heads to the kitchen and sighs at the mess her husband and kids have made. She goes to the cupboard, and a pile of Tupperware boxes fall onto her. She lets out a cuss and puts them back in neatly, making a mental note to tell Daniel about it later.

"Now, I wonder what we have in the way of food. Hopefully Daniel brought some stuff back from The Smokehouse like I asked him to," she says to the empty kitchen. She often speaks to herself and even answers back if she likes the question. She ties her black hair into a ponytail and looks in the fridge. Rifling through it, she gathers some turkey, sides, and one of Daniel's strange concoctions: blue jelly. He's always inventing new things, and it always goes down a hit. It's one of the things she admires most about her husband.

A few hours later, Loraine has set the sizeable dining room up, making sure to use the good plates and cutlery. Loraine loves to host people, and this room is her pride and joy. The walls are covered in expensive decorative floral paper, and the chairs are wooden high backs with deep red cushions. The table, which is of the finest mahogany, easily seats all the guests, and there is even space for more if needed. She has placed a fresh white cotton tablecloth on the table and even put a red table runner down the center. In the middle of the table, there are bowls of salad, potatoes, an assortment of dressings, and of course, the turkey and strange blue jelly that seems to wobble on its own accord.

"Dinner is served," Loraine says from the dining room door. They all burst in like it was feeding time at the menagerie, but when they see how impressive it's decorated, they stop and take a breath.

"Wow! This looks amazing." Væson is the first to speak, stepping into the room, their sock clad feet being hugged by the brown shag carpet, a luxury they have never felt before.

"Oh this, I've just whipped it up, that's all. It's the least I could do after my husband's performance today."

"Loraine, please! I'm being serious," Daniel says, still protesting. In return, his wife glares at him with a look so fiery, it could put you in critical condition.

Daniel's eyes move to Væson. "Ok, fun times over now, just you know... do your thing."

Væson, who for some reason is now wearing glasses, takes them off and says, "Dear Daniel, I haven't the faintest idea what on earth you are talking about. Now, I think we should sit down and enjoy this bounty of food your wife has made."

Daniel growls in frustration and turns to his kids, "Junior, Skyla, you've got my back right?" His big eyes try to plead with his offspring.

"Oh, father, maybe you should take some medicine. You had an awful fall earlier and haven't been the same since," Danny Junior says. Never in his life has he spoke like that before, but his dad can tell he's mocking him. Væson has managed to get them all in on the joke without Daniel knowing.

"Daddy, I think Danny here is right. Maybe you should rest after dinner."

Loraine shoots her husband another look, and Daniel looks back at her with hurt eyes. He's feeling desperate now, and there's a small part of him that is starting to believe them.

Væson is the first to take a seat, and as soon as they sit on the soft cushion, they let out a sigh of pure enjoyment, bouncing on it a few times without anyone knowing. They then lock eyes on the blue wobbly substance in the center of the table and wobble along with it. "What. Is. That!?" Væson asks, mesmerized.

"That is jell-o," Loraine says, confused. She had assumed everyone knows what jell-o looks like, even if it's a different color.

"Jell-o," Væson repeats, making every letter count. They go to touch it, but it's Ignatius who taps their hand away with her own.

"That's for dessert." She gives Væson a look, then softens when she looks to Loraine. "Sorry, sometimes they can be a little much."

"Don't apologize, Daniel is much the same." The look she gives her husband is another that could kill. She is wholly embarrassed by this situation and hopes that Ignatius doesn't think any less of her or her family.

Over dinner, Daniel tries a few more times to egg Væson on to turn into their true form, mostly in the hopes to reassure himself that he isn't crazy, and almost does it when he says, "Gee, you're right, Væson isn't an alien. If they were, they'd be from Mars like all the cool aliens."

Væson's cheeks turn a deep red, and fire flashes in their eyes. "Mars people suck. Ok!?"

"Oh, and how would *you* know that?" Daniel asks, his hands folded into a pyramid, a smile blooming on his face. It's a look that says 'gotcha'

"I know that because, well, science. Obviously."

"Obviously," Danny Junior chimes in.

"Yep, seems obvious to me, too," Skyla adds.

Ignatius smiles, trying not to laugh, and nods her agreement, too, leaving Daniel red-faced.

The plates are as clean as a whistle, a sure fire sign that dinner was a roaring success. Seeing this, Loraine smiles with pride and takes the plates into the kitchen.

"Ok, what is going on?" Daniel says, eyes wide, almost crazed.

"Relax, have a bit of fun," Væson says, levitating off their seat.

"Oh, great, you couldn't do that an hour ago, could you?"

"Actually, I could, I just chose not to."

"Not cool, Væ, not cool."

"Relax, take a chill pill," they say, coming down and sitting like a human again just as Loraine walks back in.

"Right, who has room for dessert?" Loraine asks, looking at Væson in particular.

"Væson's arm shoots up in the air like a rocket and they bounce on the seat, only stopping as they earn a look from Ignatius.

Loraine scoops a portion of the wobbly blue substance into everyone's bowl, and when it comes to Væson's turn, they wobble with it. This time, they go one step further and stick a finger in it, becoming transfixed at how easy their finger disappeared yet at the same time became magnified inside the stuff.

They eat a mouthful of the blue jell-o and are delighted at how it slithers down their throat, scooping more and more into their mouth. They finish before anyone else has really started.

"Wow, what is this stuff again? And is anyone else like, turning slightly blue?" Væson extends their hand out, inspecting it, making it turn a brilliant azure. This goes unnoticed by Loraine who is preparing a small speech in her head. Daniel misses this, too, but Ignatius and the kids notice and try not to laugh.

"I am sorry again about my crazy husband. I hope this hasn't deterred you from keeping our company in the future." Loraine says, mostly speaking to Ignatius. Daniel has his head lowered, moving his jell-o with his spoon around the bowl

"Sure! Sure, but I better let you know, your husband isn't crazy." Væson smirks, changing tactics, seeing as she missed them turning blue.

"Well, not completely crazy, just... a little-"

"Not at all," Væson cuts in. They roll up their sleeve and push a button on their wrist, and almost instantly, they are transformed. "See... not crazy... Surprise."

"You're a... a... alie..." Before she can finish her sentence, she faints. Daniel catches her before she hits the shag pile carpet.

"Huh... I'm sure she'll be fine. Do, uhm, all humans faint when they see something strange? Is it like cats and cucumbers?" Væson asks, grabbing Loraine's legs and helping her onto the sofa with Daniel.

"Some of us are just a little more delicate to shock, that's all. How did you react to seeing a human for the first time?" Ignatius asks.

"Well, I didn't faint, that's for sure. But one time, I think it was the second time I escaped the facility, I met this wild bunch of people, and I'm not even sure they knew I was real. Fun times, fun times," Væson reminisces, drifting off into a distant memory.

Chapter 12

Væson and the Hippies of the 60s

It was the dawn of the 60s, and the start of a crazy fun time for a lot of Americans and other humans around the globe. Væson knew very little of this while they were stuck within the dull walls of The Facility. They knew they had to find a way out – any way out. The tests were, once more, having less and less effect on them, and The Facility workers had no idea.

To Væson's delighted surprise, they escaped in pretty much the same fashion as the first time from The Facility. It seemed that lightning did indeed strike twice.

This time, when they were a safe enough distance away from their prison, they transformed into a slim, long-haired, and shaggy bearded, psychedelic looking hippie. They'd been captivated by the look when they spotted them on TV a few weeks back. The Facility experimented on their brain matter and what it found engaging on the screen. It turned out that Væson's mind lit up like a Christmas tree when it saw bright colors and people having fun, something The Facility took to mean Væson enjoyed the fragility of humans and was concocting plans to destroy them. In reality, all Væson wanted to do was hang out with them.

Instead of heading back to Las Vegas, Væson ventured the other way, and soon enough, a van with painted flowers and a suspicious amount of smoke pulled up beside them. The door slid open, and one of the six passengers asked where they were headed.

"Anywhere the road takes me," Væson said.

"Right on, man. Hop in. We're going the same way," a girl with the flower-crown and flowy white dress said.

"Groovy," Væson replied and hopped in with the help of some of the passengers.

"Groovy? I like the sound of that. Groooooovy? Yeah, I dig that a lot, man," said one of the other passengers.

There was a haze of smoke inside the van and some funky music playing on the stereo. The driver turned around to greet the new passenger. They had a floral headband on and were sporting the longest brown hair and beard Væson had ever seen.

"Good timing man, dig the outfit, too. What was that word you used? Groovy?"

"Yeah, groovy. Like this van is groovy, and all of you are groovy, too," Væson said.

"Choice words, man," said one of the female passengers, twiddling her hair as she spoke.

"Hey, just a thing, I'm not a man, that cool? I mean, I am, but like, I'm fluid, if you dig what I'm vibing?" Væson tested the waters, hoping to not be kicked out of the van. They were sort of aware of hippies and their lexicon, but it didn't hurt making sure to plant their flag in the first instance.

"Hey, welcome to the club. We're all the same here. We don't like labels. In fact, we rebel against them and the man that puts them on us, you dig?" replied the driver, only half keeping their eyes on the road.

Væson relaxed. "Oh, cool, great... groovy."

They drove for what seemed like hours across the desert, until they ended up at a ramshackle building in the middle of nowhere. The white paint was fading from years of harsh sunlight, and the grass surrounding the area was akin more to a mushy meadow. Between the two trees was a flower-patterned bench swing. It looked like the perfect home to Væson, and that's exactly what their fellow passengers called it. As soon as they got out, they ran to it with joy. Someone pulled out a guitar and played it while they walked up to the porch steps, then sat down, strumming away. Væson watched it all with fascination.

"Come on, man, come and join us, welcome to our slice of paradise!" said the driver, putting an arm on their shoulder.

Væson allowed themselves to be led inside the house, which was a mishmash of styles and cleanliness. Some of the walls had circular holes in them, and in the center of the living room was an assortment of cushions and magazines. Fabric had been put over some lamps to create a certain ambiance.

"So, um, any of you know how to play poker?" Væson asked the driver, Oculus, not really knowing what else to say.

The room was heavy with smoke and strange smells, and someone had changed from playing the guitar to strumming a sitar outside. By the sound of it, there were a good many of the hippies who considered themselves singers, but the local cat choir wouldn't even take them.

"Only game we play here is strip poker. Same rules, except you pick some cards, and then you strip. It's revolutionary, man."

For the first time in their life, Væson was lost for words. "... That's nice. And um, what happens after you all strip?"

"Then the *real* fun begins, man," Oculus said with pride. He looked barely out of his twenties but seemed to have risen to leader status within this little... now, what was it, in fact? Væson wasn't too sure, but whatever it was, he was the leader of it. For some reason, Væson felt a stab of jealously for his status. There was no way he wanted any of this, but he wanted to be loved and wanted friends, and it seemed as though this gang had it all.

Over the next few weeks, Væson immersed themselves in this little hippie-groove vibe. If they had known any better, they would have known what this really was – a cult. Væson kept hearing Oculus talk about 'The Coming', and for the most part, Væson thought it was another sexual thing. It was surprisingly easy to rise up the ranks, and within two months, he was second in command, right in the inner circle.

In one of the rooms in the ramshackle house was a door marked 'private'. It struck Væson as a little curious, but they hadn't had a chance to investigate further yet as Oculus had started to stick to Væson like glue. When he was around, that was. For whatever reason, he was fascinated with the human mimic and his strange way of speaking. The door was innocuous enough. It was just a plain white with a golden doorknob. The sign was done in bubble letters and had an assortment of flowers all around it. A simple door, but it kept calling to Væson, and there was something *off* about Oculus, too. He would go off meditating for hours on end, but no one knew where he was on the compound. He would often lock himself away in the private room. He was seldom seen, and the others were on too many drugs to notice his absence most of the time. When they did see him, it was like a hero's return, and they would rush to his feet and kiss them endlessly. They didn't even care that sometimes there were bits of toe jam in between his toes, which made Væson question even harder just where this leader went. Some of them even bowed down to him, and as soon as he gently touched their heads, they fell to the floor and rolled around in ecstasy - or on ecstasy.

Væson was sat on the swing chair out front, taking in the afternoon heat when they spotted Oculus coming over the hill and towards the compound. Oculus gestured to Væson to come and meet him at the top of the hill, and the leader of the hippies put his arm around them.

"Look at it." He nodded toward the surrounding.

"At the sky?" Væson asked, a little confused.

"All of it, man. One day, we will ascend upwards and leave our human vessels behind. Our time is almost here, but we must make our final preparations." This was the first time Oculus spoke directly about any of this, and it shook Væson, mostly because they hadn't a flipping clue what he was going on about.

Væson decided to scan his mind to try and glean some information... any information, really.

Not long now until I slaughter them all in the name of the good one. He has promised eternal happiness in the next life. Væson will be my first. They deserve to experience the joy of it all before any of us.

Væson's three hearts all skipped a beat, and their eyes widened to an even more unnatural size. Oculus didn't notice, as his gaze was transfixed outward, towards some sort of upcoming rapture destination. There was no doubt that this guy was a whole sandwich short of a picnic.

"Oh. Ok... and when is this all going to be happening? Groovy as it sounds, it'll be nice to plan for it," Væson suggested, keeping his voice calm.

Oculus gripped Væson's shoulder tightly and said, "Sooner than you can imagine, man, sooner than you can imagine."

I can't tell them that it will be tomorrow. Their minds need to be pure. I'll announce a special gathering tomorrow afternoon. We will soon have everlasting love and eternal happiness. I can already feel it radiating from me. I've waited so long for this. The time is almost upon us.

Væson's hearts threatened to burst right out of their chest, and they flopped onto the floor like a fish gasping for air. For the first time, their hands became clammy, and a strange, smelly liquid came rushing out of their pores. Why didn't they think to turn their super computer brain on earlier? Had this place dampened their abilities like The Facility? Maybe it was something to do with that strange lingering smell or the skittles they kept giving them. Thinking about it, those skittles always had a strange taste. They had stopped eating them a few days ago, and that's when their head became an uncontrollable magnet to their thoughts again. If Oculus had been around more, maybe they would have seen the signs earlier.

This human skin is malfunctioning! Why is it so fragile at the worst possible time! Væson panicked. The pros and cons to M.O.R.K.-78 advanced tech was that it was extremely good at what it did. Take this instance, for example. When Væson switches to human form, like his fellow Morkians, their genetic make-up mimics that of the human, too. They had never truly realized just how vulnerable this human suit was, falling at the smallest of hurdles. It took many hundreds of years to get this right, but the results are outstanding... if a little sweaty. The only thing they couldn't seem to mimic from the humans was their eyes, but after all, the eyes are apparently the window to the soul - and a human soul and an alien one are completely different. Still, it's close enough for most humans to not be able to tell the difference.

Then an idea struck them that was so far-fetched, it might just work. But they had to wait until the gathering tomorrow night to execute their plan. If all went to plan, everyone would live to see another day, including the crazy hippies who weren't like the ones they admired on TV back in the far away land of The Facility. They had no idea how long they'd been here. Time had become such a loose construct, it didn't even enter their consciousness anymore. It could have been three weeks, three months, or even just a handful of days. It didn't matter to Væson. It was just an observation they had made and would be something they would eventually report back to their home planet... If they ever made it back, that is.

The next morning dragged more than any day they'd ever experienced outside of The Facility walls. They spent most of their day sat on the swing, kicking up clouds of dust with their sandal clad feet. Their long, brown, bell-bottomed trousers were caked in dust, but they didn't care. There were a million thoughts racing through their head, hoping their plan this evening was going to work. If it didn't, they would soon be meeting their best friend and co-pilot in the afterlife center, getting ready to be redistributed and flung among the stars into a new life. A new life that Væson wasn't quite ready for. Their alien body was still good for a few hundred years, and there was too much they hadn't experienced yet. *No, tonight must work. Tonight will work.* Væson was the superior being here, and tonight, they were going to prove it.

Chapter 13

Væson Saves the Hippies

T he musician hippie had gathered everyone around a campfire when the sun started to set, and they were singing some kind of song about a sandman. Væson tapped their feet in the dirt to the rhythm. They had no idea what the song meant, but it was a song that spoke to them. It sounded familiar, too, as if they had heard it before, long ago. A tear rolled down their face without their invitation, and they wiped it away. Then, as if a bolt of lightning had struck their memory, images of Jenson came flooding into their mind. The memories made them laugh and cry for a good while, but the strange part was, some of them didn't feel like memories at all, but events that could still happen.

"I will find you, Jenson. In this life or another. In this world or the Dreamland. I will find you," they said to the sky.

A light touch on their shoulder made Væson jump a few inches off the swing, and they turned around to see the maniacal smile of Oculus. He was dressed in a white robe with a solitary flower etched on the upper left breast. His once long, flowing hair and beard was now shaved, giving him an unrecognizable look. The only reason Væson was sure it was him was because they scanned his mind and could tell by the eyes. Those once kind eyes now had a look of murder in them. There was something behind his back, too, that he was holding with his right hand. Væson couldn't make out what it was but was on high alert to the potential danger.

"It's showtime, man. Are you ready?"

"Ready... for what?"

"For ascension and enlightenment, my friend. It's time," he said in an eerily calm voice. He took Væson's face in his right hand and smushed their lips together in the process.

"I guess so," Væson mumbled.

"Good, man. Here, put this on. You're gonna need it." He handed them a robe of their own that must have been the thing he was holding behind his back.

Væson put the curious looking robe on as instructed, then followed Oculus down to where the hippies were singing a song by an artist Væson would soon come to love: *Elvis*. It was another toe-tapper, and for a moment, Væson forgot how much the hippies couldn't sing and about their impending doom.

"Gather around, man. Our time has come," Oculus addressed his flock with open arms.

They all stopped singing, and the guitarist stopped mid-strum in an unintentionally comedic way. A buzz of excitement hung in the air. Some of them bounced up and down and others shoved their tongues down each other's throats because seemingly, that's the thing to do when you're about to die – not that they knew that.

"Follow me, everyone. Our groovy time on this earth is coming to the next step," Oculus continued in that strange voice.

Væson wondered why no one had mentioned his harsh, new look, but then they remembered they hadn't either. They were becoming more and more human every day by the looks of things, and not in a good way.

Oculus lead them all to the top of the hill which seemed to have been transformed into some occultist's wet dream. There were six flame torches on either side, at least five foot in height, and at the peak was a small platform. To the left of the makeshift platform was a banner of some sorts with the words 'Groovy Ascension' written in bubble writing and adorned with flowers in every hue. If what all this entailed hadn't been leading to mass murder, it would have actually been pretty *groovy*, in fact. And, for a moment, Væson was captivated by the glitz and glamour of it all.

It had the same effect on the rest of the hippies, too. They held onto each other while pointing and looking, wide eyed, and chatted amongst themselves about what all of this could mean. Excited by the prospects, every single one of them was higher than Mary Poppins' umbrella, so they weren't alert to impending danger. In fact, some of them thought the fire was some kind of special effect. If it were in touching distance, they would reach out and grab it, a fact that Væson was so sure of, they would have put their ship on it.

"Gather around, all of you," Oculus encouraged them. "That's it, come closer, closer, right up to the edge of the stage. There'll be plenty of time for you all to step onto the stage, don't worry." The crowd did as he said with minimal fuss, and some of them were vibrating with excitement.

"The day has finally come, and you have all been so patient. This evening, your patience will be rewarded with everlasting love and happiness," he said. He looked almost twice the age he was yesterday, his formerly youthful, brown eyes now those of a serial killer, set deep against his tanned skin. The hippies whooped and cheered at what he had to say, and Væson focused their mind on the task at hand: save the hapless hippies from a strange high hippie who wants to kill them. None of this was in any syllabus back on M.O.R.K.-78.

"Væson, my groovy number two, come up here and join me, man," Oculus called to Væson. "You will be first. You are to be the one who leads the way. The rest of us will follow you, and I shall be last, following on from behind."

Væson stepped up onto the platform in their strange white gown and looked down at the expectant eyes of the hippies below. They were pretty much salivating at all of this, with no idea what was about to happen. The irony of it all was that neither did Oculus. His world was about to be turned upside down and spat out... If all went according to Væson's plan.

Until that moment, Væson didn't see the table at the back of the platform with the array of pointy instruments laid out on it. Oculus walked over to it and picked out one of the longer, pointed ones. It looked like it could go right through Væson and come out the other side drenched and dripping with their galactic blood.

"Væson, dear friend of ours, do you have any last words before your immaculate ascension?" he asked, not expecting a response.

"Actually, I do, yeah. First of all, all of this is dumb. I mean, it's so unbelievably dumb that you'd have to be high for months on end to even buy into this rubbish..."

Oculus burned a hole through Væson, turning love into instant hate with their stare, almost like a deer in the head-lights moment. Oculus tried to remain calm outward, but inwards, his blood was turning into lava.

"Don't speak such insolence, man. You have no idea what you're talking about. I'm the one who has had the voice speak to me. I'm the one who knows the next chapter-"

"Oh, give it a rest!" Væson interrupted. "The only voice that has spoken to you is the one you made up. You're nothing but a poser hippie on a gap year trying to rebel against his rich parents. You're not even called Oculus. You're called Tarquin!"

The crowd gasped at this revelation and Oculus – or Tarquin – bared his teeth.

"Don't you dare use that name... It's lies!" Tarquin snapped.

"Oh, so. I'm assuming the fact that you wet the bed up until the age of fourteen is also a lie. And that you slept in your parents' bed until sixteen is another lie, too? How about the fact you killed the family dog and your pet fish? Oh, and the fact that you jack off into your mom's unmentionables is also a lie, correct? I mean... that's gotta be... right?" Væson gave Tarquin a satisfied grin. Despite knowing this, Væson had hoped even until the very last moment that Tarquin could and would change. It's this that separates them from most humans. They will never give up on finding the good in people.

Tarquin charged at Væson with the blade in hand, but they held out a hand which stopped him in his tracks. The hippies watched in wonder, none of them knowing whether what they were seeing was real or some kind of Off-Broadway production. Væson lifted Tarquin into the air with a flick of the wrist, and a puddle appeared at the crotch of his gown, yellow liquid gushing down his leg and onto the stage like a waterfall. He begged and pleaded for Væson to put him down, and after a moment, they obliged by dropping him on his head unceremoniously.

"H—How...This isn't possible!" Tarquin stuttered.

"Not for humans, no, but... I'm not human!" Væson said with a wry smile and tapped their wrist, revealing their true form.

One of the hippies in the crowd, the one who never spoke, reached for something in their back pocket.

The rest of the hippies looked on with amazement. The guitar man bowed first, and the others followed, even Tarquin. All except the silent hippie. Væson didn't notice until it was too late, but it seemed as though they had taken Væson's true form as some kind of intergalactic messiah, someone who would lead them to the promised poppy field lands and LSD laced tress of whatever they believed in.

A dart found its way into Væson's neck, and they dropped like a sack of potatoes. Moments later, their world faded to black. They didn't hear the gunshots or see the slaughter of the unfortunate hippies; at least The Facility gave them that mercy. Ordinarily, this would be out of the jurisdiction of The Facility and would be down to the FBI to take down cult leaders, but The Facility had become twitchy and had jumped at many shadows and false leads the past few weeks. Procedure also didn't call for a whole cult to be killed, only their leader, and even then, only in extreme circumstances. But this was The Facility, and nothing was beneath them. They were like a wild and hungry dog backed into a corner, baring its teeth at anything and everything. The irony was lost on The Facility that they were more like a cult than the hippies.

The next time Væson woke, it was back in the awful surroundings of their soul numbing cage at The Facility, and they wept once more, with no one around to care. It was beginning to feel like no matter how hard they tried, The Facility would always find them. The punishments inflicted on them by The Boss were more excruciating than ever, and at one point, The Boss had been so boisterous in his demand for answers that he had almost killed Væson when he gave them one too many volts of electricity to their skull. The marks from that incident are still there as a stark reminder to Væson that not all humans are good and kind.

Chapter 14

Accepting the Alien

"So, what you're saying is you were part of some kind of sex cult that wanted to murder you and everyone else in it?" Ignatius asks, dragging Væson out of their memories.

"Yeah, that pretty much sums it up," they say as if it was the most normal thing ever.

"What happened to the hippies? I didn't read about any of this in the papers or history books," says Daniel, scratching his head. His wife, Loraine, is still zonked out on the couch, and the kids have joined them in the living room because they were fascinated with the story. They shouldn't have heard most of it, but they're grown up enough to understand. That's what Daniel says, anyway, whenever he puts on Evil Dead or The Shining for them at the ass-crack of night.

"I'm not really sure. They probably died or got jobs as accountants. You didn't hear about it because The Facility made sure it didn't happen... officially, that is." Væson still had no idea about the gunshots and the bloodshed, and that was another small mercy.

"They can do that?" asks Danny, his eyes wide with amazement but his voice filled with disgust.

"They have the power to do anything. They have more power than the President!" Væson exclaims dramatically.

"How can that even be?" Skyla asks, not believing it. To her, the President is the most powerful and greatest person in all of the United States. Well, in her eyes, only coming second to her librarian, Mrs. Vanholt.

"Well, the President doesn't know The Facility exists, for starters—at least I don't think he does. If he did know, I'm sure he would deny it, anyway, like a true politician. I don't know how they rose to prominence, but I do know they have the power to do a lot of things, and they work underground– in places you won't believe exist."

"They've gotta be stopped." Skyla states in a defiant tone. She looks a lot like her dad but has all the grit and determination of her mom. She even tucks a strand of her auburn hair behind her ear, just like her mom does when she's in full 'let's take on the world' mode.

"Yeah, I'm sure they do, but I'd rather stay alive, in all honesty. I've messed with them for too long, and I'm not going back this time, that's a promise," Væson says with gritted teeth.

Loraine stirs from her position on the sofa and sits up with a yawn and a stretch. She blinks a few times, trying to adjust to the familiar surroundings with unfamiliar people. She holds her head in her right hand as if she's stopping her brain from falling out of her ear.

"Oh, jeez, don't faint again. It's a whole skit, and it just takes it out of the both of us. Yes, I'm an alien, yes, I have amazing azure skin, yes, I do have sexy eyes, yes, I can talk, and *no*, I'm *not* from Mars. Mars sucks!"

The words swim into Lorain's conciseness and try to float out. She attempts to understand what this blue creature is saying, but it cannot be possible. Yet here it is, in her living room, talking to her and telling her it's not from Mars for some reason. She holds onto the sides of the sofa to try and stay grounded because at the moment, she feels like she could just float away.

"You're... an alien.?" she asks, words hanging in the air. Coming out of her mouth, they sound like they don't belong to her.

"Sure am. The name's Rumvæson, but my friends call me Væson or Væ. Before yesterday, I didn't have any friends, but now, I have at least three, and I'd love another one." Væson reassures her with a smile and an extended hand, hoping she'll shake it. For a moment, she just stares at it, and they are about to take it away when she takes their hand in both of hers.

"It's nice to meet you, Væ... I'm Loraine."

She lifts herself into a more comfortable position on the worn sofa and observes them properly for the first time. They really do have amazing eyes and wonderful, cobalt skin. It's like some kind of special effect. She takes her hand and touches their face to confirm they are real. Their skin is warm to touch, and Væson holds Loraine's hand in their own. She feels even more warmth, like someone had put the heating on inside her body, but it isn't' uncomfortable; it's nice and peaceful.

"Yep, I'm real! Oh, I can also read your thoughts and do lots of other neat tricks. Stick around long enough, and I'll tell you about them. Now, who's hungry? Because I could eat a cow! You don't have any cows, right?" Væson asks, levitating off the dark grey rug with excitement.

"Not a whole one, no!" Daniel chuckles.

"Well, I'll go with anything right now. You can all cook, and I'll wash the dishes!"

"You're volunteering to wash the dishes? Dude, never do that!" warns Danny, putting a hand on Væson's shoulder in a way humans do when they bestow great truths on people.

"Trust me, it's no hardship. They like it," Ignatius clarifies.

Danny stares at Væson in confusion and curious fascination, then says "With all the powers you have, you choose to take joy in washing the dishes? Dude, if I were you, I'd shoot them with lasers or something." Væson rolls their eyes at Danny Junior, patting him on the back with his long, blue hand. Amusement trickles up their spine. Of course lasers would be his first thought, and how cool would that be? But as much as their amethyst eyes seem all-powerful to humans, they're simply decoration on their already captivating form.

"Of course! It's like giving my fingers a personal bath, and trust me, the way I do it, you'll understand why it's great." Væson ruffles Danny's jet-black hair.

"You're weird, dude!" He laughs, rolling on the floor in hysterics as Skyla and the rest of the Cummings clan watch on. Once he starts laughing, it's hard for him to stop.

"And you're trash at Mario Kart... and short," Væson counters and levitates around the living room, being careful not to bang their head on the faux crystal chandelier.

"Væson!" Ignatius seizes at the name in anger.

"What? What'd I do?" Væson pleads their innocence.

"You can't be rude in a house that isn't your own, even I know that!"

"Rude? I thought we were saying facts about each other. My bad..." He leans closer to Ignatius. "Does he not know how bad he is at the game or how short he is?" This is one of those *harsh truths* they'd learned but aren't' too sure if it's more honest or harsh.

Ignatius stifles a laugh. "I'm sure he does, but you can't just say stuff like that. You're apt to hurt people's feelings."

"Urgh! Humans are so temperamental," Væson groans.

Lorain gets up from the couch and stares at Væson not because of the comments but to try to get her head around the fact that a real alien is in her house. She reverses out of the room and into the kitchen, not taking her eyes off them. She resists every urge to pick up the wall phone and call everyone she knows. She would be laughed out of the town and sent to Pembroke Asylum where the rest of the nutjobs are. No, she would not want to be locked up in there. Just the thought of it sends a shiver down her spine. It is the worst place you can end up in, and if you're lucky to get out, you're never the same. So, instead of picking up the phone, she picks up the cookbook and flips through some recipes. This time, she doesn't have Daniel's leftovers from The Smokehouse, but she is just a great a cook as him. She would say better, but that's just the competitive side of her rushing out.

"I'm cooking for an alien," she mutters to the pages, shaking her head with an amused smile pulling at her lips. *How ridiculous.*

Loraine flicks through the book, trying to determine what would be most suitable for Væ. She settles on a lasagna, which is one of her favorites, and if the alien doesn't like it... well that's tough titties for all she cares; but then the magnitude of the event takes over again, and she has a stern talk with herself. She also gets out a few cokes from the fridge and puts them on the table, along with a couple of Twinkies and Junior Mints. As she puts her plastic farm animal clad apron on, she wonders if she might be the first human to host an alien for dinner. She's technically done it twice now, if you count the one where she didn't know of Væson's true nature.

"Looks like I'm hosting a party for junkies!" she says, exhaling deeply and running a hand through her infinite black hair which she ties up into a messy bun.

The array of sweets looks absolutely ridiculous on the huge mahogany dining table with huge, ostentatious flowers. If her mother could see this, she would roll her eyes and walk out with her pointed nose in the air. At least the dessert, a traditional English trifle, is a recipe she picked up from the British expats, Mark and Sharron Smith. That in turn was adapted by

S. REED

Daniel's British friend, Harry before finally being tweaked again by herself. She is known throughout the neighborhood as the "hostess with the mostess". Ignatius often hires her to do the catering for her audacious parties, and even though Loraine would refuse payment, Ignatius would still shove a couple of hundreds into the palm of her hand with insistence.

When she's done, she calls them all in. The kids are excited about the 'junkie spread' as much as Væson is, who literally levitates with joy at seeing all of the foods they'd seen in their books at home. The sensation of overly sweet and sugary flavors that fills their mouth is like nothing they've experienced before, and they aren't shy about saying it.

"Mom! You never normally let us have snacks at the dinner table. What's changed? Not that I'm questioning this. Far from it. You're a rad mom, Mom," Danny Junior says as he rakes another Twinkie from the center of the table, sucking out the cream in the middle first and then devouring the outside before his mom can even answer him.

"Sometimes, change is as good as a rest. That's what they say, anyway. That's part of the reason, at least. Now, if you're all quite finished, I'd like to bring out the main course."

Goblets of drool are hanging from Væson's mouth. They can smell the main course from the kitchen and are lazily levitating off the chair, as if being drawn by the smell.

Loraine comes in, opening the swing door to the dining room with her shoulder while carrying a literal silver platter that's big enough for more than in attendance. On it is her famous lasagna, and smoke billows out of it in tantalizing tendrils. Rich smells of the freshly squeezed tomatoes, the slightly burnt at the edges cheese resting on the top and in every other layer, and the meat cooked so perfectly enters the nostrils of all in attendance.

Once again, Væson is the first to dig in as they dive their fork into a corner and scoop out a good-sized portion. They

112

plop it on their plate, and a bit of the sauce splashes onto their face. They recoil slightly from the heat, not realizing it will be a prelude for the actual contents. They are thinking with their stomach not their brain when they pick up a corner piece with their fork from the plate. Before anyone can warn Væson about how hot it will be. It's in their mouth, scorching their insides like the sun. They do their best to swallow it with tears streaming down their face. They drop the fork, and it lands on the rest of their lasagna. Their vibrant blue hands fly up to their face and try to fan the heat out. The rest of the table watch on in hysterics. Danny Junior in particular has doubled over again and falls off his chair, which makes him laugh even more. Skyla is the first to offer some refuge by handing them a glass of water from the jug on the table. Væson downs it in one go.

"Wow. That's hot. And not in like a sexy way, but in a 'wow that's hot' way. Phew!" They say with a weak voice. Skyla pours them another glass, and they gulp at it a little more conservatively this time.

"You should really blow your food before putting it in your mouth," Skyla says in her matter-of-fact tone.

"That's information I could have had a few moments ago," Væson says, stroking their tongue with their hand.

"Are you sure you're not from Mars, Væ?" Danny Junior asks, easing himself back on his chair, wiping tears from his eyes.

"How dare you. If I were from Mars, that would have eviscerate my insides, and I'd be rendered unconscious for three weeks. Puny Mars creatures. Pah." They stick out their chest and beat it with their left hand. "I'm a Morkian. We are strong, fearless and brave."

"And forget to blow things when smoke comes off them!" Danny Junior says again in jest with more laughter bubbling away at the surface.

Væson blows on their food while giving the whole room a

little too much eye contact. The smoke from the lasagna drifts up and away into the high vaulted ceiling of the dining room, and by the time they're done blowing it, it has a small carpet of spittle on the top.

"I think you can eat it now, Væ," Daniel says with a warm smile and gives them a nod, which Væson returns.

"This is a lot better when there isn't a fireball for taste. Most excellent, in fact! I can really taste the cow and the cow's food."

"You mean vegetables?" Ignatius asks, taking a sip of her water.

"Yeah, those," Væson replies as they gather another slab of the food onto their fork before blowing it intensely. They manage to finish it all without burning their insides again and lick the plate clean.

"Looks like someone enjoyed that," Loraine says with a smile. She's still wearing her apron, and her hair is in that same, messy bun. The compliment warms her insides, and she files this memory away as a proud moment.

Loraine gathers up all the plates and puts them on the side of the sink, then comes back into the dining room with the English trifle. Væson's jaw drops a few inches shy of the dining table as they say, "What is that!?"

"It's a traditional dessert from a country called England. Our British friends taught us how to make it, and we jazzed it up by putting toffee syrup on top." Daniel explains, leaning back in his chair and unbuttoning his trousers. A sigh of relief escapes him. "Much better, now I've got room."

Væson watches in fascination, then looks down at their own trousers and unbuttons, too. "Wow, you're right, it *is* better. Good one, Dan. You don't mind me shortening your name, too, do you?"

"Not in the slightest. In fact, it's totally cool." A warm glow fills his insides, and a smile breaks out onto his face. He's got a real alien friend and one that gives him a nickname of sorts, too. If only his younger self could see this, he'd flip his lid in excitement. As will all his AOL friends, but he will never tell them, not if it means threatening his friendship with Væson.

"Good. Now, what's in this trifle? More meat?" Væson asks hopefully.

"Ew, gross, no. You don't put meat in a dessert." Skyla puts a hand to her mouth as if she is about to gag at the thought of it.

"Well, you should. I bet it'll be fantastic." Væson says, levitating on their chair before settling down again and scooping a spoonful of the creamy dessert into their mouth. "You know, it's a lot better when you don't need to blow your food."

The discussion over dinner is filled with questions about M.O.R.K.—78: what life is like there and what they've been doing all this time. Warmth spreads over Væson's chest. This is the humanity they saw on TV shows; the friendship they craved and searched for each time they escaped their prison. People who accept them as they are—in all of their alien ways. Unlike those fiends at the facility. Every time they'd misgendered Væson was a dagger in each of their hearts; though they never let it show on their face. They had tried hard to keep their personal life and knowledge a secret, giving them just enough to stop them from torturing their pet prisoner.

Soon, discussion turns to what Væson is going to do next and how long they are going to stick around, and Væson shuffles uncomfortably in their seat. They haven't thought much further than tonight as every time they lay down plans, The Facility finds them and takes them back to the pokey prison cell.

"You can't live your life in fear, Væ, that's not healthy. You have friends now, and friends don't let people down or put them in trouble," Ignatius says defiantly. A sweet and tender aching envelopes Væson, and tears threatened to spill from their deep purple eyes.

"You'll really look after me? Even though you know the

dangers that come with looking out for me? Wow, humans *are* crazy," Væson says after a moment. This time, the tears do fall from their eyes, leaving a shiny track down their cheeks..

"You got that right!" Daniel says proudly.

"What do you think the rest of the neighborhood would think about me being, well... an alien?"

"Well, Carol will try to call The Facility in the first instance. As for the rest, I'm really not sure, and I don't want to find out either," Ignatius says.

While Væson and their new friends are discussing their future, The Captain is striding up and down his office, muttering to himself and knocking random things off his desk in rage like a big angry cat. A few days have passed since his pet escaped, and there have been no sightings at all, which is unusual – too unusual. The thought comes to them that someone has killed the little blue bastard, but that only enrages him more. *He* wants to slaughter the alien, and if someone else beats him to it, he'll kill that person for stealing his dream away from him. He sits back in his chair and seethes. His mind is so focused on catching the alien, he has started to neglect his appearance and his diet – unless you count a diet of whisky and bourbon.

"I'll get you, you little blue bastard, even if it's the last thing I do!" he shouts, laughing like a loon in the night while pouring another shot into his eye. He's done it so many times now, he doesn't even recoil from the sting anymore.

PART II

Chapter 15

Movie Night

The day is still young when they finish their food, and Væson is keen to soak up as much human interaction as possible. Over the course of the meal, Loraine cautiously accepted the fact that there is an alien in her house and moved away from the thoughts of 'what will the neighbors think?'

Væson shows their dishwashing trick like a magician, their audience is amazed. Even though Ignatius has seen it already, she still marvels at the way the suds form by themselves in the sink and the faucets turn themselves on. How the scrubber scrubs the pots and pans to look brand new, and how the cutlery and plates march to their correct places. It reminds her of some sort of elaborately choreographed dance. While all this is going on, Væson sits on the kitchen chair and conducts the whole thing with a smile on their face. Once it's done, the kids clap and cheer. Væson takes an exaggerated bow from their seat which garners more applause.

"So, what else we got for entertainment around here?"

Væson asks after absorbing all of the plaudits they thrust at them.

"I vote movie night!" Skyla suggests.

"We've seen all of these, though." Loraine gestures to the stacks of DVDs and VHS tapes piled neatly on the shelves.

"But Væ hasn't," Skyla persists.

Daniel sniffs the air in exaggerated inhales. "I smell a movie night."

"Yeah, yeah, that's what we're talking about," Loraine says in frustrated jest. It seems as though Væson's arrival has brought out the fun and happy Loraine, and it warms Daniel's heart to see it.

"Not just any movie night... a Blockbuster movie night," Daniel implores with an ear-to-ear grin.

The kids bounce up and down in excitement, and Væson joins them.

"I have no idea what is happening, but I want to do it," they say, linking arms with the kids and letting out a high-pitched cheer. "What's a Blockbuster?"

The rest of them laugh, and Daniel puts an arm around them, the way a father would do to their son when they are about to bestow a huge secret upon them.

"Væ, Blockbuster is the greatest place that humans have created. It's a place filled with every film imaginable."

"And you can buy popcorn!" Danny Junior interrupts.

"And sweets!" adds Skyla.

"And don't forget video games," chimes Daniel.

"And it's all overpriced," Loraine states flatly.

Daniel takes in a sharp breath. "You bite your tongue, madam! Blockbuster is *not* overpriced."

"So... it's a place where you get to buy these things?" Væson asks, levitating over to the shelf to inspect a DVD.

"Well, you can buy them, but most people rent them for a small fee-"

"And if you're late bringing them back," Loraine interrupts, "which you *always* are, you have to pay a hefty fee, and it is often more expensive than it would be to buy the darn CBD or whatever the infernal things are called!"

Daniel gives a small snicker to his wife's mispronunciation of DVD and thinks that if they sold CBD, then Blockbuster may be transcending a whole new market. "Me and Harry have an understanding now, though!"

"Oh, I'm sure you do," She puts her hands on her hips, giving her 'the look'.

After a few moments of awkward marital silence, Ignatius says, "So, we're going then, right? I'll drive! Væ... mind doing the honors and turning into your human form? I dunno how the geeks will take looking at an actual alien."

Væson salutes her and does as she requests. Moments later, they are all piling into the minivan and heading towards Blockbuster. As they leave Poppy Field Lane, Darren waves at them from his security both.

Halfway into the journey, Væson blurts out the most hated question proposed by kids: '*are we there yet?*' Ignatius lies that it's still a little ways away, but in truth, it's a forty-minute trip one-way and they have to drive to the neighboring county of Bats Cove, which isn't a place you'd want to stay for too long. Some people say it's haunted, but that could be because it's the location of Pembroke Asylum *and* Stone House Prison, not to mention the biggest graveyard in all of the East Coast. As they drive through the center, Ignatius tells them all to lock the doors, which they do without hesitation. Thankfully, Blockbuster is on the outskirts of the town. Væson marvels at the dilapidated ruins of the shops and at the people shuffling about on the street. It looks like the rest of the county has forgotten all about them, and what's worse, it looks like they are glad about it.

A short while later, they pull up outside the store. The huge yellow letters are lit up, bathing the parking lot in a tinted glow. Væson gasps at it and the constant stream of people going in and out of the store.

"Are you ready to have your mind blown?" Daniel asks.

"...Not literally, right?" Væson asks in a small voice.

"No. It's just an expression. Don't worry about it. This place is amazing," Daniel reassures his new best friend.

They walk in and are instantly greeted by the smell of popcorn and noise of hustle and bustle. The overhead tannoy tells the patrons to "Make it a Blockbuster movie night" intermittently, and the sounds of movie trailers play from multiple tv screens in corners of the store. It's almost a sensory overload. To the left of the entrance, where the registers are, Harry shouts over the desk to Daniel to greet him, and Daniel waves back to him.

Væson's eyes are even wider than normal as they try to take it all in. Rows upon rows of shelves stuffed full of DVD's and VHS tapes all organized into different categories. As they walk farther into the huge store, they notice on the right-hand side, just before the bank of registers behind the huge blue and yellow desk, is a wall of a thing called 'Pick'n'Mix'. Væson stares at it, fascinated.

"What *is* that?"

"That, my friend, is the wall of candy. We pick those out once we've found a movie to watch," Daniel explains, putting a hand on their shoulder and smiling while gesturing with his other hand like a game show host revealing the prizes up for grabs. Væson laps it up and at first is so excited, they don't know what to do but stare in cosmic wonder.

After about thirty minutes, they have all picked out different films that they want to watch. Among the array of films, Væson picked out *Edward Scissorhands* and Ignatius chose *Batman Returns*, a personal favorite of hers that she'd watched at the cinema at least three times in the first week of release.

"Does this person really have scissors for hands?" Væson asks, starring at the cover, then at their own, human mimic hands in disappointment.

"Nah, it's just some movie magic and special effects," Danny replies, not knowing he's just shattered a piece of wonderment that was residing in Væson's hearts.

"Oh, so humans aren't born with cool looking blades for hands?" Væson asks, feeling a little cheated by the cover.

"Not that I know of, but I'm sure it'll still be a great film. My friends at school have all said it's awesome," Danny continues, taking the box from Væson's hands and flipping it over to the back to read about it. He, too, is fascinated by the cover and his friend's hype about the film. He hangs out with the movie geeks and most weekends, they catch the latest movie that's in the cinema (travel permitting), and if they want to watch certain "R-rated" films, they know someone who will sneak them in. This was one of the films that he missed when it was at the cinema, and his friends still haven't forgiven him for it, especially since they all wanted to dress up as the titular character last Halloween.

"Can we go back to the wall of sweets now? I'd very much like to try them." Væson's eyes focus on the array of backlit colors, their feet dancing on the spot—inching toward the wall. Their new friends laugh and lead them over to the huge wall of sweets. Væson has never seen anything like it. They're completely and utterly enamored by the whole thing. Their eyes threaten to pop out their head and saliva piles up in their mouth. They flick some away with the heel of their hand.

"You can try one if you want," Daniel says.

"Not before we've paid for them, Daniel! Don't encourage bad habits," Loraine scolds.

"Relax, everyone does it. Besides, it's all part of my and Harry's understanding," Daniel reassures her half-heartedly, flicking his head toward the clerk with a wink.

He picks out a fizzy cola bottle and pours a handful into Væson's hand, who puts them into their mouth without being warned to take just one at a time. Their tongue is instantly bombarded with flavor and sourness, their eyes water, and a shiver goes up and down their spine. The reaction makes the others laugh, and Danny Junior in particular bends over, hands on his knees and tears freely falling from his face. Væson's tongue feels too big for their mouth, and they have a hard time speaking for a good couple of seconds. When they finally get their composure back, they say, "*Wow*! I'd like some more of those."

"You're not meant to eat a whole handful like that, dude. They're too sour," Skyla says.

"Here, you gotta try these too, they're called *flying saucers!*" Daniel offers, handing them another handful which Væson takes and scoops into their mouth in one go. This garners the exact same response, and once more, their friends are laughing with tears in their eyes.

By the time they are ready to check out, they have three hefty bags filled mostly with sour candy and two bags of popcorn.

"Can I offer you anything else?" Harry asks.

"Nah, I think we're good, thanks," replies Daniel.

"And you've got your Blockbuster card with you, right? Don't worry if not, I can just search you up on the system."

"Nah, nah, I've got it here somewhere," Daniel insists, sifting through the cards in his wallet. "Ah, here we go!" He plonks the card on the desk, and Harry swipes it.

"Got a couple of late fees on here, bud. I'll just wipe them off for you, don't worry about it. Try and bring these ones back on time, though, ok?" Harry says, knowing that won't happen. "I'll even extend the time on them for you, so you have a whole week to watch them all, ok?"

"Great, thanks, you're the best."

"I know, I know." Harry says bashfully.

"Listen, next time you're at The Smoke House, your meal is free." Daniel says, batting away the protesting from Harry and ignoring 'the look' from his wife.

"Enjoy your films!" Harry calls after them as they exit the store.

"So, what did you think of the place?" Ignatius asks as they climb back into the car. She's been a little quiet this whole time and was trying not to feel so sour about not being the main person in Væson's life.

"I thought it was the best place in the whole world!" Væson announces.

Here's the thing, though. When you've had a tough life and you dare to forget about it and be happy for the briefest of moments, life comes back around and shrouds you with even more darkness and even more pain. It's life's way of punishing you for daring to be happy, to be daring enough to break the vicious and barbaric cycle of life. Væson is as complacent as are their friends. It's why none of them noticed they had a stalker the whole time they were in the store. And why would they? They were too busy daring to be happy, daring to fucking live, to even notice Carol and her beady eyes the whole time they were in there. Her interest was piqued when Væson said, "I wish my flying saucer was this tasty," while at the Pick 'n' Mix stand. Sure, it was perhaps a throw away comment, but Carol isn't going to let it go. She would be a perfect employee for The Facility.

As the car leaves the parking lot, Væson sticks their head out the window and waves goodbye to the store, whispering promises of next time.

"I think we may have a movie addict on our hands!" Daniel says, giving them a gentle elbow in the ribs. He had chosen to sit in the middle seat on the ride home, which wasn't the best move as he is the larger of all passengers, and it leaves the ones either side of him jockeying for a bit of space.

The whole ride home, Væson raves about how much they loved the place and how they can't wait to go back. They must've asked at least four times if they can all go back tomorrow, and each time, it's answered with a 'we'll see.' As any youngster knows (not that Væson is a youngster, but they are in spirit), that is normally parent code for "*not a chance unless either you're good or I don't have anything better to do*." Væson files this memory away in the small section of their brain that's entitled 'happy memories with friends' which, until a few days ago, was almost barren, save for the few adventures they had with Jenson.

As soon as they all get home, Væson spreads all of the new films on the floor and stares at them, as if waiting for the films to speak back to them. When they don't, Væson opts for doing a M.O.R.K-78 rendition of 'eenie-meenie-minie-mo' called, 'which one is which, what shall I pick? Catch a rainbow, then you'll be rich'.

Their finger lands on *Edward Scissorhands*, but not without some severe cheating that goes uncontested by the rest of their friends. Soon after that, the lights are out, and the movie plays with everyone munching away at the sweets and popcorn. It's the safest Væson has ever felt and, if they are being honest, the happiest, too. They watch a further two films, and the movie night doesn't end until gone 2 a.m., by which time, only Væson and Daniel are still wide awake. At some points, Væson has to be pulled back from the screen as if they went any closer, they would be active participants in the film. During less intense bits of the movies, Daniel tries to steal bits of conversation from Væson where he tries to glean a little more life from his new alien friend.

When the films ends, Daniel says his goodbyes and offers to help carry Ignatius home, but Væson says it was all groovy and thanks him for the offer and for being a good friend to a complete stranger. Væson offers their hand to Daniel who bats it away and pulls him into a hug. Væson feels the love radiating from Daniel as they rest their head on his chest. Væson attempts to pull away after a moment but Daniel says, "One more moment. I've always wanted to wish this into existence, and here I am, living a childhood fantasy."

"It's good," is all Væson can manage. If they dared to say anymore, they would have become a bubbling mess of tears and snot, once again proving that their human skin is all too feeble, but not caring because it means they are feeling something, a warmth that they have longed for.

Væson carries Ignatius back to her home, tucks her into bed, and they once more sleep soundly on the sofa. Alfie comes in around 4 a.m. after keeping a watchful eye on Ignatius and sleeps on the floor, as if protecting the strange new thing in the home. There is a moment of understanding between the two of them, and once more, Væson tells the canine that they mean no harm to his human.

Chapter 16

Curtain Twitcher

At the exact moment Væson is carrying Ignatius home from the movie night, Carol gets up for her routine night pee, and it's then that she sees it, the very thing she wanted to see while she was stalking them at Blockbuster. Her eyes widen as she attacks the window ledge to get a closer look. Her mouth hangs agape in shock. This is it. She wanted to see something out of the ordinary, but this... Ignatius's' cousin isn't exactly carrying Ignatius, but rather, she is hovering just above his shoulders. Carol squints and blinks the sleep out of her eyes just to make sure she is seeing what she thinks she sees and even pinches herself to check she isn't dreaming. *No.* What she sees is real and *ungodly,* she thinks. Upon reflection, it could have been a trick of the lights, but she doesn't buy that excuse for one moment. She also has no intention of letting on with what she saw but vows to keep a closer eye on Ignatius and her *cousin.* She knew there was something strange from the moment she saw him but couldn't put her finger on it as she'd gotten lost in his eyes that seemed impossibly big.

"What on earth are you hiding this time, Ignatius?" she says to the empty landing.

Crawling back into bed, Carol snuggles up to her husband. Nothing makes her happier...or hornier than gossip. The juicer, the better. Some even think it's what keeps her young. Others say it's what keeps her relevant. Some of the younger residents and teenagers say that if she didn't have any gossip to dispense, she'd curl up in a big ball and die. That is sometimes greeted with cheers of "good riddance."

Carol wakes up early the next morning in an effort to see what is going on at the beachfront house, but it is annoyingly silent for her liking. She decides that the first course of action is to make coffee. When she is on the hunt for a scandal, everything else goes out the window. She considers it her duty to inform the rest of the neighborhood with all the facts as soon as she knows them... or makes them up herself, without a care in the world about who she hurts in the process. She makes her way downstairs and into the stillness of the sickly pink kitchen, fumbling to find the light switch. It's always strange, seeing your home in the dark. No matter how many times your mind memorizes the layout in the day, at night, it becomes something entirely new, and things are always a little farther away than they are in the light.

The kitchen is Carol's most garish room, showcasing tasteless tat over an otherwise sophisticated style. Absolutely everything is pink from the kettle to the toaster to the oven mitts. The only things that aren't pink are the frilly white curtains, the bowls, the cutlery, and the trims of the cupboards. Adorning the wall opposite the kitchen window is a cuckoo clock, and every hour, a pink owl waddles out and screams a hoot, never failing to make Frank jump and curse under his breath, each time garnering a rueful look from his wife.

She whistles away a tune she hasn't heard in the longest of times, a song about a sandman, as she prepares an early morning coffee – she was going to jog first, but her morning senses caught up with her morning gusto and put a stop to that post haste. There's an extra spring in her step as the day promises to bring great revelations. It's certainly going to be a monumental day for her as well as the town. She's like a detective embarking on a brand-new case, one that would define her career. While the coffee is percolating and creating its sweet smell, she starts making some dime stack pancakes, just the way her mother taught her. It's a generations old recipe, only to be made when there is a scandal afoot.

The smells of the cooking and the coffee make their way upstairs and into the bedroom where Frank is still lightly snoring. After a few moments, the aromas invade his nose and stir him awake, instantly putting a smile on his face. He puts his dressing gown on over his pajamas and makes his way downstairs, that same smile on his face. He's still feeling the effects of last night, too. It's nights like that, where she and him combine as one hot sticky mess, that make him forget what an utter bitch she can be. He is completely submissive to her, especially in the bedroom, and that's the way they both like it. She wears the metaphorical trousers and cracks the literal whip, a cat o' nine tails, to be precise.

There are more secrets that Carol is hiding, too, and they're a lot more deadly than a kink whip. There's a reason why Væson picked up on her prickly aura and why Carol demands she has a tight grip on the town, and it has to do with one word: murder. She's gone to devastatingly painful lengths to cover up what she's done and sure, the thrill of it was intense, but the fact she could and would be put behind bars if she was ever found out drives her and the dictatorship she leads. In her control room, there's a secret drawer in her desk, and if you hit it a certain way, damning evidence will fall out and reveal her true past that entwines the fate of her and Ignatius.

Chapter 17

The Smoke House

The early morning sun slides through the blinds of Daniel and Loraine's bedroom early the next morning. The brightness invades their corneas, forcing them both to pull the light pink duvet up and over their head, but the solace is only momentary as their 3 a.m. alarms buzz them into immediate action. With sleep crust still in his eyes, Daniel gets up and snaps off the alarm clock, which doubles as a radio, on his side of the bed. Loraine does the same on her side. They stumble around like zombies looking for a brain buffet. They greet each other at the foot of the bed and give each other a tired kiss. Drool strings from their lips as they part and sluggishly wrestle to the bathroom.

"You shower first, I gotta use the porcelain throne." Daniel's voice is heavy with sleep, and Loraine grunts a form of reply and makes her way to the shower cubical.

The days Loraine isn't at her remedial job that she hopes she can one day quit, she is helping Daniel run The Smoke House, and when she isn't around to help, she enlists the help of an autistic teen, Ryan. He is often picked on at school for the way he speaks and for being the smartest in class. A lot of the time, he doesn't realize they are teasing him, but the times he does, it feels like a dagger of shame in his heart. Sometimes, he reacts before he thinks, and that's apt to getting him in trouble. He loves his job as a newspaper delivery boy, though, and the mornings when he rides around the neighborhood on his red and silver bike is one of his favorite parts of the day. His mom, Liz Anders, works at the local GP as a receptionist, and his dad is out of the picture since divorcing her. They had fights over how to raise Ryan, and Liz grew tired of his form of discipline, smacking him until he cried and learned his lesson. He didn't believe autism was real and just though that he was making the whole thing up to be able to get away with his bad behavior.

Back in the Cummings' household, Daniel is just about ready to start the day thanks to a warm cup of coffee. Loraine is with him at the kitchen counter. It's the only time of the day when it's just the two of them, and they revel in the peacefulness of it all, not needing to speak, positively enjoy each other's company.

"Another cup of coffee?" Loraine queries, disturbing the silence, Daniel nods from his side of the counter top. He's wrapped in a pleated, checkered blanket he got from the couch as the house hasn't quite warmed up yet. He feels the cold more than anyone despite his slightly bigger frame.

She fills it up to halfway, and he puts a splash of milk in. Loraine always thought that was a waste of coffee doing that, but it's an argument she can't be bothered with these days.

In about an hour, they will be opening the Smoke House for the morning rush, but this time is their quality time. There is nothing finer in this world than being in the company of the one you love. You don't even have to fill the comfortable silences as long as you can feel their presence.

"Got many coming in today, do you think?" Loraine asks,

handing Daniel a fresh cup of coffee in his favorite Star Wars mug.

"Oh, I think so. It'll be the usual lot, plus a few others. The day has a strange force about it, I can feel it," Daniel says wistfully.

He's prone to get these feelings and more often than not, they are proven right, which is why Loraine doesn't bother sighing or rolling her eyes. "What kind of feeling?"

"I can't say for certain yet, just something strange. I don't know if it's a good or bad strange yet. Only time will tell." He takes a sip of his coffee, being careful to blow it first as an image of Væson from the night before comes back to him and a smile breaks out on his face.

"Well, let's hope it's something that can help with our restaurant. The winter rush will be here soon, and we can't do this all by ourselves, even with Ryan, Junior and Skyla's help." Worry flashes in her eyes. She's already stretched as it is, and they can't afford to lose any time from The Smokehouse, not now that it's finally starting to break even.

Daniel closes his eyes, as if sensing something, or at least trying to sense something. He is silent for a good long while. When he speaks again, it makes his wife jump.

"Good gawd almighty, man! Don't be doing that! You'll scare me to death one of these days." Loraine clutches her chest. "What did you say, anyway? I was too busy making sure I didn't see a bright light. I'm not ready to leave this earth yet." Loraine is often at her wittiest with a fresh cup of coffee in her system.

"Oh, ohh, you think it could be something to do with the restaurant?" Loraine asks, replaying the snippet of conversation they had just had.

"I *know* it is!" he states confidently, wrapping the blanket tighter around him to stave off the chill of the morning air.

"Good or bad?" She hesitates, not sure she wants to know the answer.

"I don't know, but I can't see us waiting too long."

They finish their breakfast, and Loraine gets to tidying the kitchen as soon as her husband takes his last sip. There is a busy day afoot and no time to waste. She puts on her pinafore, 'the one that used to be her mother's before she passed, and her mother's before that. It once had a glorious shine to it, but now it's cracking through age. The words on it, although now faded through time and washes, are as prominent as ever, though, and so is the picture – it's a simple smiling woman with a red bandana with the words 'We Can Do It'. Meanwhile, while Loraine is busy cleaning the home kitchen, Daniel heads into the restaurant kitchen that's just a little ways down the street, still clad in his blanket. Thankfully he's fully dressed underneath. He starts up the grills and gets to work on the usual orders. They all come in at the same time each day and order the same thing. There are a few exceptions to the rule as always, but it's always been good practice to start things early. When Loraine comes twenty minutes later, she turns the *closed* sign in the window to *open,* and before long, people come teeming in, busy with the mornings chatter and smiles. This is the highlight of some of these ladies' day, and it's certainly a good place to get gossip. Carol has been known in the past to sit in the corner of the Smoke House and listen in on everyone else's conversation, then later use it for her advantage. It is a trick that still works from time to time, but she also has other ways now that are equally as effective.

The first ones through the door today are ones whom neither Loraine nor Daniel expected – at least on a conscious level: Ignatius and Væson, who looks like a cowboy had thrown up on them. They take a seat towards the back of the restaurant, underneath the picture of a rainbow.

The rest of the crowd is the usual assortment, and Daniel gets on with asking what they want—out of politeness, since he already knows.

The music in The Smoke House is always easy and soulful and never too loud. On the evenings, Daniel sometimes tickles the ivory, and on the rarest occasions, Loraine sings. Those are always the busiest nights, and people come from afar to hear her and her raspy tone.

"My, my, if it isn't Ignatius. What have I done to deserve this honor?" Loraine greets them with a pencil and notepad in hand and a smile on her face.

"We came for more of your incredible food, but this time, we are paying with human money," Væson says in a southern accent that she can't recall hearing much of yesterday.

"You are far too kind, young man." Then she asks, "Who is this handsome young man, and why is he dressed like a Clint Eastwood stand in?" She tips them both a wink to not alert anyone that they have previously met. Gossip is this neighborhood's currency.

"Howdy ma'am, the names Væson Feltrap. I'm this little lady's cousin," they say with a smile and tip her their version of a wink, which Ignatius laughs at once more. It'll never not be funny to her.

Ignatius then cuts to the meat of the matter, sitting down and taking a menu to hide her lips from prying eyes. "I have a favor to ask of you, if that's ok, of course."

Loraine puts a hand on Ignatius's shoulder and gives her a radiant smile. "You know I will do anything for you, what do you need?"

The rest of The Smoke House is going about their everyday business, and Daniel is making the orders and taking them to the tables, sometimes shooting a glance at his wife to see what she is doing. He can cope with the rush for now, but when it gets a bit busier, she's going to need to help him.

"Well, I think it would be good if they had a place to work. You know, to keep suspicion low. Any chance they can help out here?" Ignatius is ready to beg if she has to, but there is no need.

"We could do with the help. The winter rush will soon be upon us, as I was just saying to Daniel not even two hours ago. Væson, you ever cooked before?"

"Sure have!" they say with pride.

"Good, what have you cooked?"

"I'm known for cooking a mean steamed anus and eyeballs," they brag.

The ladies exchange a look that is mirrored on each other's faces. It's a look of both horror and a hint of inquisitiveness, but that soon fades as they begin to picture what that could look like, turning into dry heaving.

"Hey, hey, I'll have you know it is a wonderful delicacy!" Væson defends himself. Their eyes shoot to the table, a little out of embarrassment.

"What is it with your world and anuses and butt cheeks?" Ignatius asks, shaking her head. "Yet another question I thought I'd never ask."

"What is it with this world and not being obsessed with them? They are glorious! Some of us even paint them and get them out at every opportunity. Like you all would take a family portrait, we would do that with our anus. It's quite tasteful, actually... and tasty too, but we never eat Morkians... unless it's in the boudoir, of course. We take it from the bovines that have recently passed. We are very health conscious."

"In all my years, I have never heard such things, and I don't want to see such things either," Loraine says, aghast.

"It's so good though, you have-" Loraine raises a finger and an eyebrow, cutting him off.

"I was talking. Don't interrupt a lady when she is talking. That is basic human manners, and I will not be trying your anus... or anyone else's, nor the eyeballs. We cook good, honest food here, do you understand me? I am all for tolerance, but the clientele here are not, so we shall keep it under our hats for now. I'm sure Daniel would try some of your special food, though," she adds to soften the hostility. Væson respects the honesty put forward and is even a little scared of her. She doesn't like scolding Væson. It makes her insides turn into knots, but just the thought of the food sends her sick.

Væson stays silent, not really sure what to say or even how to talk to Loraine at this moment.

"How handy are you with a mop?" Loraine offers up a smile, trying to get Væson to warm to her again.

"And by mop and handy, she means the human way, not the way you do it on M.O.R.K-78," Ignatius warns with a firm stare. She's become a lot calmer since this chat and doesn't feel the same jealousness she felt yesterday.

At this comment, Væson looks a little dejected, but it doesn't dampen their spirits. "I'll give it a go. How hard can it be, right?"

"Right. And maybe later, when we have locked the doors, you can show me the M.O.R.K-78 way, how about that?" Loraine suggests, trying not to show the glee on her face. Last night, she was transfixed with how they washed up the dishes.. "Ignatius, I guess by your attire you won't be staying to help out with the lunch rush?"

Ignatius laughs and looks down at what she is wearing as if seeing it for the first time today. She is looking resplendent in ankle high black boots, black jeans, and a very expensive white jumper with a chiffon sleeve. Her hair is tied back into a bun, and her big, black glasses are resting on her head. She can't even remember how she got dressed this morning or if, in fact, these are the same clothes she wore yesterday.

She laughs again. "I'm afraid not. I'll pick Væson up just after lunch."

Væson says they will indeed teach her the proper way to

clean up once the customers have gone and will do their best to adhere to the human restrictions until then.

Ignatius waves goodbye at the door and feels a little lump in her throat. She tells herself to stop being so stupid, that she'll see them again soon and nothing bad is going to happen... but even thinking that feels like it's tempting fate.

Back in the Smoke House, Væson is trying to work out which way the mop goes. They figure it out with a small prompt from Loraine who can't help but smile. Daniel watches on with amusement between customers. By 11 a.m., there is a bit of a lull and a plethora of empty plates and tables. The back hallway resembles a mini lake, and a muddy one at that, as Væson hasn't got the hang of mopping and keeping things clean just yet.

"Væson, Væson, where are y-" calls Loraine, but before she can finish, her feet go from under her. Væson sees this just in time and stops her going ass over tit and cracking her head in the process. Of course, they stop the fall with nothing but their mind and luckily, there is no one around to see.

"It's a bit slippery, watch your step," Væson says, lowering her gently.

"I...I can see that. Now, why on earth have you turned my floor into a damn water park?" she asks, not even bothering to mention the other thing.

"I'm mopping!" Væson grins ear to ear, and they even tip their cowboy hat to Loraine as a sign of respect.

"No, you're making a mess and a fine one at that. Don't you know you're supposed to rinse the mop in the bucket first?" Loraine takes the mop from them with exasperation and does a demonstration.

"*Oh.* Now, that makes sense," they say, taking it all in.

"But of course, with what you've done to my floor, you're gonna have to get some rags and dry it all up first. You're no different from the rest. You do a job and make a job. I'll go and get you some old rags to clean this up. Don't you be making any more messes while I'm gone."

Væson feels like a naughty school child being reprimanded by the principal. It's been many moons since they were one, but the feeling comes screaming back to them as if it was only yesterday. Isn't it strange how things like that can haunt us even years later? Stranger still when you think that the person who once scolded you at school is now a can of worm food and their torment is still lingering on, making them live on in your subconscious. Perhaps the fact that both humans and aliens can be connected by one common feeling will bring both species together in the long r–n - a common ground built on past regret and the need to grow.

Loraine comes back a few moments later carrying a bundle of old rags and mutters some things under her breath that Væson can't quite hear.

"Now, do you need supervising with this, too, or can I leave you to it?" She hands the bundle over to them, hoping she doesn't sound as prickly. She has a hard time not being stern with her words - due in part to her day job where 'he's surrounded by men who think they know better.

"I got it," they say confidently.

"Sure. You said that about the mopping and look what happened." The words are out before she can process them, so she offers a smile as a compromise.

"I dry the floor with these towels. Seems simple to me," they say with misplaced confidence.

"Yes... and you have to rinse the towels into the sink. Not the kitchen sink, as that'll be a health code violation, but the sink in the bathroom. Not the customer one, but the one behind you. Once you have no more puddles, I want you to get a fresh load of water and soap, but not too much now, and clean the floor once more. Don't be forgetting to dry and rinse your mop before it touches the floor though, otherwise you'll be apt to do the whole process again."

Væson nods and Loraine leaves, but not before giving them another smile. This time, it's returned by Væson.

They manage to clear up the mess they made, but not by any human methods. Although they do try, Væson resorts to the M.O.R.K-78 way, which is much more user friendly. The floors become so shiny, you can literally eat off them.

"My goodness, now that is what I call clean," Loraine says when she comes back to check on them.

"It's ok?"

"Better than ok. I don't know why you didn't do this in the first place, but I guess that's neither here nor there..." Her left eyebrow shoots up into the shape of a bow, questioning them. "You didn't use your powers to do this, did you?"

"*Of course no*—yeah, I did. But look, it's so much easier and no one saw, I promise," Væson pleads. The truth is, they have no idea if they were seen or not.

"Well, it's too late now to worry about it, so I guess it's done. Ignatius is here, and we've closed for lunch."

Chapter 18

The Curious Past of Carol and Ignatius

To say that the relationship between Carol and Ignatius is strained is an understatement at the very least. And it started long before Ignatius turned up with her 'new money'. Carol knew Aiden Feltrap long before Ignatius did. However, contrary to popular – or Carol's – belief, Ignatius didn't steal her man or make him cheat. Carol just enjoys playing the victim and shouting down on anyone who says differently. To get the full scope of this feud, we have to go back to when Aiden and Carol first met in the mid-80s. This fact has been locked away deep in her mind——so deep, in fact, that Væson hasn't even found it; not that they would want to invade her privacy. Ignatius keeps this memory locked up partially out of spite and partially because she wants this memory all to herself. It's one of the only pure memories she has of Aiden. And would this memory help clear her name from Carol's mouth? Sure, but Ignatius can be stubborn, which can often lead to a detriment to her own happiness.

They first met in a small diner, a place that perhaps neither of them would be likely to patron now – most of all Aiden, due to his untimely death. It was one of those chromatic trailer conversion diners that had a former life as a trailer for a family of half a dozen. The waitresses all wore hot pink shirts and looked like they smoked a carton of cigarettes every couple of hours. The food, when it finally came out, was filled with enough grease to cook three more meals. Carol was sitting, needling at her toasted English muffin, slice of good old Canadian bacon, and two perfectly poached eggs swamped in hollandaise sauce. Some call the eggs benedict - but in this beaten down diner, it was called English-style. She washed it down with fresh... well, *fresh-ish* coffee. She was dressed in her finest regalia, which made her stick out like a sore thumb; it also gave her an inflated sense of self-importance— dressing better than others made her feel superior to the company she kept around her, even though her face was stained with the tear tracks from her makeup and, try as she might to get everyone to look and take pity on her, not a single soul cared. In this diner, everyone had their own problems and none of them concerned a spoiled, rich girl. That was, until Aiden walked in...

The small bell over the diner's door alerted her to his entrance. He was a few years her senior at around thirty-three, where she was in her mid-twenties, but that just made him all the more enticing. His chiseled good looks were a stark contrast to the rest of the establishment, and as soon as she saw him, she turned the dramatics all the way up to eleven. Still, no one paid her any mind... except, of course, good-guy Aiden. He rushed over like a knight in shining armor, almost slipping on the greasy floor, but that just accelerated his momentum. In one swift movement, he slid into the booth opposite her, sliding a fresh cup of coffee her way, too. It was the ultimate cheese. He was not sure what compelled him to rush to this stranger's aid. When he was younger, his parents had always told him to look after crying women; perhaps that's where it stemmed from. He was brought up to be empathetic and chivalrous. On this occasion, it certainly wasn't *cosmic force*.

"Are you ok?" he asked, looking into her watery gray eyes.

"I... I am now," she said dramatically, staring into his ocean blue eyes. For a moment, she thought she could fall right into them and swim, as if they were an ocean just for her. She clung onto his hand as he slid into the booth beside her.

That day marked the start of their courtship, and they were married the following winter. At that point, they were not living at Poppy Field Lane but were certainly searching for a place they would call home. Aiden had just gained a promotion with his work, and it allowed Carol to abstain from working herself. She had said it *'wouldn't look good'* if the wife was working as well as the husband. It was *'something the lower and middle class did'*. Aiden had already learned to not protest or rebuke anything Carol said in the year they had been together. When they first got together, he walked proud, head up and shoulders back, but not in an arrogant way. Now, due to her snide and snarky comments, he walked with slightly hunched shoulders, as if they were pinched in the middle. His gait had become laborious, though never in an overstated way. You could only spot these things if you knew Aiden before he met and subsequently married Carol. Whoever she got her claws into, she manipulated into being her little puppet, making them subservient and spineless. And curiously, she had this aura about her that seemed to feel like a leech, almost as if she oozed unknown negativity, sucking all the happiness and confidence out of him.

Before they moved to Poppy Field Lane, they found themselves in another suburb, not quite as prestigious, but exclusive all the same. At this point, Aiden was almost mute in the relationship, constantly in fear of treading on eggshells and worrying what kind of hair-brained thing she was going to come out with next. She was insanely jealous, too, and loathed the thought of another woman talking to him or even looking in his direction. The looks he got in the street – ones that used to be full of lust –were now heavy with pity. Carol didn't see it like that. Any look was a threat to her, and when Aiden wasn't looking, she would curse them out or even send them an intimidating letter if she knew where they lived. It was one of the ways in which she rose to prominence in the neighborhood. Everyone began to clamor to be by her side; not because they liked her or her hosting skills and sophisticated cocktail parties with a black-tie dress code – although that helped – but because of the fear of them being frozen out of such events. There was one such couple who got frozen out so fiercely, they left town, and no one even remembers their name or them leaving. It was this kind of iron fist ruling that put her in good stead to take over Poppy Field Lane a few years later. She was excellent at honing her craft, sharpening her claws.

Their relationship hit a huge bump when Aiden could no longer keep down his job. It was due to a multitude of factors – most notably Carol. She had worn him down until there was barely anything left in his heart and soul due to her constant hen-pecking and deliberate public dressing-downs. Onlookers would avert their eyes in case they caught her fury, but all of them looked sorry for him. If you were to look up the phrase 'perpetual state of melancholy', you would find a description matching Aiden and, if your dictionary had pictures, you'd see an image of him, too.

Aiden was called into the office one day. His heart was beating ten to the dozen, his hand practically shaking the door handle right off when he opened it. His tie was thin, worn, and lifeless; a visual representation of the man it was hanging onto. He had become so thin and frail, he looked like a sack of bones in a loose-fitting suit. His boss sat behind a grandiose desk, not even looking at him as he walked in. Instead, he was going over a financial report. Aiden hovered by the door, and he would have gone unnoticed if he didn't feebly clear his throat and say, "umm, you wanted me... to see me, I mean." Looking down at his worn shoes, he didn't look like a man who was dealing with hundreds of thousands of dollars' worth of accounts. It was hard to believe he was the same guy who walked into that diner so long ago, with the chiseled jaw and good looks.

"Aiden... Jesus, look at you," his boss said in a disgusted tone. He didn't care for anyone who didn't have a three-piece pinstriped power suit with immaculate hair. He was also a horrendous chauvinist, and his views on women would have looked out of place, even in the 1800s.

"Look, I'm going to make this short and sweet. We're restructuring, and we're moving on without you. Quite frankly, when you walk into a room, the lights go dull, and you just suck all the happiness out. Not to mention that you make the room look poorer. So, with immediate effect, you're fired. Clear your desk as quickly as you can, and don't make me get security." With that, he turned around, not wanting to lay his eyes on the poor and destitute looking former employee.

Aiden left his office within the hour, holding back tears; not for losing his job, but because he had to go home and face his wife. He knew she was going to fly off the handle at him, maybe even hit him. She'd done it before. That night, to avoid telling her the bad news right away, he stopped at a seven-eleven, bought a pack of cigarettes and smoked the whole carton. He contemplated downing a six pack of *Budweiser*, but that was a step too far, and she *would* beat him if he did that. He'd never been a smoker before, so smoking a whole pack took a while. He didn't even know why he did it, especially when the coughing fits started after the first drag.

Ignatius came into this story when Aiden was out at a lowkey party in a local bar... ok, so party was a strong word, but maybe guys' night out without the 'ball and chains' was more accurate. This was shortly after the firing incident which, as suspected, did not go down too well at all; especially since they had to live off their savings until Aiden got a new job. It was the first time in as long as Aiden could remember that he half-smiled. It took him most of the first hour to stop looking over his shoulder, expecting to be reprimanded for saying something out of turn or being corrected on an already accurate story. She corrected him often when it didn't show her in a good enough light. The bar was heavy with cigar smoke and the cackle of old man laughter. The smell was a mixture of hardwood and ale with the hint of piss from the elderly gents in the corner sitting by the slot machine. Aiden was with a group of four other friends, all his age and all happily married. They had grown up with him and noticed his decline. His hair was also prematurely thinning, and they couldn't see what he saw in Carol. This night, they had a plan to ambush and question his motives and to try and get him away from her. They had indirectly been trying for months, making comments here and there, but he wasn't taking the bait or getting the hint. Their hope was to get him to a place like this where he could see how other men were and how happy they were, with the faintest of hopes that he would perhaps meet someone else here.

As the night wore on, Aiden's friends got louder and more drunk, reciting old stories and adding bits here and there to exaggerate an already dull one. Some became more bullish in their attempts to tell Aiden to find someone else, and one of them directly said she's the worst thing that ever happened to him. Aiden, still stone cold sober, decided that was the time to move away from the bunch and propped himself up at the bar to order another soft drink. He was never too fond of alcohol and only agreed to come along because they had been pestering him for months, not to mention making some strange comments that he failed to understand. He was working around the clock to keep Carol happy and a roof over their head. This was the first night in months that he had been out with the guys, and it took him a long time to ask Carol if he could go. The trouble was, his new job was bringing him insurmountable pressure, and he was pretty close to losing it and his money. He knew deep down that as soon as that happened, Carol would be out the door, leaving just dust in her wake.

The night that he got fired from his new job was the night things finally started to change for Aiden. He went home with a heavy heart and sat Carol, who was not at all pleased to be up at this time of night listening to her boring pet of a husband, down at the kitchen table.

"Carol," he said with a deep sigh. She looked at him from across the table - not really giving a shit. "I have some bad news. And I don't know how else to say it, so I think... I think-"

"Oh, spit it out already, Aiden, so I can go back to bed," she scolded.

"I've lost my job. Again. But I know another one is just round the corner, so don't worry. I'll look after us, I promise." His eyes darted down in shame, and he picked at the cuff of his sleeve, which was already becoming threadbare from excessive nervous picking.

Carol got up from the table without a word and went upstairs, leaving Aiden dumbstruck in the kitchen. A short while later, she came back down with a pre-packed suitcase and a perky smile. "I knew this day would come, when your spine would crumble and you'd become a useless worm 'kin. You don't deserve to be in my presence anymore. You're not good for my image. Luckily for you, I've already found a charming new man, and he has no trouble keeping his job down... or his penis up, for that matter." She added the last bit in out of spite, but it seemed to have lit a fire inside Aiden and suddenly, years of built-up rage poured out of him.

"You know what? Thank fuck. Everyone has been trying to tell me for years what a vindictive bitch you are, but I was too blind, too beaten down to see it. I'm just glad the trash is taking itself out because it was starting to stink."

Now it was Carols turn to look utterly dumbstruck. She left the house quicker than a bat–out of hell - and they didn't see each other for a good while after unless it was about divorce proceedings. The invisible string that bound them together would see them meet up a few years later in Poppy Field Lane: a place they would both call home but with different partners. Carol would already have the neighborhood in her vice-like grip and seeing him again would bring a chill down both their spines. As soon as she left, his heart got lighter, but the adrenaline wore off quickly. He needed to get out of the house, and the first place he thought of was that bar he went to with his friends a few months back. It had recently become his fortress of solitude. Carol didn't care as it made her sex sessions with her new –over better - she knew where he was' but he didn't know nor care what she was doing.

"Going to stay on the soft drinks all night?" a woman asked from behind, startling him.

"Oh, oh... I'm not much of a drinker," he replied, still looking into his glass of juice.

The music in the bar turned to a popular power-ballad, and a couple of guys (that on this night he didn't want to call his friends as they were being hugely embarrassing) started singing along, all of them off key. But that didn't stop them, and within a few moments, others had joined in for the chorus.

"I can see that," she said once the signing had died down a bit and took a seat next to him. He looked at her, not really taking her in, but when he looked again, he was in love with her from that very moment.

Eight months after Carol left him, he had a rugged and devilishly good look about him, and the bags beneath his eyes had started to disperse. He was mending on the inside, too, and no longer felt like he was breeding anxiety spiders. You could say that he was happy... or almost happy, anyway. His friends practically celebrated the news as if *The Pats* had won the Superbowl. He even got poached by another company, after doing so well in the job he tried to tell Carol about all those months ago. They valued him much more, the hours were less, and the money was better. And above all, he loved the job. His new position was an investment banker, and before long, he was earning almost three times the amount he was before. If Carol knew this, she would have been running back to him. Trouble was, she's like shit on the sole of a sneaker: once she's in your life, it's hard to get rid of her, and she leaves a god-awful smell. Other, less kind people have likened her to herpes as she keeps coming back. But that's not quite true. At least with herpes, the outbreaks are less severe each time... with Carol, they're worse.

"I've seen you in here a few times this week. No wedding ring, so you're not hiding from your wife. Not unless you take it off, but there's no prominent mark on your finger, which means you were married, but I'm going to say you went your separate ways and she's still alive. Also, no red veins on your nose, so you're not an alcoholic... like your friends over there," she said, hooking a thumb in their direction. "And you don't look like a perv, so why are you here?"

"Are you some kind of shrink?" he asked, only half joking.

"Just observant, that's all." She smiled at him, taking her time to appreciate his tortured beauty.

"And you think I'm worth observing because...?" he asked defensively, an old habit leftover from his time with Carol.

"More so than the rest of the crowd, yeah. Let me buy you a drink, non-alcoholic of course," she offered.

"A gentleman never lets a woman pay. Drinks are on me." he countered, giving her a smile. For the first time, he noticed what she was wearing, and it struck him as rather odd but in the best possible way. She was casually dressed but wore accessories that elevated the whole look up to almost high fashion. Not that he knew what that was, but he could tell she was confident; it was all in her voice.

"I'm not a damsel that needs saving, but I will let you buy the first drink. If you're as interesting as I think you are, I'll buy the next one. Sound like a deal?"

"I don't think I could say no even if I tried, right?"

"Nope!" She laughed. "I'll start with a scotch on the rocks."

Aiden liked her instantly, and this brief exchange only made his feelings for her grow. Yes, she was upfront and told him what she wanted, but not in the same, obnoxious way as Carol did. Her eyes were kind, too, and the smile, well, Aiden would be thinking about that one long into the night. They talked and drank (mostly non-alcoholic in both cases) for hours. He saw his friends leave and waved at them, but they were far too drunk to even know who he was. They were trying their best to hold each other up while simultaneously screeching the words to *Livin' on a Prayer*. Ignatius and Aiden chatted as if they had known each other for a millennium. They would have talked longer, but at around 3 a.m., the barman had no choice but to kick them out as he had to close, so they exchanged phone numbers on the sidewalk, the moon illuminating their faces, and they both had matching smiles.

The next morning, they both met up for a coffee at one of the local shops and chatted some more. It was there that they discovered they didn't live too far from each other, and they had similar interests jobwise, too. They spent the whole Saturday together and even made plans for an 'official' date the following day. Aiden was nervous about asking the question as he didn't want to ruin the magic or come off too needy, but when he asked, there was no thinking time at all; she jumped at the chance to say yes, as if she had been waiting since the moment she met him, which of course was true.

They both got dressed up for the date as previously

discussed, and Aiden had booked one of the most exclusive restaurants in the city. He had to grease the wheels to get such a good table on short notice, but it was all worth it. The atmosphere in the place was the complete antithesis of the one where they had met just a few days before. It had felt like they had been together for years, and Aiden thought he could see himself marrying her. But this time, it would be different, as both parties were equal. There was no power grab, no mind games, just two people enjoying the hell out of each other's company. Ignatius, on the other hand, already considered him her best friend, or at least one of. But that didn't stop her mind thinking of wedding bells either. She had every intention of growing old with him, and she couldn't wait. Never in her life did she expect to fall so madly in love with a complete stranger, let alone dining in a fancy restaurant with him, but here she was doing just that, both of them with unspoken wedding plans on their mind and laughing over dinner while the rest of the patrons looked on, some even tutting at them. They weren't being loud, but some people couldn't stand jovial behavior. At one point, a woman who looked like she sucked lemon for a living, judging by the wrinkles around her lips, loudly tutted and would have gone over to them if it wasn't for the raised eyebrow firm on Ignatius, almost daring her to come say something. Aiden saw this and had to stifle a laugh, making a mental note not to get onto Ignatius's bad side. The silver haired woman retreated and turned her chair at an angle in such a hurry that she hit her shin on the leg of the table, thus knocking some of her wine into her food. She ate the rest of her meal in silence, which was a relief to her husband, who would hear about this incident for the rest of the week, with added hyperbole.

The music in the establishment was also a complete one-eighty from the one they first met. The off-key and wildly drunken tones of the bar had made way to a crooner on a small stage. He came down from his flamboyant stage every so often to serenade the diners. None of them took much notice and would have preferred to be listening to him from a distance, but when he came over to Aiden and Ignatius's table, Aiden, to everyone's surprise, joined in. They made a nice sounding duet, and Ignatius was mesmerized by it. The crooner hammed it up. Not wanting to be outdone, Aiden hammed it up even more, and they sang their way to the stage, belting out a couple of Frank Sinatra's classic songs. The whole restaurant began to ripple with excitement, and when Aiden finally got off the stage, he was greeted with chants of "more, more, more" by the patrons and even by the crooner. After very little consideration, he obliged, but this time, he took center stage, and the crooner played the piano. There was also a trumpet player, and the whole evening was transfixed into an impromptu and magical time that none of them would forget. Ignatius watched on with glistening eyes that were so full of love and admiration, they almost burst.

To say that they were soulmates was perhaps stretching it a bit, but their love was pure and genuine. Ignatius had given him back the one thing that Carol took many moons ago: his confidence. And now, they were both reaping the rewards. Within a year, they were married, both extremely successful in their respected fields and had put a down-payment on a house in a very exclusive area: Poppy Field Lane.

Chapter 19

Won't you be my neighbor, Carol?

The sun was a hot ball in the sky, threatening to burn anything in its path if it stayed there for too long, but the certainty didn't perturb Ignatius and Aiden's mood on moving day. How could it? The house was like something out of their wildest dreams, and they never failed to realize how lucky and privileged they both were to be in such a position.

Ignatius was dressed in sweats with her hair tied back into a high ponytail, her ringlets threatening to burst out of the band. It looked out of place in the neighborhood, but she didn't care two hoots, especially since she was carrying heavy boxes from the moving van and into the new dream house. The thought of her attire didn't even cross her mind until a woman in leopard print Lycra came bounding up to her.

"Hi, I'm Carol. You must be our new neighbor!" she said enthusiastically, sticking out her hand - trying to establish dominance right away. She was always the first to greet the new neighbors and did it so she could get a read on them and see what information she could get out of them to use later. Using off brand products? She'll spin a story about how you're broke and struggling to make ends meet. Everything she did was designed to break people down and make them as submissive as her husband.

Ignatius, not wanting to be rude, jostled for leverage with the box to free up a hand and shake this *Carol* woman's hand.

"I'm Ignatius, nice to meet you," she said, wanting the conversation to be over with already.

Carol continued to shake her hand, and when she let go, almost a second too long, she noticed a wedding ring, one that was almost double the size of her own.

"And whom may I ask is the lucky man?"

"What? Oh, my wedding ring. I'm sure you'll see him around. Now if you don't mind, I'm pretty busy, as you can see, so if there's nothing else, I'd like to get back to it, please."

"Hmm, charming, well, there are other things to discuss and such, but it will just have to wait until later. What time is good for you and your husband?"

"What is this, some kind of cult?" Ignatius asked nervously, taking a few steps closer to her house and wondering where in the world Aiden was. "Maybe later when the van has gone. I don't know," she added in an effort to sound less harsh, with a pitch to her voice so high, it sounded as though it was dipped in sugar., all in an effort to sound a little less brash. This woman just brought it out of her, though. Ignatius took an instant disliking to her and her *door-to-door* salesman spiel.

"Cult?" Carol laughed as if this was the funniest thing she had ever heard, but inside, she already wanted to slap the uncouthness out of this vile woman with the man's name. And what on earth was she wearing? She desperately hoped she was going to unpack a mirror. If not, Carol would go out and buy her one, and a large one at that, too. As soon as she was done listening to the rudeness of the woman, she was going to get right on the phone and tell all her girlfriends about her and make sure they all kept an eye on her. She could feel that this woman was going to be trouble, and she was going to be sure to make her toe the line as there was only room for one Matriarch in Poppy Field Lane.

"No, no, we're not a cult. We are the epitome of high society. What we do and what we say is often reflected in the local news. Everyone wants to live in Poppy Field Lane as I'm sure you know, but not everyone can. They lack a certain, shall we say, decorum."

Ignatius rolled her eyes and headed up to her house, hoping that her husband would be there. She had to tell him about what just happened. Oh, she was going to have some fun with this woman, that was for sure. She hated uppity bitches who thought they were better than everyone else. She hated uppity men, too. Things were certainly going to change in this town.

She managed to find Aiden in the kitchen, and she recounted the strange encounter with their new neighbor, telling him she was going to be having some fun with her at every chance she got.

"Give her some time to get to know us, at least first. We don't want the whole neighborhood to hate us," he said, brushing a blonde ringlet of hair out of her eyes and kissing her cheeks and then her lips.

"Oh come on, where's the fun in that? I'm sure she's just a desperate housewife with too much time on her hands. I'm sure she'll be a mainstay at all of our soirées."

"Soirées? I don't think this is the place," he said, laughing.

"Well, that's another thing I'm going to be changing around here, then," she declared, joining in the laughter.

"I don't think this place is ready for you!"

With boxes strewn around them in the kitchen and in every room in the house, they forgot all about that for a moment, his hands reaching the back of her hair. and kissing the side of her neck. His soft red lips then reach her scarlet red ones, the world around them dissolving. He then hoisted her onto the kitchen counter and kissed her neck with deep passion. One hand was grabbing the back of her head and the other was fumbling for her bra strap under her jumper. Her hands were busy, too, as they worked down to his belt buckle and undid it with swift dexterity. She reached into his boxers and grabbed his already hard dick.

"Yoo-hoo, excuse me! Oh good gracious…" said a voice that sounded just like Carol.

When Ignatius turned around, she found it *was* Carol, and anger rose in her so quickly, it scared her a little. Unfortunately for Aiden, she turned round with such velocity that the hand holding his penis gripped a little too tight and he let out a little yelp. She made a note to make it up to him later, but right now, she had some laws to lay down.

"What the fuck are you doing in my house? Get out!"

"How… how rude! It is most unbecoming for a lady to use profanities!"

"Well, tough shit! I ain't no lady, so you better get used to it. Aiden… This is the woman I was telling you about, Carol. She's our new neighbor, but you can add the prefix of nosey to it, too."

Aiden and Carol saw each other for the first time in what had been years, and they did a double take.

"Carol?"

"Aiden?"

"Oh, great, you two know each other? This should be easy. Goodbye now, Carol."

"You look… well," Carol said through disbelieving eyes. If he looked like that when they were together, she would still be with him now, but this *skank* by the name of Ignatius had taken him. Oh, there was going to be hell to pay for this.

"You too," Aiden lied. There was so much make-up plastered on her face that the cracks in her Botox were showing.

"Wait... Is this the crazy bitch you were telling me about all that time ago at the bar?" Ignatius asked, not caring at all about the consequences.

"I beg your pardon?" Carol said, blood rushing into her cheeks.

"No need to beg, I don't treat people like you treated Aiden." Ignatius said with a wry smile. She already had Carol's number and was dialing it incessantly. It was like a cat playing with a blind mouse.

Carol had nothing to say. In fact, she didn't say anything and left the house in such a fluster, she ran into a few boxes on her way out.

"Watch your step now," Ignatius called after her.

The door slammed shut, and they both burst out laughing.

"What are the odds of that happening? Please tell me you'll be nice to her... She's, well, she's crazy. I don't want you getting caught up in her crazy world."

Ignatius smirked, which told him everything he needed to know. The next few weeks were certainly going to be a test, but he was certainly glad he was on the side of his *loving* wife and not of the *suppressive* one. He felt infinite sorrow for the poor chap who wound up with her and thought to himself that he would end up in an early grave.

Chapter 20

Væson Goes Shopping

A few days have passed since Væson's first stint at The Smoke House, and they have gotten the grips of it a little more than the first day. In fact, they have become so used to life in Poppy Field Lane that they are sat at the kitchen table in Ignatius's home, mulling something over, but they just can't quite articulate the words yet.

Ignatius notices something is on her visitor's mind but is waiting for them to tell her what it is, so she makes herself busy by preparing another pot of coffee. The radio is on in the background. It's some upbeat number from an American band, and she taps her foot away to the beat.

After a few more agonizing moments, Væson says, "Umm, would it be alright if I go... if I go, shopping today?" It's something that has been on their mind for a while now, ever since they found out about the existence of shopping back when they first escaped from The Facility. They're not even sure why they're so nervous about asking, either. They're like a sixth grader asking for their first sleepover. Well, they knew *of* shopping from the shows they watched back on M.O.R.K-78 but didn't quite understand the complex joys of it until they came face to face with it. And they've never been on an actual shopping spree like in the movies.

For a moment, Ignatius is stunned by the simplicity of the question and almost bursts out laughing as she thinks it's a joke, but then she looks into their amazing milky way-colored eyes and sees that they are welling up, but why? From embarrassment, perhaps? She isn't sure. She stops what she is doing and puts a hand around them, pulling them into her chest. Væson is unsure how to react at first but then puts an arm around her.

"This is a big deal for you, isn't it?" she asks after a few moments of holding them, letting go to look into their eyes again.

"It's something I've wanted for the longest time," they say with longing. There is so much innocence in them. Despite the hyper intelligence, there is so much practical knowledge they don't have, and they're eager to learn, eager to grow.

"Are we talking about grocery shopping or Mall shopping?"

Væson's eyes light up. "Both! Yes, that would be the best... Can we make a day of it?"

"You want me to come with you?" she asks, touched by the thought of it.

"Of course! You are my best friend, and I have read countless books and watched infinite films that tell me that your best friend should always be there for you," they say in pure honesty that warms Ignatius's heart. She hasn't enjoyed someone else's company this much since her time with Aiden.

"You really aren't human, are you?" she says, smiling.

"What gave it away?" They wink and smirk.

"Your empathy and honesty," she replies without missing a beat. It's true, but saying it out loud confirms how much she actually likes her new alien friend. She can see them being friends until the end of her life. She hopes so, anyway.

Væson tries to get the discussion back on topic as there is too much soppy mush in the air. "So, you'll come with me? Are you sure you're free today?"

"The benefit—well, there are many, actually—to selling your billion-dollar company is that you have all the time in the world to go shopping and not have to answer to anyone. As soon as we've finished our coffees, we can go to one of two places: White Plains or The Hamptons. But if we go to The Hamptons, we'll have to stay over for a few days."

The billion dollar company in question was, ironically to Carol, a makeup line that was used almost exclusively by celebrities and high(er) society people. Ignatius had done an internship one year at a fashion house and excelled quickly, learning what she needed to start her own company. Word got out fast about a young rising , and clients were clamoring to use her products. She moved into clothing shortly after that and then sold both of them when a stupid amount of money was thrust upon her. Truth is, she wanted to spend more time in the 'real' world, anyway, and the offer came at the right time.

"And that's a problem?"

"Not in the slightest!" she says, putting the coffees on the kitchen table and taking a sip.

Today is going to be a good day.

The journey to the grocery store fills Væson with the same excitement as the trip to Blockbuster. Once again, they are literally hovering with anticipation in the passenger seat.

"Hey, Væ," Ignatius says as they go past the exclusive yacht club that is centered in the town enclosed around Poppy Field Lane.

"Yeah?" they ask as they look out at the boats bobbing on the water, the sun shining down on them, giving them a dazzling haze.

"Do they not have malls and grocery stores where you're from? I mean, what makes this all so exciting for you?" she asks, briefly taking her eyes off the road to look at them. Their boot clad feet are on the dash, eyes looking out the window and cowboy hat firmly on their head. She's not sure anyone else could pull off this look, and perhaps part of it is due to the way they carry themselves.

"No such thing as malls or grocery stores on M.O.R.K.-78. We've all heard about them, though, and all of us have wanted to enter one."

"How do you all get your food and clothes, then?" she asks, perplexed.

"We have everything delivered to us via an intricate series of tubes which takes around four seconds from clicking buy to being delivered."

"Holy shit, that's dangerous!" She slams a hand to her mouth in shock. They are now driving through the town center. To their left are high boutique buildings, and to the right, the lake gives way to a dog park and lush green playing fields.

"Dangerous how?" Væson asks.

"I would spend too much, too quick. So if you have no stores, how do you order your stuff or go for a meal?"

"Oh, we have restaurants, of course, and little side shops, but they're seldom used. You know the thing you have here, the umm, what's it called? The internet, that's it, we use that."

"That slow dial-up thing?"

"Trust me, with our technology, you'll soon have super-fast internet. We call it fiberoptic broadband on our planet, and everything will literally come to a standstill when it stops. Luckily, that's a rarity, as every business relies on it."

"That sounds a little silly, putting all your eggs in one basket."

"Eggs? I'm not talking about eggs... In-ter-net, not *egg-ter-net*. You humans really need to listen to the other side of a conversation," Væson says in relative disbelief.

"No, no, it's a saying. It means, well... It means, hmm, how can I put this? Sort of like saying don't rely on just one thing in case it falls apart."

"Human language is strange," Væson declares.

"Well, I think it's just the English variant, in all honesty."

"See, there again, why did you have to say all honesty? Surely you would be wholly honest, anyway. Why the need to state the fact?"

"That's the English variant for you again, and the fact that most of the time, humans aren't honest."

"Oh, I believe that! You and the rest of the residents of Poppy Field are the exception though, of course... In all honesty."

"Now you're just pulling my leg!"

"I am NOT! My hands are right here, look..." Væson says, a little shocked at the accusation, and stretches their arms out as some kind of proof.

Ignatius laughs and explains that it's just another saying. This goes on for a little while, and by the end of it, Væson grasps the English language a little more. In fact, more than they ever have from a textbook or scan of the human brain.

When they pull up to the grocery store, Væson's jaw drops to their chest. It's everything they dreamed of and more. Ignatius watches on with a smile on her face and once again, she wishes she saw the world through their eyes, akin to a kid at Christmas. And speaking of, there are already some holiday decorations outside, but they're the spooky cousin of Christmas: Halloween. When Væson locks eyes on them, they shrink away and let out a little scream. Ignatius can't help but laugh.

"What the hell is that?" they shriek, pointing at a ten-foot tall female vampire decoration. Its eyes seem to follow Væson, and that slight smirk is all too terrifying. Ignatius continues to laugh.

"That's just a Halloween decoration, nothing to be scared of." She tries to sound reassuring but is laughing too hard.

Væson looks at more spooky decorations and listens to the spooky sounds and after a moment, they get used to it. They edge closer and closer to the decorations, and Ignatius already knows what's going to happen but remains silent. Væson makes a tentative beeline to a huge bowl of candy. A witch is guarding it with her hand outstretched over the bowl. The wait for what is about to happen is almost too agonizing for Ignatius, and she feels bad... almost.

Væson stretches their hand out to the bowl, and as soon as their hand touches the brightly colored candy, the witch cackles into life and grabs Væson's hand. Its animatronic head goes back and forth, and Væson jumps so high, Ignatius thinks a rocket had been strapped to their ass. The scream that follows is deafening.

"Mother cock-sucking whores antelope ears!" Væson says in machine gun fire.

The incident has drawn a small crowd, and they are all laughing, including Ignatius, but then she does feel bad and rushes to his aid. They are shaking like a leaf in a fall breeze, and she finds it hard to stop the waves of laughter.

"Di...Diii. Diiid you see that!? It tried to grab me. It DID grab me!" they say once their breath is back.

"Relax, it's just a robot. It's on a sensor. Just a silly Halloween decoration. It's not going to hurt you. Excellent choice on the swear string, though!" she says, smiling, still trying to hold back laughter. The small crowd has dispersed into the store now.

"Just a robot, eh? I'll show that hunk of metal who's boss!" they say as they stride back up to it.

"Væson, wait, no!" Ignatius shouts but to no avail.

Væson goes up to the witch once more, this time with balled-up fists. As soon as they are in range of the sensor, the witch cackles again, scaring the shit out of Væson, who in turn screams and runs back. But this time, they are laughing a little bit, too.

"Oh, I'm going to get you... one day!"

This time, Ignatius does laugh.

She's worried this could go on for a while, so she grabs them by the hand and gets them to walk the other side of the witch. As they enter the store, Væson flips the witch off and puts their thumb to their throat. That gesture means the same on M.O.R.K-78 as it does on earth, and Ignatius laughs again.

As soon as they both enter the store, an old man with a flat cap who looks like he has a taxidermy collection greets them warmly with a smile full of yellow teeth. The sight, mixed with the strange colored smile, makes Væson jump, which isn't too hard to achieve as they are already on edge from the witch. They have to fight down a scream but ball their fists just in case the old man tries to do something funny. Ignatius pulls them further into the store.

When they enter the center of the store, the anxiety that Væson was feeling dissipates into pure joy. They see rows and rows of fruits and vegetables, and they pick some of them up, inspecting each one with curious eyes. They even try to bite one but are stopped just in time by Ignatius.

"You can't just eat the stuff; you have to pay for it first. Didn't they show you that bit on M.O.R.K-78?" she asks, a smile curling her lips. "Listen, you wait here, and I'll get us a cart. Do not eat anything, I'll be less than a minute."

She leaves them, and they stare at the people passing by with carts full of produce and other items that the patrons deem essential. One woman, in a pink power suit jacket coupled with a pencil skirt and kitten heels, is busy deciding which type of melon is the juiciest. Væson goes up to her cart and riffles through it, not knowing any better. They pick out a banana and look at it as if it's the most peculiar thing in existence. The pink power suit woman turns around to see the stranger rummaging in her cart and she screams, making Væson jump and squeeze the banana so hard, the innards of it seep from the sides and some even hits her in the face. For a moment, she doesn't register this, but when she does, she takes a manicured finger and wipes it off, then inspects it and screams.

"They're my bananas!" she screams hysterically.

Væson, unsure what to do, tries to hand the woman the mushed banana but she swipes it away and screams again.

Ignatius sees this and runs with the cart to Væson's aid.

"I'm so sorry. Excuse them, he's not from around here," she says, pulling them away.

The power suit woman is still screaming about her banana and wiping bits of the fruit from her face as shoppers actively skirt around her in case she screams at them, too. The shouting has caused the manager to come over and see if she is all right, but by the time he comes to see what all the fuss was about, her 'assailant' is nowhere to be found. To calm the power suit woman down, the manager promises a discount on her shopping for a month. That shuts her up pretty quick and she goes about her business pretty robustly after that - as if nothing had happened. Unbeknownst to her, though, she still has bits of dried banana clinging to her face. Some people she passes by gawped and laugh - but the woman is in a world of her own.

At the other end of the store, by all the beverages, Ignatius says, "I thought you knew better than that, Væ!" She tries to be serious, but the image of the banana sliding down the hysterical woman's face is too much, and she cracks.

"I thought they were for anyone, unless she just really likes bananas. Humans are strange," they say, laughing now, too.

Once they both recover from the incident and are sure power suit woman isn't looking for them, Væson finds time to stare at the seemingly never-ending rows of neatly stacked items and the autonomous way that the shoppers go about picking them.

"Does this live up to your expectations?" Ignatius asks, watching them stare at everything with those big, innocent eyes.

"More! I knew it was going to be great, but this, this is..." Væson can't quite finish what they are trying to say.

"...America." Ignatius finishes. "I'm curious. All those months you spent away from the, umm," she says the next bit just below a whisper, just in case there are prying ears around, "facility, didn't you make your way to one of these? Or even to a mall?"

"Vegas had everything I needed. Well, the casino did, and when I was out again, I tried to remain inconspicuous. And you gotta remember, it was a kind of cult as you all say, and the people tended to do the shopping for us. The other times, I was barely out long enough, but when I was, it was teeny tiny shops. Back on M.O.R.K.-78, when movies showed this kind of a place, it looked like some magical yet primitive playground for adults. We thought the same about the malls, too, and loved every moment of it. When, well, if I return to M.O.R.K.-78, I might even be hailed as a global treasure. Wait, I might even get an award! Ooh, can I have my picture taken in the store!? They'll need proof! I mean, they could just download my memories and see, but this is so much cooler, and authentic," Væson says excitedly.

"You want me to take a picture of you posing in a grocery store?"

"Not posing, per se, but yeah!"

"Guess we better get ourselves a disposable camera, then," she says with a smile. She is glad to be sharing this moment with them and is still a little surprised that she hasn't gone mad at the thought that an alien from another planet is quickly becoming her best friend.

They fill the cart with non-perishables and snacks as they make their way to the cameras, where they grab a whole bunch of them. Ignatius has to explain to them that they have to come back here once the film inside it is full so they could be developed; a fact that almost blows Væson's extremely powerful mind. The magic camera box is both primitive and on the cusp of great technology. Væson holds one of them in their hand, still in the packet, and is fascinated.

"Such an ingenious invention in a teeny box. We haven't heard of these before. What do they do?"

"You're from a planet that is so advanced, you could wipe Earth out in mere seconds, and you don't know what a camera is? You are an enigma, you know that, right?"

"I do, I do... now tell me, what does this thing do? You called it a camera, right?" They say the word camera delicately, making sure to feel each letter in the word. They wonder why they haven't come across this contraption before, either on M.O.R.K-78 or here on Earth, and they doubt it's a new thing. Perhaps it was just a small oversight or called something different. Whatever the reason, they are fascinated by it before they know what it can do.

"Wait, you should know what it is. You asked for a picture to be taken of you not even thirty seconds ago!" she says, confused.

"I meant with a pen and pencil or a painting. All humans can do that, right?"

"No," she says, laughing. "And besides, that would take ages! A camera takes a picture of a moment you want to remember or cherish, and then you can take it to a mall, and they'll develop it, and you'll be able to hold onto the picture and frame it or put it in an album or even in your purse or wallet, like this." She pulls out an A5 print of her wedding day photo. The creases show it has been folded and unfolded many times, and the faded red shows that she kisses it goodnight every night.

Ignatius hands the picture over so delicately, it might have been a precious gemstone, which in fact, to her, it is. They hold onto it by the edges as they can sense how precious it is to their human friend. They trace the edges with one of their fingers lightly, feeling the emotion and the love from that day and almost feel overwhelmed by it.

The only word they can mutter is, "wow," and they hand it back carefully. Once back in her possession, she stares at it, like she always does, taking in every inch of Aiden's face, taking in his smile and his eyes, and just like every time, willing him to jump out of the photo and hold her just one last time.

"How did he... How did he, umm, stop existing in this world?"

Ignatius looks at them for a moment, ignoring the passersby in the supermarket. "I told you already, didn't I? He died in a fire." In her mind, she had always suspected one person and one person only; but with no evidence, there was no crime.

"Yeah, you told me, but I just can't wrap my cranium around it. Are you sure he perished in a fire? Did you see it?" They levitate, a nervous electricity surrounds them, and a hand strokes their chin in deep thought.

The pure question is as blunt as a battle-worn axe and just as cutting. The overhead speakers add to the bizarreness as they play a Christmas tune, even though it's not even Halloween yet. The Christmas decorations around the store outnumber the Halloween ones almost 3:1. It's often the way with stores. Before people have had the chance to digest one holiday, they're already trying to shove the next one down their overstuffed throat.

"Of course I didn't," she says, trying to decide whether they are being serious or not. She runs a hand through her hair and crosses her tanned hands against her chest defensively.

"Then how do you know? On my planet, we don't determine the cause of death until we are absolutely certain, and there is normally a witness, too, but that's because most of our kind die of old age, surrounded by loved ones, not because we have an inordinate number of murders or foul play. Like I said before, we are a peaceful species. Not everyone in the galaxy is, though, but we keep ourselves to ourselves, gathering data and just enjoying our beatific planet."

There is a lot to process in Væson's statement. Ignatius picks at the part that makes her wince first, getting it out of the way like ripping off a band aid, but in this case, the skin was still raw and weepy.

"I saw the coroner's report. I even saw the photos. That's how I know." This is a topic she doesn't want to discuss and has shut herself away from. The pictures still haunt her at night sometimes, and she tries to numb the pain with her parties and copious amounts of alcohol.

"But you didn't see the body of your husband in person? Strange. Perhaps it was fake?"

"Fake? Why on earth would it be fake?" she protests, almost laughing at the prospect.

"Well, did he have any enemies that he needed to get away from?"

"None that I know of." she states with wavering confidence.

"Any people you know that might have wanted to cause him harm?"

"Other than Carol? No. But even she isn't that evil. And besides, she loved him. She didn't want him dead... Me, maybe, but no, not my Aiden."

"Ok, then do you think the death was meant for you and not for him?" Such a simple question, yet no one prior to this has even thought of asking it.

"I... I have no idea. No. I don't know... I have always been told it was a freak accident." Her mind starts to spin in wild circles, overthinking ever scenario that had led up to that moment. She has done it a million times before, but not like this, not with such renewed purpose.

"You know, I could always scan Carol's mind and see if she did it," Væson says, shrugging. While they have been talking, they have absentmindedly moved to the top end of the store by the fridges, and a waft of cold air lands on their skin. Væson recoils at the feeling and swiftly moves away from the coldness, Ignatius follows, keeping pace.

"You could do that?" she asks, not wanting to sound too optimistic but also not wanting to open this door.

"Oh, sure. It'll be easy. I can do it right now if you want. Just point me in her direction."

"But... If you do this, and you find out that she has done it, there would be no way to prove it. It would be pointless in the long run, right?"

"Never fear, I'm sure there will be something in her mind that will tie it all together. Maybe she kept gasoline recites or anything that ties her to the building at that time. Then we can tell the, what are they called here?"

"The police?" Ignatius offers.

"Yeah, that sounds right. Them," Væson says in earnest. "We can tell them!"

"I still don't think they'll listen," she says, downbeat, not wanting to get her hopes up.

"Why are humans so defeatist? This is surely worth a shot to find out the truth. So, let's pay for these amazing treasures, go to the mall, buy some more treasures, and then confront that bitch, Carol, the murderer who fried your husband!"

Ignatius blinks at them, not once but twice. It's like she has just been hit by a mac truck, and then the craziness of the statement hits her, and she laughs and laughs like some kind of strange being has put a spell on her. Oh it is so great to laugh. She is finding laughing with Væson so much easier and life is becoming a joy once more. And once more, she gets a wave of guilt about not wanting to let them go.

Without talking, they both head to the cashier line. Væson is their upbeat self, humming a tune that is all too familiar to them. It's a complete contrast to Ignatius's face, which is stoic and deep in contemplation.

"Next in line?"

Væson looks around, not sure where the sound is coming from.

"Next in line? Hello, 'scuse me, next in line?" the persistent voice says again.

"C'mon, move it, you're holding up the line, Jesus almighty!" complains an extremely well-fed man with an unkempt beard. The voice that is coming from just behind Ignatius's ear makes her jump and whirl around, right into the stench of the guy's breath.

She apologies and moves to the cashier who has been beckoning them. With the help of the bagging assistant, they're out of the store and onto the mall in mere minutes.

Chapter 21

Mall Thoughts

The drive to the mall from the grocery store doesn't take too long, and they can see it, the crest of it, anyway, from a good ways away. Its white domes glisten in the mid-morning sun, and as soon as Væson sees them, another wave of excitement washes over them. They stick their head out the window, face fighting against the g-force like an over-excited dog. The only thing that's missing is their tongue hanging out of their mouth. Ignatius looks over and can't help but laugh at them. How could she not – they are the epitome of joy and looking at the positives that life has to offer. She strives to be more like them, like she was once, until Aiden died and knocked the life out of her. Her parties are still there, but they lack the normal sparkle and pizazz. Væson is the spark to everything, and it isn't lost on her just how important this life form from M.O.R.K-78 actually is.

Ignatius parks towards the back of the parking lot, a trick she had learned from Aiden. He told her that the further back you park, the less likely you are to have someone park next to you or worse, hit their door onto yours.

THERE GOES THE NEIGHBORHOOD

Throughout the journey, Ignatius's mind has been on that of her husband and Carol. She replays every last conversation with her late husband, with Carol, and with everyone else she can think of. But there is no way she can connect the two. No way Carol hated Ignatius enough to kill her husband, but then she remembered that she perhaps wasn't trying to kill Aiden, but her. Is that more plausible? Well, it certainly may have been. But she has a husband of her own. Sure, he's a boring, wet fart, but she still has one, and what would she have done with Aiden? Wear him down again?

She sits in the car for a moment, staring absentmindedly out the windshield her seatbelt still on. Væson looks at her with electric anticipation at the prospect of going into the mall and taking more of those picture things with that magic camera. For a moment, she looks catatonic, so they do what surely every self-respecting person does in this situation – they poke her in the eye.

"Ow! What the hell did you do that for?" she cries, immediately coming out of her glazed look and putting her left hand over her left eye, the other eye giving them a disdainful look.

"I had to reboot you! You were just staring off, right into the distance. I thought you were broken! I have to say, though, I got results," they say with pride.

"I was *thinking!*" she snaps a little harder than she wants to. The pain starts waning in her eye, but she still holds her hand there for sympathy.

"Maybe don't do that, or think more often? I don't know, but you sure need practice by the looks of it. The top of your head was all wrinkled, too."

"Thank you, thank you very much for your insight."

"You're welcome!" they say with even more pride than a moment ago.

"I was being sarcastic!"

"*Oh*, is that person a slow thinker, too? If so, that was a great impression!"

Ignatius slaps her forehead with her right hand and sighs. "You're impossible, you know that, right?"

"I'm *Væson*... Don't *you* know that?" Væson asks, confused.

This goes on for a little longer than it really should until Ignatius realizes that this time, Væson is on the wind up. While she was driving, they learned to do this from their previous misunderstandings in the car, and now it's paying dividend, at least for Væson who is in howls of hysterics. Tears run down from their eyes that are impossibly big to be human, and she looks at her intergalactic friend and can't help but join.

"I'm sorry I got grouchy. This whole Carol thing has thrown me through a loop. If I find out she killed my Aiden, I... I don't know what I'll do. I might have to kill her, too!"

"That's crazy talk!"

"No, that's redemption talk," she counters.

"That sounds like a great name for a vigilante. You know, someone who is above the law but is all dark and mysterious and brooding."

"You mean like Batman?"

"Yeah, but without the gruff voice and nipple suit," Væson says, laughing.

An idea formulates in Ignatius mind, and she tucks it away, right at the back, in a locked drawer where no-one can access it. It's where she keeps her darkest secrets, and not even she dares to look at them. It's also the place where she has her darkest ideas, too. When Væson first searched and scanned her mind, they saw it, too, but it looked ominous. The thick silver chains wrapped tight around the tall gray filling cabinet was something they hadn't seen before nor wanted to see again. It gave off an odor, too, one they weren't familiar with. It was the smell of rotten memories and dead dreams. It was filled with all the

THERE GOES THE NEIGHBORHOOD

things she had hoped to do with Aiden as they grew old together.

They both exit the car and head into the huge mall. The white domes on top of the building looks even more impressive close up. The neon sign reads, "*White Planes Mall - Open Late!*". The letters are huge and inviting, and Væson stares at them in wonder.

"Can you take a picture of me in front of this?" they ask, a little shy.

"Of course!" she says, smiling.

The two of them get a few funny looks from passersby, but Væson doesn't notice, and Ignatius doesn't care. *Why is that so many people think they can judge others for doing no harm and take the mic out of people's hand for doing something like this?* Ignatius thinks, still not caring. It's something that's always boiled her piss and, in that respect, she isn't as carefree as she claims to be.

Photos taken and one happy Væson later, they head inside the 'holy mall'. It doesn't have as much Halloween tackiness as the grocery store, but it has a few creepy paper bats and jack-o-lanterns hanging from the balconies, but nothing, as far as Væson is concerned, is going to jump out at them and scare the living daylights out of them. In the mall, despite the lack of Halloween decorations, they don't elect to play Christmas music like in the grocery store. It's full on in the Halloween spirit and is playing *Monster Mash*. Væson's hands begin to involuntary click in time with the beat, and their shoulders start to shimmy. Ignatius looks at them and laughs.

"I can't help it!" Væson says with a cheeky smile and before long, they are full on dancing to the song. People stop and stare at them, but not in a rude way. Væson is busting some serious moves and once the song ends, they take a bow, and the audience of about thirty claps, then waits a moment to see if they are going to do any more before dispersing to go about their day. Ignatius has the smart thinking to take a few snaps of them in action and hopes they will come out well.

"Having fun?" she asks, smiling and putting an arm on their shoulder.

"The most! The mall is the best. And that song! I want to hear it every day." They start to hum it and snap their fingers again. They already memorized the lyrics, and it's now playing on repeat in their head.

"Where do you want to head to first? This place has everything from clothes shops to movies... and trust me when I say this, I recommend the clothes shops," she says, looking them up and down, taking in all of their faux cowboy chic.

"Movies! That's a movie place, right?" Væson asks, pointing to a cinema.

"Yeah, but I really think you should get some new clothes first, to blend in, if nothing else. Not that I want you to blend in, but you know, better to be safe than sorry."

"Movies."

"Sure... But after, clothes shopping. It'll be fun! And we can even grab a bite to eat," she says, trying to keep her mind away from Carol, the murderer – *possible* murderer. Can't be tarring her with that brush just yet. "And look at the size of this place. If we don't get done what you want to do today, we can always come back, don't worry."

Væson looks up at the three-storied-mall with fascination and sees everything they have ever dreamed of and more: the confectionary stores, the places where the humans get their hair chopped off, the place where they pay people to draw on them permanently with needles, bookstores, clothing stores, and home furniture stores among many others. They see the moving stairs transporting the humans to different levels of the mall. They also see that the neon, pink and white color scheme continues indoors, too. In the center of the mall is a humungous and wildly ostentatious fountain made of marble, and the center has a golden light which makes the water look like liquid gold. There are a bunch of teenagers hanging out by the fountain, drinking cola from a fast-food cup, probably chatting about how many people they've kissed or got to third base with, but all of them exaggerating. Others, who are hanging by the fountain, are tossing pennies into the water, making a wish. Væson spots an elderly lady and her husband, hand in hand, both hunched over from age and wrinkled as prunes, toss in a penny and then kiss. They already have everything they could ever want, but they are wishing that others have some of their happiness, too. The fountain serves as a great meeting point. It's so large, it spans all the levels. It's the biggest one Ignatius has ever seen and the only one Væson has, outside of Las Vegas. You can access it and sit on it on all levels due to the bespoke design of it. If it was anywhere else, it might've been considered gaudy, but not here. Not in the White Plains Mall.

Væson watches the humans for a little while longer, and Ignatius does, too. They watch people go about their business, sometimes in groups of three and four, mostly sticking in their own age groups but all of them in their own little world. Ignatius thinks if Væson was to transform into their true form right now, no one would bat an eyelid, not a single one. She takes some comfort in that, but also some horror. The world is becoming something she doesn't like. It's becoming a world of *me first*. Væson, on the other hand, is transfixed by it all and resists the urge to scan a few minds as they go past. They don't want to invade the humans' privacy any more than they have to, but... it would be good for their mission. They think about asking Ignatius if it's ok but get sidetracked by the sheer magnitude of the mall. All their life, they have wanted to come here and now, here they are, in one of the best ones.

"Do people live here?" Væson asks with hope in their eyes.

Ignatius laughs. "No, don't be silly. Where would they sleep?"

Væson points at a shop frontage called 'The Bed King' and says, "There?"

She looks over to where they are pointing and can't help but laugh even more. Væson's keen and innocent eyes strike again.

"Well, I guess they could stay there, but it's against the law."

"It's against the law to sleep in a shop?"

"Yeah, of course. What if people steal when they're in there?"

"And what if people don't?"

"I'm sure people would steal. Trust me. You said it yourself, humans are bad."

"But they're not given the chance to be good."

There it is again, that innocence, but... they are right. People aren't given the chance to be good when they are always perceived to be bad. The trust and honor system is negated by this very thing.

They hit a few clothes shops, and Ignatius buys Væson a raft of new outfits. She used to do this with Aiden, and a few tears prick at her eyes during some moments. She makes sure Væson doesn't see, though. This is their time, and she wouldn't let anything get in the way of that. She allows them to have just three cowboy style items that they relentless insist on having, and also a kilt. Væson's fashion sense is bold and certainly unique. There is no way Ignatius is going to dull their sparkle. The people of Poppy Field Lane have tried to do that to her, but they failed, and they'll fail again with Væson, too, if Ignatius has anything to do with it.

Chapter 22

Carol's Crusade

W hile Ignatius and Væson are busy having a whale of a time at the White Plains Mall, Carol is playing detective. She can't get what she saw out of her head and has devised a plan to expose the vile woman and her... what did she call the man? Oh yes, her *cousin*. She is in her strategy room, and on the boards are ideas upon ideas of Christmas related things, but on her desk is something else. It's a single sheet of paper with two words on it:

Ignatius
Foreign?

She had come to the conclusion that the pretend cowboy is quite possibly from another planet when she saw the thing levitating Ignatius the other night. She racked her brain all day about it and thinks that the only way a person could be that happy that they practically levitate is because they are a foreigner or good heavens above, a gay! It must be noted that despite Carol being evil - she's not known for having too much common sense. When Carol is on the trail of something, logic often stays at home along with her decency. There is no room for either in Poppy Field Lane in Carol's eyes. Unless of course that foreigner is mowing her lawn or cleaning her pool. Thankfully, Carol is the only person who holds those archaic and downright retched views. Her cronies, however, are guilty by association for not putting her in her place.

Frank knocked timidly on the door a few hours ago to give her a cup of coffee on a literal silver platter. He's back again now with another coffee, and this time, a small smattering of cookies. His knocks sound like a gust of wind has picked up a couple of feathers and brushed them lightly across something. Only the finely tuned ears of his wife can hear them.

"What, what? Come in, quickly," Carol snaps from the other side of the door.

Frank comes in, head down and eyes looking at his feet and not at the boards on the wall. That isn't for him, and he wants to be out of here as soon as possible. The room makes him uncomfortable, like it's hoarding power or something. He can't put his finger on it and doesn't even want to. He hands her the tray, but she says, "Don't give it to me, put it on my desk. For goodness sake, can't you do anything?" She looks at him and sees that he is looking at the floor, and her heart sinks for a brief moment. She lifts his chin with her white gloved hand and makes him look her in the eyes. "What's wrong, dear?"

The question makes him flinch, as if she just hit him, which wouldn't be the first time. He is a beaten down and broken man, with nowhere to go and no oomph to rebel. On the outside, people think of him as just being boring. If only that were the truth. The man is a shell.

"N...Nothing, my wife. W-what would you like for dinner?"

"Oh I do hate it when you stutter... It makes you sound so simple. Please do try and stop that," she says, no longer looking at him but over him, at the board. She strokes his cheek gently with a gloved hand, the way one would perhaps stroke a skirting board to see if it's dusty.

Before Frank speaks, he tries his best to be stutter free. "Sorry. I will work on it."

"Good. See how much more eloquent you sound now? You practically sound British! Dinner tonight will be beef bourguignon with a fine wine. I trust you have the ingredients?"

"Yes, my wife," he says monotonously and exits the room, shuffling his feet along the beige shag pile carpet as he closes the door behind him. Carol doesn't even glance away from the boards. She doesn't realize that the way she is treating him is abusive and wrong, she just sees it as being a wife in control. Like a real woman should be... in her eyes, anyway. She walks over to the silver platter with the biscuits and coffee lovingly arranged on it, and she takes one, not caring to notice they're in a heart shape and not realizing that they're her favorite kind— the ones that are only available from two towns over. It's these small details that if he soon stopped doing would become noticed. But because they are a daily thing, a *loving* thing, it goes under his wife's radar. On one occasion, Frank thought about putting ricin in her coffee. Everyone would think she died of a strong flu and fever and not because of a husband who was pushed over the edge one final time. That was in his weak moment, though, a few years back. There is no way he could contemplate such things now. But love does strange things to the mind, it makes you do things that you wouldn't normally do. That's why there are so many songs on the subject.

Carol goes back to her boards that detail her Christmas fair spectacular. It's broken down into who is doing what and when and at what time and at the precise section of the green, too. She wants this year to be bigger and better than ever before, and there is no reason why it wouldn't be. After all, she is in charge, so in her mind, it's going to be perfect no matter what.

She has given herself the best position at the fair, too, like always. There are plans to have a giant Ferris wheel in the center of the green, decorated in gaudy Christmas things. She has also planned for a plentiful amount of faux snow, which will complete the winter wonderland aesthetic. She steps back and admires her work again. To her credit, it looks like it really is going to be one of the best events this neighborhood has ever seen.

Once the lovingly arranged biscuits have been devoured by the black heart of Poppy Field Lane, she goes to the pure white wall phone and dials the number of Kent Barret, the local GP, in an effort to find details about Ignatius and her 'cousin'. Again, sound logic stays at home.

I n the souls vessel of Carol's home, or as others call it, the Neighborhood Watch central, or as Ignatius now calls it, the home of the murderer (probable, not wanting to get ahead of herself. but that's a bit of a long title, so ends up calling it *that bitch, Carol's*), Carol is eating dinner with her husband. They are sitting at the opposite ends of the impossibly long table. The only noise is that of the grandfather clock in the corner of the room and the sound of chewing.

"Don't chew so loud, Frank. What are you, an animal? Or an uneducated oaf? I'm hoping you're neither."

"Sorry, dear." Frank says and ceases his 'loud' chewing in an instant.

"There, much better. That wasn't so hard now, was it?" As she says this, she smirks and cocks an eyebrow at him. The devil doesn't wear Prada, after all. It wears florescent lycra and a shit-eating grin.

Chapter 23

Closer

Back at The Facility, The Captain is once again pacing his office. He looks like he's aged a few years in the space of a few days. The pressure is mounting on him to find the *little blue bastard,* and not only that, in a couple of days, he's meant to show off his little secret to some of the darkest minds in the world. He's even meant to show them what powers they have and the technology, too. He's cast his net far and wide but to no avail. If he had hair, it would be gray from the stress. Dark circles hang from his eyes like shopping bags, and he's been pulling all-nighters at The Facility. He has forgotten the art of self-care and showering, but no one dares to tell him how much he stinks. Some of the people have tried to coerce John Mercer to tell him, but just the thought of it almost made him piss himself. No, they have all decided to just let him stink. It's better that way. If any of the darker minds want to bring it up, then more power to them.

His office almost mimics that of Carols, with the strategy boards and even more papers on his desk. In the center of the boards is Væson's picture. Three, in fact. One is of their alien form, and the others are when they worked at the Casino in Vegas and when they were a cult leader. There is no direct correlation to any of them, and if you didn't know any better, you would not think they are the same thing, making the search for the *little blue* bastard even harder. None of them can notice their inhuman eyes, which is probably why Væson has been able to stay out of their traps for so long and so often. None of his team has been of any help at all, and he has murdered a few of them in cold blood when they didn't give him a satisfactory answer.

One thing is for sure: if he doesn't find the *little blue bastard* by the end of the month, the darkest minds would rip his head off and shit down his neck. The Captain rubs a lot of the darkest minds the wrong way, and they're looking for any excuse not only to get him out of the way, but his entire family, too - and that includes the ones who have never worked at The Facility. He's always been one giant rose thorn in their backside and that of The Facility, and to be rid of him would be like finally scratching an itch that's deep inside a cast. The Boss is of course oblivious to how much he is hated by the darkest minds and by the rest of The Facility. He truly thinks he's untouchable, but recent events have left them angry with him, and they're waiting for him to fuck up big time. They're pretty good at making sure people don't exist anymore—wiping them clean from history.

Every time the phone rings, he lets it go to his answer machine as he doesn't want to deal with the constant barrage. There's no space left on the machine, so he's probably missed a hell of a lot of important information. He doesn't care, though. If they try to say anything, he has a pre-loaded excuse... *'I've' been busy'* or *'that's why I have a secretary. If she doesn't do her job, I don't get the information.'* Then he envisions blowing her brains out with his .45.

There is a timid knock at the door to his office, and he flies from his chair and almost rips it off its hinges. The momentum launches him right over the door knocker, the intruder to his faux-peace, his right-hand man, one very timid John Mercer. He is already on the verge of pissing himself before he sees The Captain.

"What in the fuck do you want?" The Captain demands.

John Mercer is shaking like the preverbal leaf. He looks worse off than The Captain does. He has huge black pouches under his eyes that are so big, a joey could squat in there. There are also indents on his hooked nose thanks to his glasses. This is the absolute last place he wants to be, and all his concentration is spent on willing himself not to piss himself.

"Umm, umm, well... We may have some news," John says, trying to spit the words out as fast as he can, but they get stuck like a bottle neck in his throat. His cheeks are turning red, and for a brief moment, he thinks of himself as that kid in school that he used to be, the shy timid one. Not much has changed now; he's still being shouted at, berated, even, but now he has a voice. It may only be a small one, but he still has it. The trouble is, whenever he encounters The Captain, it vanishes like a fart in the breeze.

"What do you mean, *may have*? Either you do, or you don't!" The Captain snaps. A bead of sweat runs down John's forehead, and it isn't due to the air conditioning not being on. He rocks back and forth in his boots that are so well polished, you could see your own face in them. John is so preoccupied with his own worries that he doesn't even notice that The Captain is out of sorts. If John was a viper, or a shark, he would capitalize on this, but instead, he is a mere sheep and not in wolf's clothing.

"Well, umm, you see... We know categorically that the subject isn't in Nevada. In fact. It is nowhere near here."

"And how the flying fuck is that good news?" The Captain yells, swaying again. This time, John does notice it, and his eyes widen. In that instant, he sees that he also has blood shot eyes and has patches of beard all over his face. This is most unlike him. The Captain sways again, and this time, John manages to catch him before he falls to the ground. The Captain's physical and mental state is much worse than was whispered about.

"Get the fuck off me!" The Captain says, slurring his words.

John politely takes no notice but instead guides him over to his chair and sits him down.

"It means, that..." John starts but then stops, noticing The Captain's eyes closing. His breath smells like the sewers of hell, but he braces against it. "It means, maybe you should get some rest, and I'll brief you when you wake up. By then, we should have even more promising news for you."

John leaves the room in a hurry, giving The Captain no time to tell him to stop and get back here. In fact, as soon as John leaves the room, he puts his head on his desk and falls right to sleep for the first time in days. He doesn't wake up until a good few hours later, in a pool of drool that follows him as he brings his head up. The sun has given way to the moon, and there is a chill in the air. A moth is flirting with his desk light, and he reaches out and grabs it with his bare hands, turning the goth butterfly into dust. He looks down into his hand, sees the results, and a smile stretches across his face for the first time in a long time.

As the clock strikes past 10:35 p.m., Carol is hunched over the windowsill in her bedroom. The curtain twitching at a minimum, this woman is a pro and would win gold at any Olympic games. Her binoculars are trained on Ignatius's house, but to her vexation, the blinds are drawn again. *This is most unlike that wretched woman*, Carol thinks. She is trying to gather more evidence on her neighbor, but little does she know, she could soon be hoisted by her own petard. The insane amount of coffee she has drunk has worn off, and she is trying to fight the effects of caffeine withdrawal. You know the feeling you get when you've had so much coffee, it's made you able to practically *smell* colors? Well, she's past that bit now and in the state where it makes you drowsy. She wrestles with her eyes, trying to strain them open. For one maddening moment, she has the urge to stick matchsticks in her eyes in an effort to keep them open, but then shudders at the thought. Eyes freak her out, but the thought of it jolts her awake for a moment. Her head is swaying back and forth, almost in time to the light snores of Frank. Each sway becomes more pronounced, and her eyes grow heavier with every second. Then, as if her head was tied to an invisible string, she bounces her head off the window and falls to the floor in a floral pajama clump. The sound doesn't wake her husband, and the pain doesn't wake her. If it wasn't for the giant egg forming on her wretched head, you could almost say she looks peaceful... and nice.

"Bingo!"

"Shh, you'll wake her up!"

"Not a chance. That stuff I put in her coffee, his too, is from my home planet. She'll be out for hours. So will her husband. Poor guy. I bet it's the most peace he's had in years."

"I bet. Poor soul. If she treats him even half as bad as she treated Aiden, then he has no life at all," Ignatius says from the bush underneath Carol's window. They are both dressed in black, with camo paint on their faces for dramatic effect... Væson is the one who insisted on this outfit, but Ignatius didn't put up much of a fight.

About an hour prior to this, Væson covertly brainwashed Frank to slip something in both of their coffees. It was so simple to do, it was borderline pathetic. Nonetheless, it gave Ignatius a fit of the giggles when she watched the vile woman's head smack off the windowpane. She even made a joke about what a *pain* she was, but it flew over Væson's head, and she had to explain it a good couple of times. Too many, in fact, and the joke was dead and buried by the time they got the punchline. There's a saying among comedians, "Some jokes you can resuscitate." But not that one, apparently.

Ignatius slides the window up and crawls inside, being mindful not to stand on the clump called Carol. Væson practically dives in through the open window and combat rolls to the other side. It's done so majestically, so soundlessly, that Ignatius just stands there for a moment, totally amazed. There seems to be a growing list of the things her new alien friend can do. At the end, Væson does what Ignatius is quickly beginning to call their trademark bow, and she claps silently. She then scans the room and gets her senses, her eyes adjusting to the dim lighting coming from the hallway through the crack of the door. Ignatius notices how tidy and precise the room is. There is a glass of water on her bedside table, a lamp, and some reading material. She can't quite make out the title but is sure one of the words said *Town*. Carol is known for her history, so it may be a book on undiscovered towns or boring towns to visit. Ignatius doesn't know nor care. On Frank's bedside table, there is also a glass of water and a lamp. However, instead of a book, there is a book of puzzles. The light shines more on his side due to him being closer to the door. Ironically, Carol wanted him on that side of the bed in case an intruder ever tried to break in. She obviously forgot about windows and intergalactic aliens.

"Right... Are we gonna do this?" Ignatius asks, sounding unsure.

"Only if you want me to. Once you know the truth, there's

no going back. You'll have to live with this, you know that, right?" Væson reminds her gravely.

"I know. That's what makes this so difficult." She puts her hands on her hips and exhales. "This could change my life – almost certainly will, in fact."

"Just say the word, and we can get out of here. No one knows we're here right now, anyway. I will say this, though. I think you owe it to yourself to find out the truth." They put a tentative hand on her shoulder, and Ignatius grabs it gratefully.

"Fuck it. Let's do it," Ignatius says, this time with a little more conviction. Then she adds, "Yeah," but that's more for herself. One final push for her subconscious.

"Alrighty then! No going back now. We're about to enter a world of truth, and what you do with this truth must be taken seriously. You may find out that she has in fact killed your husband, by mistake or not. For the sake of us, you cannot retali-kill her, ok? We will have to be smart about this and play the long game."

Ignatius nods, but she fights against every instinct to comply to this. Væson doesn't need to read her mind to tell either. It's written all over her face.

On the bed, Frank is still snoring quietly, blissfully unaware of what is going on.

Væson stands over the incapacitated Carol who is in the downward dog yoga position. A sound emits from her ass, quickly dispelling the rumor that women don't fart.

Seconds later, Væson is rummaging around in Carol's head, and it only takes him a moment to realize how insidious this woman truly is.

Back on M.O.R.K-78, President Œstegen is sat in their office. They are at their cylindrical desk which is in the center of the room. The walls are floor-to-ceiling windows with the most beautiful vistas of the planet you could hope to imagine. Part of it overlooks the rolling hills with the blossom trees, although these are no ordinary ones. They would make the ones in Japan look rather plain and un-interesting. These are almost double in size and spectacularly more vibrant. If they looked out the opposite window, they would be greeted with a bird's eye view of the main city, Pækern. They would see dozens of Morkians going about their day, some on foot or hovering, others in sleek electric hover cars. Some even choose the hover boards and bikes. It's fast paced, it's lively, and it's, well, practically perfect. But not quite. Œstegen is trawling though some digital screens on their interactive desk. Once they find the one they want, they zap it up into the middle of the room, making it bigger. It's a picture of Væson and Jenson. Jenson's now in black and white with the words "Peaceful Rest" stamped on his picture in sorrowful black writing.

"Come on, Væson, finish your mission and come home," they say to the room. They might be as old as time, and they may even look it, too, but they still have a zest for life, and they vowed that they would not die until Væson came home. It's strange. Only a few years ago, when they first became President, Væson was unheard of not only by the President but by the rest of M.O.R.K-78, too. But since Œstegen became aware of Væson's plight, they have done everything in their power to make it national news. Often, the headlines are offering huge support for their lost citizen. Whenever Væson has the chance to update the President, they in turn would share it with the rest of M.O.R.K-78 and you can guarantee that everyone would be tuned in to watch it. Parties are held so they can watch them together, wishing and hoping that Væson is on their way back.

They are utterly fascinated by the news that Væson brought with them, and although they live in a relative paradise, some even wonder why Væson is trying to come back. There is a whole universe out there, and Væson is stuck on one of the best planets. It just happens to be a little dangerous, too. It was the first time some of them have ever seen updated footage of Earth, and everyone was transfixed by it. Some places have even gone to the lengths of making huge banners with Væson's face on them and the words "M.O.R.K's Hero" emblazoned on them in big letters.

However, not everyone is quite so enamored with Væson's antics. Flagant is sat in his own office that is the absolute antithesis of Œstegen's. Where the President's is light, bright, and airy with cutting edge designs and views to die for, Flagant's is dark and dreary. It only needs a bit of rain to match their dower mood, and you'll have a case of pathetic fallacy on your hands. They, too, are pawing over documents that contain information relating to Væson and Jenson. Flagant is trying to do everything in their power to pin the murder on the President, and then they would swoop in and act like the hero who thwarted the *nasty and vindictive* President who has overstayed their welcome long enough. They are hoping that Væson is already dead, along with Jenson, but while others are celebrating the news and the video footage of Væson in a mall - information on this alien planet can travel at hyper speed, especially when it becomes a national interest - and other stinking human places, Flagant is turning a deeper shade of sickly yellow. They shake their head, and their long jowls smack from side-to-side, making a horrible wet sound. Their perpetually hard face narrows - which in fact is their normal and rightful expression - into a scowl, and they smash their hand through the glass table, making it gush with purple blood. They let it trickle for a moment, then they lick at the wound, like a stray cat in an alley would lick at rainwater from a drainpipe, before healing it completely. Not many Morkians are feared, but Flagant certainly is. When they hover, their weight drags them down, and it makes them look more like a slith-ering slug, which adds to their demeanor. When they speak, their teeth protrude out of their gums like jagged mountains, and some have even debated whether they were deliberately sharpened, which they were. If Morkians knew just half the things they have been up to, Flagant would be feared an awful lot more. And now that they know exactly where Væson is, it's perhaps time to pay them a visit.

Chapter 24

The Truth is in there

Væson sees it all in vivid and living color, rich in dirty and heinous detail. The urge to recoil from it is strong, but they persist for their friend, the one who trusts them to tell the truth, no matter how horrible. Væson has never seen a murder before and seeing this drains a lot of the color out of their normally vibrant skin.

"What? *What is it?*" asks Ignatius with a shaky voice. She knows already but has hoped that by saying the words, the trouble would just melt away. That saying them out loud would diminish the impact and soften the blow. It doesn't.

Væson can barely hear the question as they are still wrapped up in the memory of Carol, watching the events of the murder through her eyes, feeling how she felt at the time, or more to the point, not feeling.

The fire was indeed meant for Ignatius.

Carol had planned it all perfectly, or thought she had. She knew Ignatius was supposed to be in the building alone at that time. The building in question was an almost derelict house that Ignatius and Aiden had just bought and had grand designs to turn it into a luxury boutique hotel just on the outskirts of town. The views were stunning, and it backed onto a lake, but the water was not enough to save the flesh of Aiden being burned. Carol acted alone, that is what Væson can categorically find. She hid this all from her husband, Frank, too. Something like this would eat a normal person from the inside, but Carol felt vindicated by it. A repetitive mantra rattles around in her skull saying *'if I can't have him, no one can. I'm glad he's dead, and I'm glad she's alone. She'll die alone.'* The mantra is spiteful, and Væson can tell she doesn't care at all.

Væson sees how she made it look like a gas leak, and when the oven was turned on, Aiden was hurtled to the other side of the kitchen his final thought was of his wife, Ignatius and he was no longer scared. The only mercy was that Ignatius didn't see him like this. Someone had heard the explosion and saw the flames that were licking away at the abandoned house. The fire department came quickly and tackled the blaze. They were the ones who found Aiden. Carol watched it all from her vantage point across the road. Væson can almost feel the corners of her mouth turn up into a smile, and that perhaps is the most disturbing thing about it all. She didn't give two shits about what she had done. She didn't even know who she had just killed in cold...warm blood. When she arrived, the lights were already on in the property, and she had just assumed it was Ignatius, seeing as it had been her routine for the past week or so. When she saw the blaring lights and heard the screams of the fire engine, she walked off, and can you believe the bitch was humming? And not some melancholic song either. She was humming an upbeat pop song, *'Disco inferno!'* To add vinegar to the wounds, she did a little shimmy as she walked away.

Væson is pulled out of this memory and dragged back into the stillness of the room by Ignatius shaking their shoulder vigorously.

"Did...Did she do it? Did she kill my husband?" Her eyes are desperate and on the verge of tears.

Væson doesn't know the proper procedure for this kind of situation, but they recount a few times when they have seen people crying on TV after being given bad news. they embraced the crier in a hug, and that is what Væson does. Ignatius knows all too well what that means, and she weeps silently in their warm embrace.

They both stay in that position, frozen in the moment. Years from now, when Ignatius picks apart this tapestry of a memory, it will be frayed from years of playing it over. It's the moment she found out what had truly happened to her husband, and she has been living right next to the woman who did it.

Væson motions for Ignatius to go on without them as there is something they need to do. Ignatius, who is deep in thought, nods and walks the long way back along the beach. Væson makes their way into Carol's inner evil sanctum, runs their fingers along the big, important drawer, and gives it a stern whack. The thing they'd been looking for reveals itself immediately.

Væson shuts the secret drawer up, sticks a finger up at Carol's control board, then leaves the room in silence to go back to her house. It takes all of Ignatius's strength to not beat the evil out of her. To not grab her by her hair and smash her face into the radiator over and over. Revenge would be sweet. Retribution would be sweeter.

In the kitchen, she puts on a pot of coffee. They are silent until the fresh coffees are steaming in front of them. Væson gives her a baleful look, one that conveys the complexity of alien emotions. She can tell they don't want to tell her but are compelled to by loyalty. She reaches her arm over the table, and Væson squeezes it gently.

"I'm sorry you had to see that," she says after a long while.

Væson shakes their head and says, "No, I am the sorry one.

You lost a husband in such an evil and brutal way. We will take her down. You will have your redemption, I promise."

"Are you saying you found something that connects her?" Ignatius asks with hope.

"Sure did. Or, at least, I think I did." A bloom of a smile rises in their face despite the circumstances.

"Just for the record, I don't want to know what you saw... I... I just want confirmation that she did it. I want to hear you say with a gut full of honesty that Carol Lilinster killed my husband, Aiden Feltrap. Once I've heard you say it, we'll get the bitch dead to rights."

"I, umm, thought we weren't killing her?"

"We're not, it's just an expression," she says with a wide-eyed gaze. She is lost in the myriad of ways she could kill her, and to hell with getting caught.

"*Oh*, ok. In that case, Carol Lilinster killed your husband, Aiden Feltrap. I'm so sorry," Væson says, shrinking their head between their shoulders. They are back in their true alien form, eyes as big as saucers, full of tears for their friend. Ignatius's eyes, on the other hand, are full of white-hot fire and determination. It's a look that is so intense, it could surely open the gates to hell, and Væson is too scared to look at her. They know she wouldn't hurt her, but those eyes, there is something in them, something that scares them to their very core.

"Then let's get her," she says finally. The room has been so silent that hearing her voice makes Væson jump. All this time, Alfie has been sitting beside his human, and they could feel the change in Ignatius. If it came down to it, Alfie would defend his human until their very last breath. Alfie doesn't understand what was going on but knows it's pretty serious by the stance of Ignatius and the temperature she is giving off. He thinks he heard them talking about murder and his old human, Aiden. He was a good man, and he loved him. He used to look forward to greeting him when he got home, and one day, he didn't. Alfie

looked everywhere for him for days, in between comforting
Ignatius. Alfie would dart from room to room, tail hanging low,
ears up in anticipation. This would go on until he searched
each room in the house for days on end. Then he would wait by
the front door, tail swooshing languidly from side to side on the
floor, waiting in the hope that Aiden, their best friend, would
return. Then one day, she told him that he's not coming back,
and Alfie howled long into the night. For the people who say
animals can't feel anything, this would have been a smack in
the face on an icy morning. Alfie licks Ignatius's dangling hand,
and the wet warmth makes her jump before realizing what it is.

"Sorry, boy, I didn't know you were there," she says,
scratching in his sweet spot, just behind the ear. His back paw
goes up involuntary, and his head cocks to the side and into her
hand.

"He knows you're upset, but not quite what about. He
thinks it's like last time, your sadness, that is. And he says you
have the color burning red inside you."

Alfie cocks his head the other way to look at Væson, then
remembers that the creature can hear his thoughts and starts to
wag his tail excitedly.

"He wants me to connect you to his mind. Is that ok?"

"Of course. You want to talk to me, boy?" she asks, holding
his big Labrador head in her hands.

Alfie wags his tail even more. Væson thinks that thing could
take off like a helicopter at any moment and connects the two
of them before that can happen.

*I will protect you, human Iggy. I love you. No matter what, I
will keep you safe,* Alfie speaks into her mind.

*I know you will, boy. That's why you're the best, but you know
what? I'm the one who'll always protect you. You and Væson over
there are all I class as family now, and no one is going to bring either
of you harm.*

We trust the alien?

More than anything. They're gonna fix things. Remember Aiden? My husband and your best friend? They know who took him away from us!

Alfie turns his head to look at Væson, who twiddles his fingers in a wave-like fashion. Alfie's tail wags again.

Aiden coming back? Aiden here soon? Alfie pads the floor with his paws in excitement, and seeing this rips open Ignatius's heart. She strokes his ears with the back of her hand, just the way he likes it.

No, boy. He can't come back, but we can get retribution.

Alfie cocks his head once more and then understands. He lowers his head and looks up with only his eyes, giving him a sorrowful look. Ignatius draws him into her and hugs him tightly for fear of losing him, too. She couldn't bear to lose either of them. They are all she has in her whole life now, and she wouldn't even let *cosmic force* rip them away from her.

Ignatius gets up and puts some food and fresh water in Alfie's bowls, and Alfie thanks her with his mind. It has opened up a whole chasm of possibilities for them both now. Alfie is thinking of all the ways he can now communicate with his human and not having rely on guess work. He can even tell her that he doesn't actually like the 3 a.m. walks as he's dog tired at that time. But right now, there are more important things afoot... *apaw* in his case.

"Right now, I think we have to remain completely normal... or relatively normal. Don't raise suspicion, and don't let on that we know what that evil bitch has done. If she finds out before we have a chance to execute our retribution, she'll run a mile, and then we'll have no chance."

"Don't worry... She'll never escape from me. Once you're embedded into my memory, it's very hard for you to lose me... so just a heads up if you're planning on running away from me," Væson says, trying not to sound too serious, but they actually mean it. They want to spend the rest of their life with her ... and the dog, too.

Ignatius grips her alien friend in a loose bear hug, "Remember what I said, you're family now. And family stick together no matter what," and then she releases them. Væson is relived for two things: firstly, being let go of the bear grip, and secondly, being told once more that they have a family here on earth. They say friends are the family that you choose, and this is certainly true in this instance.

"I have the beginnings of a plan, you know, on how to catch her and make her confess. If this goes well, we won't even need the evidence you gathered in her mind, but we'll have that as a backup, just in case."

"As long as it doesn't involve killing, I'm all for it. You humans are obsessed with killing each other. It's very uncouth, I must say."

"No killing, promise. I will say this, though: she loves Santa, but he's gonna put her straight on the naughty list when he finds out what she's done."

Væson laughs. "It's a lot more complicated than a list, but I appreciate the sentiment. See how much better I'm getting? Pretty soon, I'll be able to interact with any human and not cause any suspicion at all."

"You know, maybe it won't be such a bad idea after all if people saw you as your true self... Just hold off a little while longer."

"You're not afraid of what people might think of me?"

"Not anymore. If they can't accept you for you, they don't deserve to be in your company, anyway. No longer will your sparkle be diminished by other people's prejudice. You can have a big reveal, very soon."

Væson nods eagerly at the thought of this. They could be their true self again, after weeks of wearing plaid shirts and cowboy boots. Not that there is anything wrong with that, but there is nothing like being in your own skin, literally.

Ignatius tells Væson the plan, and they salivate at the thought of it. Yes, it's risky, yes, it's dangerous, but it's surely going to be a lot of fun... if they can pull it off.

Chapter 25

Energy Blips

December 3rd.

I t's been a few months now since Ignatius and Væson discovered what Carol had done to Aiden, and they're not the only ones who've been busy.

A few days ago, John Mercer burst into The Captain's room without knocking – something they would have never done a few weeks ago, but since The Captain took to nursing bottles, they had become more malleable and less feisty. And infinitely more stinky. Roles had almost been reversed now, especially since one day, when The Captain was asleep, John had replaced his bullets with rubber ones, which took the threat instantly away. However, that is beside the point. When John came bursting through the door, he came bearing tremendous news.

"I know where it is!"

The Captain lifted his head from his desk, brining thick goblets of drool along with it.

"Who? Who?" he asked, fuzzy headed.

"The little blue bastard!" John said with a smirk.

The Captain sat bolt upright to attention.

"Where?! Where is he?" he demanded, voice filled with fury and anticipation.

"New York City. And pretty soon, we'll know the precise location, too. Seems our little friend has been causing energy blips. At first, our guys didn't know what they were, and then I matched them up with the readings we had when it was in our captive care, and they had the same genetic signature. It's still too wide to triangulate, but we're working on it. We'll have it back in time for Christmas. You can mark my words."

For the first time in months, The Captain's head cleared, and a smile broke out on his face. It didn't look right on a face like his. It looked like it was made of knives. He rubbed his hands together and cackled. It was strange and tinny, like something was trying desperately hard to crawl out.

That was a few days ago.

Today, on December 3rd, The Captain is once again clean shaven and sober, *mostly*. Something is different this time, though. He is working side by side with John, as if he's treating him like his equal. Neither John nor anyone else trusts him, but it's certainly a pleasant change of pace to the last few months and years under his stewardship. Deep inside The Captain's brain is a battleground of bad and evil, both of them tugging him in each direction. People say there is inherent good in everyone. That's not quite the case with The Captain.

"We're coming for you, you little blue bastard. And when I find you, I'm gonna string you up by your space balls and set fire to your ass. I'm gonna make pain your new mistress - as you beg and squeal for mercy and plead for me to make it all stop. And I'm gonna make you wish you were dead like that other space scum." The Captain doesn't realize he is saying this out loud, and John has to stifle a giggle despite the circumstances, which actually makes it funnier. Laughing internally, John realizes that it has been a good long while since The Captain has made him piss himself. And the funnier thing is that The Captain doesn't realize that while he has been treating John like his equal, John has been having plans of his own. He is doing what some call *the long con.*

The dark minds have postponed their visit on the remit that they are going to be promised something revolutionary in return. They are a little perturbed that they can't oust The Captain yet, but their interests were piqued when he told them it would advance the military by almost three hundred years.

On the war board, they have triangulated Væson's position even more, and it looks as though they are going to get to the alien before Christmas. In fact, the date that is written on the board in red ink is *15th December.* The very same day as the fête on Poppy Field Lane. What will be in store for everyone is going to be a different *fate* entirely.

In the deep catacombs of The Facility, scientists and army personal are busy trying to make sense of the precise location. They also had people on the street taking random citizens, forcing them into their van and interrogating them. In some cases, they even tortured them a little bit, but they did that mostly to the punk rockers and leftover hippies. Once they were finished interrogating, they used a piece of Morkian technology and used a memory wipe on them, which made them loose a whole day. They could have set it to anything they wanted and made it more specific, but they felt no need to do that. Despite their best efforts, no interrogation proved fruitful. The hippies were high and refused to talk to *the man,* and the punk rockers either spat in their faces or relished the pain. They wore it as a symbol of standing up to *the man.*

Today, the non-descript van is parked opposite a lake in the middle of an affluent town. The usual Facility goons are in it, twins by the name of Irwin and Jenkins Schmitt. They are identical, and both have shiny bald heads and muddy brown eyes. Irwin is ruthless, Jenkins is sinister. Both are stupid. Some people say they share the same brain cell as well as DNA. Unluckily for the twins, the brain cell they share is only half of one. Before they got this job, they were wrestlers, wrestling for a small promotion down in the south. One of The Facility heads was in attendance and liked the way they looked. They were meat mountains, muscles on muscles and athleticism through the roof... They just didn't make for very good wrestlers. After the show, The Facility head came up to them, and much like one of the biggest wrestlers, *The Million Dollar Man,* Ted Dibiase would say, he made them an offer they couldn't refuse - because "everyone's got a price". Ever since, they've been in the security division... and the torture one, too.

They are watching the high society gentlemen and ladies go about their business. Some of them are on their yachts again, others are ordering assistants and what looks like au pairs to carry the bags for them, but one group interests them the most. It's a group of about five or six, rollerblading... trying to, more like, by the lake. One of them keeps falling over. They are wearing jeans, a cowboy hat, and a checkered shirt. The others are encouraging the guy. What makes it strange is that the guy is in his early-to-mid-twenties, but they are treating him as if it was his first time on rollerblades. They were told to treat everything as suspicious, so that is what they do. They had an old woman in the van the other day because they spotted her jogging down the street. This was also in the radius of those energy blips. Irwin and Jenkins didn't understand what that was and just followed the orders from above. They don't care if they are the good guys or the bad guys, or as referred to in their old world, the *faces* and the *heels.* Back when they were wrestling, they preferred being the *heel,* which is the bad guy. They would flip the bird at the fans and insult their mothers, run the town into the ground, that kind of thing. This is real life, though, and if they are heels in that, too, then so be it. As long as the cheques keep coming and they are still allowed to beat people up, then it's all good with them.

Irwin and Jenkins watch the group for a little while longer before Irwin says, "That look suspicious to you?"

"A grown man just learning to rollerblade? Yeah. But the guy isn't green." Obviously forgetting that they had an old woman in the van the other day, it's clearly Irwin's day to share the half brain cell. "We were told to look out for a green alien."

"I thought it was a blue alien?" asks Irwin, confused.

"Wait, there's more than one alien?" Jenkins asks, also confused.

"Maybe that's why there are so many energy blip things? They never told us it was an invasion! I didn't sign up for this."

"Guess we can just fuck this shit and go back to wrestling?"

"What if they come after us? I don't wanna be strung up by my balls! That's all they talk about at The Facility."

"We could change our names. How about you be Jenkins and I be Irwin?" He says this like it's a revolutionary idea.

"You idiot! That's just swapping our names, not switching them...We should switch clothes, too, and get wigs! I've always wanted hair."

"Me too!"

And with that, the two of them leave their van and The Facility life and go back to wrestling. Despite their best efforts to disguise themselves, The Facility doesn't care to investigate their disappearance. There are bigger things afoot than looking for some rouge henchmen.

Chapter 26

Rollerblading

The group that Irwin and Jenkins saw is in fact Væson, Ignatius, Daniel, Skyla, and Danny. When they found out that Væson had never rollerbladed before, they jumped at the chance to teach them. They waited for a day that wasn't as frosty as the previous ones, as that could have been a death trap waiting to happen. Thankfully, the park by the lake has some sort of heated tarmac mechanism and heat lamps above. Oh, how the other half live.

Væson has seen it on TV shows and in movies and always wanted to try it. They have their own version on M.O.R.K.-78, but they added their own spin where you can hover. The Morkians find the wheels a little primitive and restrictive and only use them to recreate some of the scenes from films, or in roller derbies, which is another thing they got from Earth. It's a sport they take very seriously, and to be a top-level athlete in it is akin to having celebrity status. Of course, their rules are a little *different* and much more intense. It's the global pass time, too. Most of the little Morkians want to grow up and be a roller derby champion and play in the big leagues. Another huge sport is wrestling, but with a lot less scripted promos and more scripted violence and mayhem. It's one of the few times that Morkians would entertain that side, but it's all in good fun. Væson did suggest wrestling to them, but they all said they preferred to watch it than partake in it, so rollerblading it was.

At first, Væson was like Bambi on ice, skidding and falling heavily to the ground. They have grazed their shins and elbows a few times, but thanks to their regeneration ability, that healed in mere moments. They also refused to, at first, anyway, download the information. They wanted to learn like a real human, with practice and bruised elbows.

Skyla dashes by them apologetically does a perfect spin, and off she goes. Væson tries to do the same but spins right into the fountain and falls into it. Væson's friends rush to them with great concern, but when they pull them out of the fountain, they are in fits of laughter, instantly quelling their friend's alarm bells. Even Ignatius laughs, for the first time since the discovery of what Carol had done to her late husband. It's a good distraction to act normal in a town that has every beady eye on you, watching your every move like a kid would do with their ant farm. She just hopes they don't pull out the magnifying glass on a hot day and scorch her.

When Væson gets out of the fountain, they are dripping wet and cold, too, something they rarely experienced on M.O.R.K-78. They have also never seen snow or ice, so it's all new. The cold wind slapping on their wet body and clothes is the first human experience they don't like. Their teeth start to chatter uncontrollably, and their lips are tuning blue.

"Here, take my jacket. I'm warm, anyway," Daniel says, handing over his oversized blue lumberjack jacket.

"I think we can call it a day right there. Let's get you in the warm with some hot cocoa and a movie. How does that sound?" Ignatius says, putting the jacket on for them.

"P...P...Peeeerrfect," Væson says through chattering teeth.

Ignatius guides them to the car and the others pile in, too. The sound of hot cocoa and film sounds good to all of them as the cold starts to seep into all of their bones. That's what tends to happen when you stop doing the thing that keeps you warm on a cold day. When Væson speaks, they notice their cold breath out in the open air and are fascinated by it—but not so fascinated to want to try it again. It's far too cold for this experiment. Thankfully, they have already gotten an action shot of them on their rollerblades, so at least it wasn't a pointless adventure.

Ignatius's home feels like a much-needed warm embrace, especially for Væson who was silent the whole car journey home. Thankfully, the journey was short, and the heating was on in the car. Their body and most of their head was almost entirely in the borrowed jacket of Daniel's, and still it couldn't keep the cold out.

"Daniel, would you mind making the cocoa while I run them a bath? You know where the stuff is, right?" Ignatius asks as they enter the grand entranceway of her home.

Daniel nods and gets to it, his kids in tow. They are keen to help as always when it comes to Væson.

Væson follows Ignatius up the gleaming spiral staircase and into the bathroom with the ornate clawfoot bath. This room alone probably cost more than some houses, but she quashed her guilt by her philanthropy work outside of Poppy Field Lane. There are times when she feels guilty about her wealth, but she has to remind herself that she earned it, and she gives more to charity than the ones who scoffed at her ostentatiousness. She doesn't give to charity to satisfy and quell her guilt (anymore). She does it as she wants to make a positive difference in the world. She also doesn't bang on about it, unlike like a lot of the people, especially Carol.

This is the first time Væson has been in this bathroom. In fact, there are a lot of rooms in this labyrinth of a house that they haven't been in yet. They are still shivering in the coat while Ignatius runs the bath. She adds plenty of bubbles and a touch of glitter, which is meant to soften the skin – a beauty treatment she swears by. Væson watches on as the bubbles foam and form like clouds. They even dip their index finger in it and are delighted at the warmth. A smile breaks out on their face, and for the first time since falling into the fountain, they feel a bit of warmth.

"Not long now, and when you come out, I'll get you a warm dressing gown and your cocoa will be ready, too. Take as long as you need. I take it you've not felt cold like that before?"

"Not ever. And you humans like it?" Væson asks.

"Oh, some of us love it. Us New Yorkers are used to it. You should see when it snows. I love it! It makes the whole place look magical. Some even throw snowballs and have snowball fights."

"Typical humans, causing pain!" Væson says, shivering at the thought of being pelted by a cold ball... for fun. They have seen that on TV too but don't want to partake in that human activity. In fact, not many Morkians do. They leave that one for the humans. There is no snow at all on M.O.R.K.-78, but there are human themed adventure parks and museum. They simulate such things and dramatize their events, but with a Morkian spin, often making it a little more exciting and using good old-fashioned hyperbole and exaggeration. It's true that as a collective, humans are seen as warmongers and primitive, but they would positively fall at their feet in awe if they ever saw one.... well, most of them.

Ignatius tests the water with her elbow, like you would a baby's bath.

"Just right, you can get in now," she says.

Væson tests it with their own elbow, and the warmth greets them lovingly. They have never had anything like this before on M.O.R.K.-78. When they bathed back on their planet, it was via power showers and quick blow dry systems. None of this stewing in your own filth malarky. But there is something about the bubbles. And the smell. And the heat. And... before Væson knows, they are dipping a toe in the bath. They don't even check to see if Ignatius has left the room – not that they care about being naked in front of people. They know it's a big no-no for humans, though.

The warmth around their toe is divine. Next, Væson puts their whole body in, and the feeling is like nothing else. One word shoots to the forefront of their mind: *exquisite*. It's like a liquid embrace. They sink into the bath, and the bubbles slosh around them, even giving them a bubble beard, which Væson finds delightful. All the coldness in their bones evaporates, and all of the built-up tension in their muscles drift away. A long sigh of relief and delight escapes their lips.

This is one thing they are certainly going to take back to M.O.R.K.-78... If they ever go back, that is. They say home is where the heart is, and right now, their heart is on Earth. Morkians are taught to leave the nest at an early age, so there would be no going back to their parents, anyway, but Væson isn't sure they could cope with not seeing them again.

Lights start flashing underwater and, for a moment, Væson has no idea what is going on. Then it clicks. It's a phone call! They lift up their arm from the water and wipe the bubbles off and see that it's Œstegen. Their heart stops for a moment, then goes back to its normal pace. It isn't every day that the President calls you... especially while having a soak in the tub!

"Væson, can you hear me, my dear Morkian?" they ask.

"I can, Mx. President! What an honor this is!" Væson gushes.

"Let me tell you, the honor is all mine. Your antics and adventures have given M.O.R.K.-78 some much needed excitement these past few weeks. Some of us had given up hope of every seeing or hearing from you again," they say, then, spotting the bubble beard, they ask, "W... What is that on your face?" The lines on their face are deep, but even the wrinkles ooze with knowledge and power and wisdom.

Væson, forgetting for a moment that it's a video camera-like set-up, is perplexed and confused about the question. Then the penny drops. It seems that all the anxiety and excitement... and being around humans for an extended amount of time has caused them to become a little lapse in certain memory receptor areas. "Oooh, they are a thing called *bubbles,* Mx President. I don't know the molecular makeup of them, but perhaps the humans are a little smarter than we give them credit for."

"And... what are you in?" Œstegen is so wholly invested in what's going on that they forget the reason for the call. They're absolutely fascinated by Væson's latest adventure, and they're seeing it firsthand. They *do* have an inkling as to what it might be, but part of being wise is not opening your mouth to say something when you're not utterly sure. It's certainly something Earth's politicians could practice... That was the concessions of most Morkians, anyway.

"The humans call it a bath. It's essentially a bucket or a *tub* filled with warm water. I must say, it's delightful. It is making my whole body relax. It sounds strange, and I have no scientific proof of this, but I can feel my worries and stresses melting away."

"Is that so?" The President says in wonder, hiding the fact that it was just as they suspected. "And how long are you required to stay in this, this *tub?*"

"That is the beauty of it. I can stay in here as long as I so desire. These humans are quite good at this relaxing thing. Perhaps they're not as war happy as we initially pegged them for."

"And how would you dry the excess water off?" they ask, knowing the answer but wanting to hear it from Væson first-hand - it's their time and their story.

"I believe I will be given a towel and a thing called a dressing gown from my human. She is so delightful. She's the one who's been taking the pictures and keeping me safe and teaching me all about Earth. I have learned more from my time with her here than I have in my whole time on Earth."

"And you still feel safe? That is most important. M.O.R.K-78 needs their hero back in one piece. We are very close to getting you back now. Just try and hold out a little while longer."

And there it is. The news that Væson didn't realize they were dreading until it hit them in the face. They slip in the bath, and their head goes underwater. Œstegen, panicked, shouts if they are ok. Moments later, Væson emerges from the water, blows bubbles from their mouth, and wipes them from their eyes.

Væson catches their breath and gulps and splutters, trying to regulate normality again.

There is a frantic knocking on the bathroom door. "Væ, Væ, are you ok?" Ignatius calls from the other side of the door.

"Y... Yesss! S..Sorry," they say with an effort. Then, with more normality, they add, "I'm ok now, thank you."

"Ok, well, if you need me, just shout, ok?" she says.

Œstegen's eyes are filled with shock, and their words are shaky. "Væson, are you ok, my dear Morkian?"

"Sorry, I slipped and inhaled too much water and bubbles. That seems to be a bit of a hazard, but I am ok now. No need to worry. In fact," they say as a wave of giggles push up from their belly, "it was a little funny in retrospect."

"Funny? My Morkian, you almost drowned. How is that funny?" Œstegen asks. There is no hatefulness in their voice, only curiosity.

"I guess that's the funny thing about it. I seem to be mimicking human behavior. They also laugh at things like this, even when people fall and hurt themselves. I have to be honest; I find that funny, too. There are even shows dedicated to people filming the incidents."

Œstegen, finding this fascinating, clasps their hands together and says, "These humans, they do not cease to amaze me. Or the rest of the Morkians. Keep gathering information on them while you are waiting. I promise you, it will not be long now. Oh... and Væson, do get the chemical compound for those, what did you call them? *Bubbles?* I would very much like to try them." And with that, they are gone. An audience with The President whilst in a tub full of bubbles is a strange end to an exciting day for Væson.

There is a light knock on the door. Ignatius has all but had her ear pressed to the door, not wanting to pry into their conversation - not that she could understand what was being said anyway - but to listen in to make sure they didn't go under the water again.

"Come in," Væson says, knowing it's Ignatius.

She comes in tentatively, first popping her head around to make sure they are decent, which they are... well, they are still in the bath, surrounded by bubbles.

"Is everything ok?" she asks, sensing the room and reading their face.

Væson doesn't even consider hiding the information they just learned. "They're bringing me home soon. I don't know when, but that's what The President just said."

"THE PRESIDENT?" Ignatius asks, truly flabbergasted. In fact, there perhaps has never been a flabber so gasted. Her face turns into a tribute of 'The Scream' painting.

"The President of M.O.R.K-78, yeah."

"Does he...*they*... sorry, call you often?" More wonder rises in her voice. She puts the lid of the toilet down and sits on the edge of it.

"No, not really, but that's beside the point. I'm not going back, that's for sure," they say firmly.

"You mean you're staying here indefinitely?" she asks, not wanting to get her hopes up. They have briefly spoken about this before, but a part of her thought it was a bit of bluffing and hot air from Væson. But if they are to refuse The President, then they must be serious.

"I sure am. I mean, yeah, I'll go back there from time to time, but there is a whole universe out there. I'm not going to be confined to just one planet. Even though M.O.R.K-78 is pretty close to perfect."

"What will you do? Where will you stay?" she asks, leaning closer to them whilst on the toilet seat. She has to hold onto the side as she almost capsizes, and there is an iron guarantee that Væson would have lost their shit laughing, which Ignatius also knows full well.

"Here... Hopefully..." And then they add, "If that's ok with you?"

"More than ok! I'm sure we have discussed this before, anyway."

"We may have, but I like to be reassured. I also like to have confirmation of a confirmation, too, sometimes. So, sorry in advance."

"Never be sorry for who you are. I'm just glad you want to stay with me," she says, hoping to sound upbeat, but there is a part of her that feels like she is caging a rare bird.

Væson lifts their arms out of the tub and stretches them in an attempt to high five Ignatius, but they then spot their hands and how wrinkly they have become. They recoil and scream in horror, and the pure shock of this makes Ignatius laugh. She grabs their hands close to her chest and squeezes them. Væson is still looking at them, horrified.

"What has happened to *my hands? My beautiful hands?!*"

"Væson..."

"They're all wrinkly! How?" they persist, still looking at

them through Ignatius's own hands. They try to pull them away too, but she holds firm.

"Væson, it's ok! It's normal! Calm down," she says through tears of laughter.

Væson starts to hyperventilate, and they manage to get their hands free of Ignatius's grasp. Water sloshes over the sides as they panic more.

"Normal? How is this normal? Look at them! They look like an old ball sack!"

This really tips the lighter scales, and now she is belly laughing without apology. She attempts to tell them to breath and relax, but she's not sure whether she can herself.

After a few moments, Væson does calm down and stares at them again, this time with more curiosity. They rub their wet and wrinkly hands together, and they recoil and shiver at the texture. They've not been in water long enough to experience this sensation before and in their own skin water doesn't react this way with their body - it acts more like a waterproof suit.

"It's just your hands absorbing the water. They'll be back to normal in no time, trust me," she says, still through laughter.

Væson balls and un-balls their hands a few times, hoping that they get back to some normality, but it's far too soon for this. They start to trust what Ignatius has told them, and they calm down enough to get regular breathing back.

"I'm going to get you a towel and a dressing gown, and by the time you've had your cocoa, they will be back to normal. Ok now?" she says, wiping tears from her eyes. That was a laugh she certainly needed, and her mind is focused on this moment and not on the impending situation with Carol.

Ignatius leaves the bathroom to get the fresh towel and a fluffy, white dressing gown. She returns a few moments later to the sight of Væson still staring at their hands, which almost starts her off on belly laughs once more.

She holds the towel out for them, and they step out of the bath, bubbles still clinging to their strange and beautifully colored alien skin. They wrap the towel around themselves as Ignatius pulls the plug in the bath. The water gurgles down the hole in a mini tornado-like fashion - on their home planet they use a shower like cubical and with the touch of a button the user is instantly dry and the water disappears. This strange sight intrigues Væson so much, they are practically mesmerized by it for the duration, water dripping from their body as they watch. Then, as if breaking out of the trance, they shake their head, spraying water everywhere just like a dog, which makes Ignatius laugh. She then hands them the dressing gown, and they put it over their towel clad body.

"There are some fresh clothes on the bed in your room for you to put on once you've dried off. Or you can get into some pajamas. I put both out as I wasn't sure which you'd prefer," she says, then leaves them to it. Væson says thank you as she leaves, then heads up to get changed. The thought of pajamas coupled with the fluffy dressing gown sound perfect, and much like many scenes they've seen on TV

Chapter 27

Evening Discussions

Daniel, Skyla, Danny, and Ignatius are on their second cup of cocoa when Væson saunters into the kitchen. Their cocoa has been freshly made, and steam is rising from the cup invitingly. Ignatius hands it to them when they sit down at the table.

"Feeling refreshed and warmed up now, Væ?" Daniel asks.

"That... That was the most amazing experience ever. Even The President was impressed by it," Væson says casually.

"The President? I assume of your home planet" asks Skyla.

"Of M.O.R.K-78 - the very same, yes." Væson states matter-of-factly.

"And they were impressed... by a bath?" Danny asks, trying to make sense of this.

"Not just any bath, one filled with bubbles. Oh yeah, it was quite the sight. And then, I almost... almost, what's the word? Oh yeah, drowned!" Væson says, and then they recount the story to them, not skipping a moment and ending it on how they said to The President that humans like to laugh at such things. At this, none of them protest. Danny even smirks and laughs at the thought of Væson slipping in the bath, further illustrating their point.

The evening stretches long and is filled with laughter, cocoa, and action. The action, however, is discussed silently, in the mind between Væson and Ignatius. In the few days that they have been practicing conversational telepathy, she has become almost a pro, and her ability to send and receive the messages is sometimes on a Morkian level. They discuss in their minds what they are going to do with Carol and how they are going to confront her. Ignatius has a sudden and almost cerebral idea, and then she laughs, good and hard, startling the rest of the room.

"What on earth has gotten into you? Did you make your cocoa a little alcoholic?" Daniel asks, only half joking.

"No, no, just had a funny idea, that's all," she says, remaining coy on the subject.

"Well, care to share this information?" Daniel asks, not joking at all now, more on the lines of intrigued.

She glances at Væson who in turn shrugs.

Væson speaks in her mind, *It's up to you. Is this a case of the more that know, the better?*

Maybe? she says into Væson's mind, but she doesn't sound too convinced. *I trust them, but I don't want to burden them.*

From what I know of friendship, nothing is a burden if you do it with love, Væson says. *Friends are there to help and support and love. At least, that's my understanding of friendship. Oh, and sometimes they go on long journeys and put jewelry in fire while being chased by dragons. Although, I hope there aren't any dragons about anymore... Or Vampires, for that matter. Oh, How I hate Vampires!*

Wait... They're real!? she asks, confused.

Of course, they are! Surely when I told you Father Christmas was real, you didn't think he was the only one, right? The world and the universe are full of possibilities... I alone am living proof of that.

The thing about logic is, it's incredibly hard to argue with it. Despite this, some people do, but not Ignatius. She contemplates it and accepts it. She then says to the room, "I think we all need to talk."

"Oh no... You're not breaking up with us, are you? Look, we can change, honest. Give us one more chance!" Daniel jokes while falling to their knees and pretending to pray.

"Oh, stop it, you, and get up!" Ignatius says, laughing.

Daniel gets up off the kitchen floor and sits back in his seat. Although she is laughing, he can sense a serious tone in her voice.

"Ok, listen up, what I'm about to say does not leave this kitchen."

"Can I tell Lorraine? Or Harry?" Daniel asks.

"What about the autistic boy, Ryan?" Skyla asks.

"Where'd you learn that word?" asks Daniel proudly.

"He told me himself, when he was delivering our paper one day," she says with a smile. "So, can I tell him?"

"No, sorry. We have to keep this information quiet. Think of it as a secret because you know what? It is! And the more people know about a secret, the less secret it becomes, and then the secret fails... Aaaand, I've done that thing where you say a word so many times that it loses all sense of meaning."

"Urgh, I hate when that happens. Maybe try and say it really quickly to get the meaning back?" Daniel suggests.

Ignatius shoots him a look that says that's never going to happen.

"We're losing track here again! Ok, ok, there's no easy way to say this, but I need your word that it doesn't leave this room... aside from telling Lorraine and Harry," Ignatius says with a slight strain in her voice. Not just because she is getting frustrated, but because of the thought of recounting the story and still not being able to put her hands around that measly woman's throat. Revenge is sweet, though, and retribution... well, that's even sweeter.

The kitchen falls silent save for the ticking of the huge clock on the wall. It has one of those abstract faces where there are no numbers, just the three hands making their way around the bland, white face. It's probably meant to say time is irrelevant or some bullshit like that.

"Right..." She says, brushing her hair out of her eyes and taking a sip of her cocoa. All eyes are on her now. "I know who killed my husband. The fire wasn't an accident, and it wasn't intended for him." The words puncture the air like a knife into a balloon. All the air has been sucked out of the room, and it's replaced by a thick, black veil. "And that person lives here, right in Poppy Field Lane. We have proof that she did it, conclusive iron clad, balls nailed to the wall. We just... need help. We want to get video evidence. Daniel, do you still have your camcorder?"

Daniel, who is in a trance with the story, has to pull himself out of said trance, but it feels like being pulled out of a pool of maple syrup. "Uh, umm, yeah... sure. I've got three if that helps?"

"Marvelous! The more camcorders, the better. She wanted to be famous. Well... we're going to give it to her! I'm going to make sure the news is there too, for added proof!" She's standing now, pacing around the kitchen, ideas flitting and floating around her head like crazed loons, except she isn't crazy – far from it. She is a woman scorned. For too long, she has been a scorpion. The funny thing is, scorpions have stings, and Carol has been treating her as if she wasn't going to use it.

"So who is this mystery woman and are you sure it's her? I know you said you are, but are you *really* sure? Accusations like this can really fuck up someone's life," Daniel says warily.

"The last time I was this sure, it was when I said two little words while in a white dress standing opposite the man I loved. The man *she* killed...Carol!"

The collective air that was sucked in shoots back out again in horrified gasps. They all knew she was a vindictive bitch, but they didn't think she would be capable of murder. Ignatius tells them how she found out, and Væson helps out where possible, adding validity to the case. When they are finished, the room falls silent once more. She also tells them when this is all going to go down, and the more she thinks about it, the better it becomes. The term *hoisted by your own petard* has come to her mind before, but now... now, it has more resonance, and a smile brightens her face.

"You ok there, Ig?" Danny asks, only a little worried for her. He knows she is going to be ok, but it just seems strange to be smiling at a time like this. He is also playing fast and loose with her hated nickname. He's very sure not to add an 'I' on the end. She doesn't mind Ig too much, but Igni... she especially hates it when Carol calls her that.

"Just counting down the days, don't mind me," she says and takes a sip from her cocoa again.

Elsewhere, Ignatius and co aren't the only one burning the late-night oil. Carol is once again toiling away at her board, and credit where it's due for what she has planned for the Winter Wonderland. Even the foulest people can have a strand of kindness, and believe it or not, she does do this for the town. She loves Poppy Field Lane and would valiantly defend it if push came to shove, but no one quite knows the reason why she loves it so much. Everyone knows she loves the fortune and fame, and some have suspected that the more attention that is out on the town, the more chance that spotlight would finally fall on her, and she could write a 'tell all book' about life in the greatest neighborhood in New York. Carol has grand designs of a great book tour, too, and that would then lead to a talk show. The funny thing is, her fête has a different *fate* in mind for her, she just doesn't know it yet. She has left Frank lightly snoring away in their bed upstairs, and she gave herself a brief pause to wonder if he knew that she didn't love him anymore. In fact, she can't remember the last time she did love him. Love for the week, anyway. It's fickle and filled with an arid landscape, always waiting to trip you up and strip you of who you are. It's a game she refuses to partake in. The real kicker is, she didn't even love Aiden. She only wanted him so no one else could. Until that bitch, Ignatius, came along. That was why she had to put a stop to it. She often thinks about what she did that day, and it always brings a smile, a comfort of sorts. She wouldn't hesitate to do it again, to anything or anyone. As long as she remains on top, she doesn't care who she hurts, whose world she crumbles.

Carol goes over to her locked draw and pulls out a wooden box. It's not very big, but what's inside the purple velvet lined box is bigger than any secret. It's the truth. She puts her hands around the sides of the box and flicks open the catches. Next, she gets the key from the drawer and opens the box, revealing the charred remains of Aiden's shirt. The one she had to literally peel off his body. It was a small mercy that no one saw her doing. It's a secret that she is hoping to take to her grave. She holds the tattered fabric in her hands and clings it to her chest before giving it a sniff and putting it back. It's a strange act for someone to do who claims they didn't even love that person, but the fact that *Ignatius* couldn't have him made Aiden special, made him perfect.

She goes back to her board as the clock strikes 12 a.m. In just five short days, she will be center of attention again. Just not for what she was thinking.

The Captain is also staring at his board long into the wee hours of the night but this time, with a smile on his face. They have narrowed down Væson's location to three neighborhoods. One of them is a quaint little suburb called Poppy Field Lane.

He is going to personally bring the *little blue bastard* back to The Facility in five days' time, dead or alive. It doesn't matter to him now, just as long as the alien is in his custody. It's a trait he shares with a complete stranger. In fact, they have a lot of things in common, but they would make a terrible couple. They're so alike, they're a mirror image. Then again, they would at least like what is reflected.

For the past couple of days now, The Captain's mood has been buoyant, Not even the smallest hurdle has damned it. Internally, however, his mind is still playing a tug of war, and his sanity is falling off the precipice. He has taken to stroking his gun while in a trance, fantasizing about pointing it and pulling the trigger on the alien nuisance. Then, perhaps he would turn it on himself and go out together. Despite his upbeat demeanor, people are still scared to interact with him just in case he goes from sane to crazy on their ass. Talking to him is like a game of Russian roulette, as he has started to laugh manically while talking sometimes, and even chocking on his laughter. There was one occasion where he started chocking someone else, while laughing. He only stopped when they turned blue, and even still, he only stopped because he was pulled off his victim. It was perhaps the strangest thing he has ever done... and he's done a lot of strange things.

On his desk is a small flip calendar and on it, he has the date, December 15th, circled. That is the day he had vowed to get his hands on his so-called property.

Up in the sky, but lightyears away, are two spacecrafts. One belongs to Flagant, and the other to Œstegen. Both have the same destination at the same time, neither of them knowing the other's intentions. Flagant has grand designs on killing Væson and burying all existence of them while covering their own tracks. After all, it was Flagant's fault the Jenson and Væson crashed on Earth, and if that's ever found out, the Morkians are sure to make an example of them despite their normally reserved nature. Œstegen, on the other hand, has intentions of bringing Væson home to a tick-a-tape parade and monumental applause and celebrations that would last long into a month. Their on-board consoles say they are going to reach their destination, Poppy Field Lane, on December 15th.

Chapter 28

December 15th

Today is the day. The day that *cosmic force* would show up on Poppy Field Lane and change the lives of everyone. There's a strange atmosphere in the air, but you wouldn't have known it, for everyone in the neighborhood is filled with Christmas cheer. A fresh blanket of snow covers the green, making Carol's Winter Wonderland truly special. It's still early morning, and the robins are the first ones on the grass, picking their beaks into the virgin snow in search for an early worm.

As the clock strikes 8 a.m., a bunch of carolers, all dressed in traditional red and white Christmas garb, stride down the street, singing merrily. It's a stunt Carol pulls every year, in an effort to make everyone more Christmassy... or piss them off. You'll be hard pressed to find many people who like to be woken up that early, especially by carolers, no matter how good they are. There are just a handful of people going about their day this early. It's mostly fête people, all following orders from the barking Carol, who is insisting that every inch of the place be perfect. There are stands galore, each offering something festive, from knick-knacks for your tree and home to food and drink with extra spice for a warm kick, right down to winter wear. There is even a giant Ferris wheel, much bigger than she imagined, erected in the very center of the green. So big, you could see it from the next town over. Right in the far end is Santa's grotto, complete with real reindeer and, perhaps a little distastefully, little people dressed up as elves. She has spared no expense, and this is indeed the greatest Winter Wonderland that the neighborhood has ever seen. Darren Rose, the gate security, has an easy day today. He is to keep the barriers up and welcome everyone into the town with his soft southern accent.

Away from the green, the other townsfolk are up and busy scooping snow from their driveways. The air has a cold bite to it, so everyone who is out is wrapped up against the elements. The day is only going to get colder, which is why Carol installed heated lamps all around the fête. The woman has thought of everything. Well, almost.

The official opening of the festivities is scheduled to be 2 p.m. That's the time where she is going to stand up on the makeshift stage and literally ring in the Christmas period, complete with a giant bell. Another tradition on this oh so festive day is for Carol to drink... and drink a lot. By 2 p.m., she will be pretty much sozzled with sherries and peppermint schnapps. Frank does what he always does on this day: he sits back and watches the fireworks... After, of course, cooking the Christmas meal for them both.

At 9 a.m., The Captain is on the freeway, hurtling towards Poppy Field Lane. His ETA is at 12 p.m., unless he hits traffic. He's been driving most of the past four days and nights, with his trusted gun his only passenger and a nose full of Columbia's finest. He's only stopped a handful of times so far, often choosing a motel to sleep in when the car became unbearable. Being confined to it while being so close is maddening. The other two towns that they think the *little blue bastard* could be hiding in are still being pursued, but by other members of The Facility. There is something drawing The Captain to this town, and he just knows his prize is waiting for him there He has the windows rolled down, and the station tuned to a rock station that blasts nothing but 80s rock music. The 90s is too full of pop shit for The Captain's liking. If he could live in any time, it would most definitely be the 80s. He'd even have the hair, too: big wide perms. He is so drawn into this memory that when he draws out of it, he is fingering his bold head and thinking he still has a full volume of it. The Facility insisted on someone going with him, but he denied them at every turn. He said this was now personal, and that he would take care of it, before adding that they better have the red carpet rolled out for him upon his return.

At 10 a.m., Ignatius has a kitchen full of people: Daniel and his clan, complete with Lorraine, Harry, and of course, Væson and Alfie. She has a board of her own, and on it is their plan of action today. From 11:30 a.m., Lorraine is to start supplying Carol with drinks, and if she doesn't want any, which they all doubt, then she is instructed to spike her drinks. No one took an exception to this, especially since they knew they were trying to trap a murderer now. By 2 p.m., the plan is for her to be completely Gazebo'd, and as everyone in the town knows, once she is drunk, she's as honest as the day is long. Then it will be Væson's turn to shine, but that part is still under wraps. Danny, Skyla, and Harry are tasked with filming the whole thing, capturing every moment of her downfall, staring from 11 a.m. If they are caught, they are to tell her they are filming a documentary on her. They would watch her head swell, and she would play up to the camera. The final part of the plan is also under wraps, and that is left for Ignatius.

"So, are we all in agreement with this? Everyone knows what they're doing?" Ignatius asks, sipping a morning coffee.

She could barely sleep a wink last night. It was like Christmas, but a different kind.

They all nod in agreement.

"Even though you've gone through this traumatic roller-coaster and elaborate plan, there's still time to back out, Ig, you know that, right? I'm not trying to sound disrespectful or anything, just saying about cold feet, that's all," Daniel says, putting a comforting hand on her shoulder. "But, of course, if you're going to go through with it, we're going to join you." He gestures with his free hand to the rest of the group, who in turn smile at her.

"I didn't get cold feet the last time I said I do, and I'm not getting them now either. The bitch is going down," she says as calm as anything. She knows that an invisible string is tying her to Carol, and after today, she will be free of her. She will finally have closure on her past, thus securing her future.

Very little is said in the kitchen after that, only silent contemplation and nervous anticipation.

At 11 a.m., the time that The Captain has hoped to get to Poppy Field lane, he is changing a flat tire instead, still a few hours away from his destination. Yet that doesn't dampen his mood. The fresh snow from this morning has turned to sludge around him and is speckled in black oil and grease from the car tire. In fact, he is so buoyant in his mood and assurance that he is going to get his prize of the alien today, he is even humming a song. It's one he hasn't heard in a long time, about a sandman bringing him a dream, and what sweeter dream is there than the alien on a cold, steel table, under florescent lights, chest exposed and as dead as the dodo.

At 12:30 p.m., high above the sky are two spaceships, one at either end of Poppy Field Lane, both still blissfully unaware of the others presence due to the stealth coating the spaceships are equipped with. They wouldn't show up on even the most sophisticated radars. This is just one of the technologies The

Captain and The Facility has been hoping to exploit... If only they knew about it.

Flagant is flummoxed by the white and cold snow as soon as they tentatively step on it. "Stupid humans and their cold climate. The galaxy will be better once they're purged from existence." They say to no one but the cold afternoon air, breath coming out of their mouth in whisky tendrils. They look at it, fascinated for a moment, then try to catch it. Their teeth start to chatter uncontrollably with the cold and the snow, which is falling freely from the sky now, invading every inch of their gray space suit. It's equipped with a breathing regulator so they can easily acclimatize to the different atmospheric pressure... it just doesn't have a hood. That is an optional extra that they were too tight to fork out on. They do their best to wade through the strange, cold substance, towards the twinkling lights of the green and the huge wheel that keeps going around and around, like a moth to a flame.

Œstegen, on the other hand, did spring for the optional hood extra, but they are having far too much fun with the snow, picking balls of it up and throwing them up in the air, watching gravity pull them back down again. They even throw one up and levitate up to meet it. If anyone were to see them, they would have the fright of their life. As if sensing this, they decide to transform into a human figure. They transform into a man dressed for the cold climate, with fur lined boots, warm joggers, and a thick flannel coat. The look is completed by a hat with side flaps, also fur lined. This is the antithesis of Flagant, who is in shorts, flip flops, and a tee shirt. The only human show they have watched is *Baywatch,* so until today, they had pretty much assumed that was all the humans wore. The biting of the cold is almost insufferable, and they are cursing the humans once more.

At 11:30, Lorraine comes sauntering into Carol's vision with a warm flask. "Can I fill your cup up?" she asks with a smile.

"What's in it?" she replies, then adds, "Ah, who cares? it's Christmas, and my work is done. Hand the flask over and take the cup. I'll go directly to the source." Once Lorraine hands over the flask, which is filled to the brim with a festive Long Island, Carol swings for it, most un-ladylike. This plan is going easier than Lorraine has any hope for. Carol smacks her ruby red lips in pleasure, then goes back to the flask for more. "You absolutely must give me the recipe for this!" she says, already starting to slur her words.

Lorraine spots Ignatius from the other side of the green and puts her thumb up. Phase one is complete.

Chapter 29

December 15th – 2 p.m. The Showdown

By the time 2 p.m. rolls around, the snow is getting heavier, but there is a peacefulness about it. There are trombone players by the green's pavilion, and the carolers are bringing out their biggest hits. Everyone who is anyone is here, including the news. The size of the town has grown exponentially over the past few hours, and the jovial nature of the town is at an all-time high. Everyone is saying how tremendous the day is and how beautiful it looks. Carol is showered in praise – not that she knows it, as she is so full of booze, she can barely put one foot in front of the other. In some corners of the festivities, a few of the guests are wrestling for custody of their food with the local seagull population - and after a quick battle, the seagulls fly off with more than their fair share of food, leaving the patrons empty bellied and out of pocket.

The Captain rolls up to the street just as Carol is stepping foot on the stage.

Harry, Danny, and Skyla have their cameras primed and ready on Carol, as do the local news and their anchorwoman.

Carol taps the mic and hiccup into it. "Ooh, excuse me, that's a little festive cheer escaping me." This garners a laugh and a smattering of applause. "Th... thank you all.. for... for coming..." she struggles, then hiccup again, this time almost losing her balance. She has to hold-on tight to the microphone stand. Snow is falling all around her, and she is very lucky not to have fallen over as it's getting slippery up there. "I would just like to say... I... I... I hate you all. That's right. You're all... you're all obnoxious little pricks and none ... none of you are good enough for this town." She takes the microphone off the stand. Gasps of horror erupt in pockets of the crowd, and some even start to boo her. "Oh, shut up." This is punctuated with another hiccup. "You all know it to be true. And you know what? I only put on a show like this, in the hopes that... that some better people see it and move here, instead of you freeloaders." At this, she stops, and the reality of what she's saying kicks in. More boos shower down on her, and she tries to stop herself from saying anything more, but her mouth has become a trap door destined to swallow her whole. At this point, Ignatius stands up onto the stage, equipped with a mic of her own. These words would have never come out of her mouth if it wasn't from a little homemade sirup - that when mixed with alcohol can cause catastrophic truth telling. It's technically banned in most of the galaxies, but Jenson had gotten hold of it somehow one year and gifted it to Væson. They were always trying to give each other outlandish gifts, the next crazier than the last. One year, Væson had given Jenson a kind of light sword they had found on another planet, but after a few moments of playing with it, they found it was much too dangerous and locked it up in the attic of their spaceship.

"What are you doing here? What have you done to me?" Carol asks, scratching at her throat.

"Oh, nothing... My friend has, however. Væson, why don't you come up here?"

Væson duly obliges and joins the two women on stage. They're currently dressed as Santa—if he was on a diet, that is.

There is a whooping cheer from Harry and Daniel, and then others join in, too. Soon, the whole crowd is cheering as if this was a rock concert.

"Get off my stage!" Carol yells, running towards Ignatius, who side steps and watches Carol sprawl into the snow. She tries to get up, but Væson stretches out a hand, and then she is surrounded by a mysterious glow that keeps her in place. The crowd oohs and ahhs at this, and one or two of them faint.

Ignatius, who brings a bag up on stage, takes out the wooden box from it. The same one from Carol's drawer. At this, Carols eyes widen in recognition, and she yells, "That's my private property! You bitch! Get your hands off that!" She tries to get up, but can't due to the mysterious glow that surrounds her.

"Oh, this? It's yours? Hmm, ok, if it's yours, you wouldn't mind telling me what's in here, would you? I mean, the owner of the property is surely to know what's inside here," Ignatius says with a smile, hoping Carol takes the bait.

"Of course I know what's in there! It's part of the shirt your dead husband wore the day I blew him up and ruined your life!" she says, and as soon as the words fall from her lips, she tries to shove them back in. The crowd gasp collectively, and one or two of them even shriek in horror. She tries in vain to re-scramble her words, telling the crowd she's been drugged, that she would never do anything like that, but her protests fall on deaf ears.

The news anchorwoman runs to the stage with her cameraman for a closer look. "We are live in the normally quiet and hugely popular neighborhood of Poppy Field Lane, where the self-appointed matriarch has just admitted to a murder that was previously considered to be a tragic accident. Once again, this is Katherine Larchmont, with the breaking news of a murder from Poppy Field Lane." Her bleach blonde hair is styled in the wet look, and it's scraped back on her head. She isn't the most conventional looking TV personality, but she can sense this moment is going to make her career, and her camera-man's, too.

Ignatius pulls the tattered remains of her husband's shirt from the box, and this garners more gasps and shrieks of horror. A couple of policemen swarm the stage and put a new form of jewelry onto Carol's wrists. They escort her to the car while she confesses to even more crimes that she's committed - further jeopardizing her hopes of ever seeing sunlight or exclusive homes ever again.

The plan worked perfectly, and a weight lifts slightly off Ignatius's heart - she's long suspected Carol of being a murderous bitch, and now the whole neighborhood can see it, too. There feels like a collective calm about the whole place now, like nothing can go wrong at all.

The crowd then turns their attention back to Ignatius as she taps on her microphone.

"Now that we have that out of the way," she says with a heart beating too fast, "Væ, play us a little song. I know you, Daniel and Loraine have been practicing all week for this moment." Væson has indeed been looking forward to this moment and their first time on stage. They are a little too overzealously as they hover slightly, but it's only noticed by The Captain, who's eagle eyes pounce upon this abnormality quick as a flash.

The Captain, who is watching all of this with eager antici-pation and a nose full of coke, lurches forward. "This is it! Show yourself, you *little blue bastard!*" He moves ever closer to the stage, holding his pistol beside him, getting it ready.

Flagant is also dashing to the stage, as is Œstegen, and all of them reach it just as Væson is revealing their identity.

At the point where The Captain's, Flagant's and Œstegen's

feet touch the stage, Œstegen claps their hands together and they are all, shunted into another part of Poppy Field lane, along with Ignatius and Væson. The impact of this creates a shockwave that knocks the crowd back.

Væson looks around, and they see nothing but Christmas trees with blinking lights draped on them. It's the annual Christmas tree farm, a place where many of the residents get their trees. Outsiders do, too, and they always sells them at a high price.

Flagant, who is still shivering despite now being back in their space suit, looks around, and a gun is immediately pointed in their face. Then Œstegen also reverts into their true form, as does Væson - the gathered crowd on the green just missing their big reveal due to his immediate relocation.

"What the fuck! There's three of you!? No matter, I'll just kill you all!" The Captain say, laughing like a loon in the snowy air.

The Captain, legs wide, gun loaded and flitting between the aliens, wipes his nose, and it comes away with fresh blood. Some of it falls on the white snow. He then points the gun at Væson and pulls the trigger. The slug flies through the air and right at Væson, who falls down in a clump. It all happens too fast, far too fast for anyone to react. Ignatius screams and runs over to them, cradling her friend and weeping freely, repeating the words *no, no, no.* Œstegen is also in shock, and they rush to Væson, too, but they are already fearing the worst. Flagant, however, is laughing, much like The Captain. Two loons in the night, cackling at their dirty work. Then Flagant pulls out a blaster of their own and shoots The Captain's head clean off his shoulders, leaving nothing but smoking body. The sound of it makes Ignatius jump and cry into Væson even more.

"No one takes my job away from me," Flagant says, shivering against the cold air.

This comment makes Œstegen rise to their feet.

"What do you mean, *"my job?"*" they ask.

"I think you know what it means. No need to play dumb, and now it's your turn," they say and aim their blaster at the President, but they're too slow. For an old man, Œstegen is quicker than a cheetah and twice as deadly. They pull a blaster of their own and decimate Flagant. Now there are two smoking clumps of dust.

"I've been wanting to do that for such a long time," they say, then kneel down beside Ignatius. "You must be the lovely young woman that Væson has been telling us about. I'm Œstegen, the President of M.O.R.K-78, and it's a pleasure to meet you. I am sorry you had to bear witness to that. It's not normally in our nature to kill, but it really was a them or I situation, and I feared for my planet if they were left in charge." They stroke the head of the fallen Væson and they, too, begin to cry.

The snow is heavier now, falling in thick balls, and it's already covering up the smoking clumps. Ignatius and Œstegen, connected by their fallen friend, are so busy in their own private mourning that they fail to see Væson sit up. In their hand, they are twirling the slug that hit them.

Ignatius and Œstegen double take at them and hug them, almost squeezing the very life out of them that they thought was already snuffed out.

"H...How? How can this be? I saw you get shot!" Ignatius says in shock.

"I don't think the human bullets work the same way as ours do," Væson replies, dropping the slug into her hand.

She rolls it around in her hand, then squeezes it. "It's... It's rubber! Someone put dummy rounds in that man's gun."

"I am ever so relived at this," Œstegen says.

"Me, too!" Væson says excitedly. They had stared death in the face and lived to tell the tale.

They both help Væson to their feet, and Œstegen says, "Come, we mustn't lose another moment. Our ship is waiting for you, as is a homecoming like you've never seen before. All in your honor." They outstretch their hand to Væson, who in turn just stares at it.

"Well, come on, what are you waiting for?" Œstegen says, confused.

Væson looks at the President and then to Ignatius. "I am home." They squeeze Ignatius's hand and smile.

Chapter 30

Væson and Ignatius's Intergalactic Detective Agency

I t has been a few weeks since the events of December 15th on Poppy Field Lane, and much has changed. The world has been gifted with a story that will live long in history:, the admittance of murder by one of the country's biggest socialites. It will go on to spawn countless films and books inspired by the evils of Carol, and she will never know it, as she is facing life in Raven's Beak Asylum.

They were however, robbed of the real story that day. The existence of aliens, that headline would have pushed the murder confession to at least page ten in the newspapers. The simple fact is, humans aren't ready to know the existence of aliens, but... we are out there though. We are a friendly bunch, so if you happen to bump into us on the street, we won't hurt you, we won't probe you, or anything of the sort.

I'm sure you've figured out now who I am, and if you haven't, allow me to introduce myself: my name is Jenson. And if that name sounds familiar to your eyes and ears, it's because I dropped it into this story a few times. I was Væson's friend. Still am, in fact. I am alive and well, much to the contrary of the story.

When I crashed on earth with Væson, many moons ago, a woman found me and nursed me back to health. We lived out our days and lives until hers came to an end. I then managed to catch up with Væson and their story and watched from afar. They had a path to lead, and at that point, I wasn't to be a part of it. So, I watched and made sure nothing would happen to my friend. I was his guardian angel as you humans would probably call it. You're probably asking yourself now, so what became of the two of them, and where are they now? Well, they started up their own detective agency.

They're doing pretty well for themselves, and they both couldn't be happier. I love my friend more than life itself, but I love them enough to let them love someone else. It hurts, and time is a healer, but when you're a Morkian, your time can span several hundred years, and I'm still but a dot. I will love again, though. Much like Væson has. I still watch them from afar, keeping them safe. I don't have the courage to speak to them yet, but I will one day. You can count on that.

When I'm not looking over my friend's shoulder, I'm helping others. I'm there for the people, the humans like you who need to be comforted in their time of need. I'm not the *cosmic force*, but I am an agent of it.

A few months have passed, and Ignatius is still in awe of the fact that she is on an actual spaceship with an actual alien. It isn't Væson's own ship, but the one that used to belong to Flagant.

M.O.R.K-78 had a carnival like atmosphere for over a month, and there was a global holiday in their honor, too. They did the circuit of TV interviews and book signings, all with

Ignatius by their side. They were the power couple, adored by all.

After the homecoming parade that Væson was pretty much forced to go to by the President, they set up the Intergalactic Detective Agency with Ignatius. They specialize in finding and retrieving anything the customer's heart desires, all with a one-hundred percent success rate, thanks to Væson's truth serum, which they so handily used on Carol on that fête-ful day. Væson also no longer needs to hide behind human skin but does still dress up and morph into different species when the occasion arises. They aren't alone on the ship, either. Ignatius's dog, Alfie, is with them, often being a key to their sleuthing.

At The Facility, all events and documents relating to or mentioning Væson at The Facility were promptly destroyed. The only thing that remained of it was a little blue book entitled, *Grudge 13*. The contents of the book are top secret, and it's locked away in a safe, behind a vault, deep in the catacombs of the mysterious Facility.

Months would pass, and normality returned to Poppy Field Lane. It became an even more desirable place to live, but Carol's house remained abandoned. Some people wanted to turn it into a museum once the police turned it over, but there were too many ghosts there... and too many bodies buried in the garden. Turns out, Carol had quite the penchant for murder. Frank moved on and moved out of Poppy Field Lane shortly after and started a new life. He remembered what it was like to be happy again, too... and most importantly, to be free.

If you enjoyed this book, please consider leaving a review on Amazon and Goodreads.

ACKNOWLEDGMENTS

Thank you everyone, sincerely, from the bottom of my heart, for again trusting me with your money to tell you a story. I want to start off by saying I wrote this book midway through lockdown here in England and then 86 days later, on Thanksgiving 2020, I wrote the last eight thousand words in one sitting. (After that, I had envisioned self-publishing again, but *Cosmic Force* stepped in and I found an outstanding publisher.) I listened to one of my favorite albums in the morning, and it gave me a spark of creativity. This was my second novel, and it's much unlike my first, Kerwall Town in many ways, but in others, it's similar. Both of them center on a town that is thrust into believing in something we're all told isn't true and people have to band together to either thwart or save it. From the get-go, I wanted this one to be a comedy. I don't want to be labelled as a one genre writer, but I couldn't help myself with some of the darker bits, after all, what is comedy without a bit of tragedy?

In case you're wondering, yes, I do believe that there is other life out there. I just hope that I live long enough to see it. I also hope that they're as friendly as Væson and the rest of the people on M.O.R.K-78, that's for sure!

I honestly never truly know what to write here, I'm still learning, but one thing is for sure: I'll always be thankful for you all. You brighten up my day with your messages and your reviews and your kind words of encouragement.

Growing up, if my book bread and butter was horror, then my dessert, in terms of TV, was certainly sci-fi and aliens. I grew up fascinated by Star Wars and the Alien franchise and all sorts of space related stuff, and I still am, in fact. And when a new alien game comes out, I'm there, right away, playing it until the small hours of the morning. I also grew up in one of the best decades, the 90's. Now sure, we didn't have the music or the fashion, but we had the technology... we also had The Phantom Menace, but we'll gloss over that!

I've always wanted to write a comedy, too, and if I've managed to make you laugh or even smirk during this book, then I will consider it a great victory. Laughing is good for the mind and great for the soul. My hero, Robin Williams, knew that all too well, and if I could have a sparkle even a quarter as bright as his, I'll consider myself the luckiest man alive.

I've loved writing this story, and I'm sure we haven't heard the last from our new friends. I hope not, anyway. Perhaps one day, they'll meet some other friends of mine.

Before I continue to ramble, and *trust me*, I can ramble with the best of them, I would like to extend my thanks to some very amazing people:

First and always, TJ. Some days, I really don't know how you put up with me, but I'm so glad you do, as I would be lost without you. Thank you for putting up with my incessant puns and my relenting zaniness. Thank you for also putting up with me while I wrote this novel, and yes, I will rest a few days before I start my next, I promise. I do this all for you, and I always will. I'll love you til the end of time and beyond that too.

Vourn and Mick, you two have been and continue to be incredibly supportive, and for that, I thank you. Thank you both for letting me into your lives.

Sunjay, Charlotte, and Jess I am proud and honored to call you all my friend. Thank you all for your consistent support. I'm very lucky to have you in my life.

Liz, you're always there with a supportive ear. 2020 stopped us meeting this year, but I still live in hope of seeing my American bestie.

I would also like to thank: Jay, Viv, Tony, Collette, Wendy, Diane, and countless others, too. You are all such amazing supporters, and I am thankful that you're on my side, thank you! There are so many more, too... I'm sorry If I missed you off - but please know I'm very grateful for you.

Next, I would like to thank my beta readers and all the people who looked over this and made sure it was ready to be released to the world.

I would also like to thank everyone at Lake Country Press & Reviews for believing in me and this story. For their encouragement and their friendship. For their dedication and professionalism.

Last, but by no means least, I would like to thank you, dear reader, for sticking with me and staying by my side. Until the next adventure we have together, keep safe, stay well, and give a smile to someone. You never know just how much they might need it. And remember to look up once in a while. You never know what you're missing just above your head.

Your friend,

S. Reed.

ABOUT THE AUTHOR

S. Reed has written for the stage—writing numerous comedy plays, then watching them be performed in local theatres. He has also written for film too, mainly in the horror genre, including writing a feature film from one of Stephen King's short stories.

Most recently, he has been scaring his readers all over the world with his debut novel, Kerwall Town, which was number two in British Horror Fiction.

Reed likes to write in different genres and is crafting an interlinking universe with all his novels, so make sure to keep an eye out and pay special attention to the subtle detail he puts into his novels.

When Reed isn't writing, he's reading and gaming... anything he can get his hands on. And to unwind, he loves watching movies and tv shows with his fiancé, family, and their lovable cat and dog.

Reed and his fiancé also love traveling, especially to castles and places brimming with history. Reed particularly loves places that have a spooky edge.

https://sdreedauthor.wordpress.com